THE FANCIEST DIVE

Christopher M. Byron

The Fanciest Dive ⁓ What Happened

When the Media Empire of
TIME/LIFE Leaped without Looking
into the Age of High-Tech

W · W · NORTON & COMPANY

NEW YORK · LONDON

FIRST EDITION

The text of this book is composed in Gall, with display type set in Windsor Light Condensed and Optima. Composition and manufacturing by the Haddon Craftsmen. Book design by Marjorie J. Flock.

Library of Congress Cataloging-in-Publication Data
Byron, Christopher.
  The fanciest dive.

  1. TV-cable week. 2. Time Inc. 3. Television programs—United
States—Periodicals—History. 4. Cable television—
United States—Periodicals—History. 5. Periodicals,
Publishing of—United States—History.
I. Title.
PN1992.3.U5T8734 1986   791.45′05   85–21381
    ISBN 0-393-02261-7

W. W. Norton & Company, Inc., 500 Fifth Avenue, New York, N. Y. 10110
W. W. Norton & Company Ltd., 37 Great Russell Street, London WC1B 3NU

1 2 3 4 5 6 7 8 9 0

For Jana, who provided witness

The fanciest dive that ever was dove
Was done by Melissa of Coconut Grove.
She bounced on the board and flew into the air
With a twist of her head and a twirl of her hair.
She did thirty-four jackknives, backflipped and spun,
Quadruple gainered, and reached for the sun,
And then somersaulted nine times and a quarter—
And looked down and saw that the pool had no water.*

Contents

Introduction

ON BALANCE, 1983 was a good year for American business. The economy was strong, the stock market rose, and inflation remained subdued. In the White House, Ronald Reagan spoke of America's entrepreneurial spirit, and in homes and offices across the country a renewed energy was unleashed. In 1983, six hundred thousand new businesses came into being in the U.S., the largest number in the nation's history and nearly twice as many as in the boom year of 1973 a decade earlier.

Yet just as 1983 saw more business startups than ever before, the year also produced a record number of failures, often involving some of the biggest and best-known firms in the country. This book tells the story of one such firm, Time Inc., and a failure over which it presided during 1983: *TV-Cable Week* magazine, conceived of as a weekly listings guide for cable TV viewers. Because it survived in the marketplace for less than six months, few magazine readers knew much about *TV-Cable Week*. But within the world of magazine publishing and the media—and most particularly among the employees of Time

Inc.—it was another story. For much of 1983, *TV-Cable Week* was the hottest topic of discussion in a world that thrives on gossip.

To the business and investment analysts who tracked the project, Time's plan was the stuff that business legends are made of: bold, dynamic, in a sense even visionary. Time Inc. was already the dominant corporate power in the two most rapidly growing industries in media—magazine publishing and cable television—and *TV-Cable Week* was viewed widely as a publication that would cement that position. Company officials added to the excitement by declaring that the magazine had the promise of eventually surpassing *Time* Magazine in size, becoming the largest revenue producer in the corporation.

Yet after five and one-half months of trial by the marketplace, *TV-Cable Week* failed—one of the costliest and most surprising failures in magazine publishing history. Direct cash losses exceeded $47 million, but the indirect damage was far greater, from slippage in Time's stock, which lost nearly $750 million in market value in little more than two weeks, to the anguish and dislocation of those suddenly unemployed.

According to the press release that announced the magazine's demise, *TV-Cable Week* failed because the publication's marketing formula "proved unworkable." But an "unworkable" market plan was only part of the story. I know, because for much of 1983 I was part of the magazine's senior management team, holding the position of senior editor, and as such had the opportunity to see the untold part first-hand—the part that Time Inc.'s management did not want the public to know, the part that reflected poorly on the brass itself.

Magazine editors do not normally have access to the inner sanctums of decision making in large corporations, and generally are not very much interested in getting access either. I was different. For one, much of what I did for *TV-Cable Week* had little to do with magazine editing, but was more concerned with corporate and organizational management.

As it happened, my experience was not in television, but in

economics, law, and finance, most of which was acquired during ten years as a business reporter and editor for *Time* Magazine. Pursuing the drama of business had been my career-long calling as a journalist. Ironically, during the course of my work on *TV-Cable Week* I found myself drawn into a corporate drama the nature and size of which I had never expected.

My involvement began in November of 1982, when I was asked by corporate higher-ups to lend a hand in helping Time's new publication—still apparently in the developmental stage—to "get itself organized." There would be some modest "editing" I was told, but the real need was for someone to help organize the use of the project's editorial computer equipment, which was apparently quite substantial. There were promises of a large salary increase, year-end bonuses, and vague hints at someday perhaps succeeding the project's managing editor.

All this appealed to me. But from my first day on the job I found myself far more fascinated by the baroque world of the project itself—a world with no discernible organization or direction, but filled instead with quarreling executives, computers that did not work, and a staff that seemed to swell by the day.

Why wasn't somebody taking control? Was anybody in charge of anything? I needed answers to these questions if I were to do my job. But every briefing seemed to drag me further into the origins of the project. Inquiries about why this or that decision had been made frequently could only be answered accurately by a detailed chronology of events that stretched back over several years.

As my work continued, I came to appreciate that the real answers to what happened at *TV-Cable Week* involved some of the highest and most powerful figures in the corporation—the president of the company, members of his board of directors, numbers of his chief lieutenants. These people apparently were not simply distant observers of the project but had been intimately involved from the start—in conferences, at luncheons, in meetings. Their roles were amplified by voluminous memos, transcripts, and letters on the project, all of which were brought to my attention as my work progressed.

During those months of 1983, the executives of *TV-Cable Week* talked of their lives and bosses in ways that more normal circumstances would never have prompted. But these were not normal times. My colleagues were involved in what was turning into a multi-million-dollar business fiasco, and the pressure on them was enormous. More than once they would talk with extraordinary candor about what they had been through, if for no other reason then to preserve their equilibrium and emotional balance.

When the magazine went out of business in September of 1983, the company's brass treated me generously and quickly found a place for me as a senior editor on *Money* Magazine, another Time Inc. publication. But I was a journalist, and now in possession of what seemed to me to be an important story about the inner workings of the American corporate process. After three months at *Money,* I left Time Inc. and began work on this book.

My purpose throughout has been two-fold: to reveal the damage that can result when corporate decision makers become preoccupied with Wall Street to the expense of their customers; and to recreate the human drama of the magazine itself. Quoted dialogue in this book has been reconstructed from briefing memoranda, presentation transcripts, and the recollections of speakers and witnesses. I have sought to capture as closely as possible not only the actual dialogue spoken, but the nuances and meanings recalled by those present. Where states of mind are attributed to individuals who declined to be interviewed, I have relied for evidence upon their own spoken words to others, as well as, where appropriate, official corporate documents and memoranda.

Each principal and quoted character in this book received at least one and in some cases many requests for interviews. Some granted interviews, others did not. In some cases those interviewed were willing to be quoted on-the-record, in other cases people preferred that their remarks not be attributed to them. I have obliged. Thus the reader should not assume that any particular speaker or named individual in a scene is a "source" for that scene. The true source may in fact be an unnamed and passive observer who, for reasons of confidentiality, is not identified as being present.

The research and writing of this book has spanned two years, and one way or another touched the lives of many people. Some I feel at liberty to thank publicly for their help. In particular, I would like to thank Tony Chiu, a skilled editor and novelist, for the many hours he devoted to helping me improve, simplify, and clarify an inherently complex manuscript. He made the funny parts funnier and the sad parts sadder, and without his efforts, this book would not exist. I can say the same and more for my editor at W. W. Norton & Company, Linda Healey, as well as for my agent, Victoria Pryor of Literistic Ltd., whose faith in this effort never once wavered. David Roe of San Francisco provided a welcome perspective at a crucial moment, and for that I am also grateful. But most of all, I thank my wife and family. They alone know the sacrifices they have made.

If the reader is entertained and enlightened by the result of these labors, that is enough for me. If he comes away vowing a fresh skepticism about Wall Street and stock prices, that is even better. And if, in the end, he comes to see "management" and "innovation" as not easily linked concepts in publicly held stock corporations, then that will be best of all. In the entrepreneurial 1980s, the best ideas will continue to come from where they always have come—single, visionary individuals acting alone—and not from corporate committees. The story of *TV-Cable Week* shows why.

THE FANCIEST DIVE

ONE

A Most Boring Goddamn Résumé

N O INDIVIDUAL was more involved in *TV-Cable Week* than a young Ivy Leaguer named Jeffrey Dunn. At 24 years of age, Dunn seemed to be going on 35. Whether the effect came from the horn-rimmed glasses and the worsted-blend suits, or just the confident timbre to his Harvard-schooled voice, to meet Jeffrey Dunn at the start of his career was to meet a man who appeared marked for the fast track in business.

In the winter of 1977, Time Inc. was such a track; and though still a senior in college, Dunn was soon to begin his career as one of the company's most promising young executives. He was bright, he was ambitious, and as luck would have it, he was destined to make a favorable impression during his very first job interview, on one of Time Inc.'s most powerful— and rapidly rising—executives.

That man was Kelso Sutton, then 39, and for the past eighteen months a ranking vice president in charge of the company's six nationally circulated consumer magazines: *Time, Life, People, Sports Illustrated, Money,* and *Fortune.* These

names were as much a part of the American cultural landscape
as Exxon stations or the McDonalds golden arch, and Sutton was
involved in the business aspects of each. As the second highest
official in Magazine Group, Sutton shared responsibility with his
boss, Group Vice President Arthur W. Keylor, for the management of nearly $1 billion in revenues to the corporation, over-
seeing everything from advertising campaigns to circulation
strategies, to distribution arrangements for the magazines.

Possessing talent, intelligence, and a capacity for what his
colleagues admired as big-picture thinking, Sutton was widely
credited as the individual most responsible for keeping Magazine Group earnings growing. Among other things, Sutton had
centralized the corporation's cumbersome and widely dis-
persed circulation bureaucracy, and had gone on to raise Time
Inc.'s magazine prices beyond the rate of inflation. The fact that
readers were apparently willing to pay far more for a magazine
than had previously been thought was a discovery that soon
spread throughout publishing, even as it helped solidify Sutton's reputation as one of the most talented executives in Time
Inc.

Yet there was a certain perceived ruthlessness that made
Kelso Sutton one of the company's most feared executives as
well, and not just within the corporation. To William Ziff, the
chairman of Ziff-Davis Inc., a leading Time Inc. competitor, and
publisher of such familiar titles as *Car and Driver* and *Modern
Bride,* Sutton was a tough number, someone who "would never
forget an insult no matter what."

Inside Time Inc., the portrait was more complex. With his
superiors, Sutton often seemed deferential and even ingratiat-
ing, ready to rise and offer a chair when one entered his office.
Yet among his subordinates it was another matter. Short and
stocky, he looked "business" through and through, and stories
circulated of his ability to bring conversation to a halt by simply
entering a room. He was, in a word, the quintessential corporate politician, capable of shaping his persona to whatever the
circumstance demanded.

Like Jeff Dunn, Sutton was a Harvard man (class of 1961), and as with many Ivy Leaguers in the corporation he displayed a kind of false modesty about his accomplishments. As he liked to tell friends, taking a job at Time Inc. had somehow seemed to him an easier route to success than slogging his way through graduate school—and in the end would probably turn out to be worth more money anyway.

The vice president's office where Dunn was to have his interview was large and paneled, and faced south from the thirty-fourth floor of the Time & Life Building toward the world headquarters of the Exxon Corporation across the street and lower Manhattan beyond. As Dunn entered, trying to mask his feelings with an earnest demeanor and boot-camp erect posture, he could see in an instant that he was in the presence of power: Sutton's secretary scowled, Sutton himself scowled; here was one room into which one apparently did not bring a smile.

Nor did Sutton seem to feel the need to show his young guest much courtesy of any kind. As the seconds turned into minutes, there Dunn stood, gently clearing his throat, while Sutton, with his back to the door and his guest and his feet propped on a credenza, puffed clouds of blue smoke from a cigar while gazing back and forth from a sheet of paper in his hand to the cityscape stretched out below.

At last, Sutton wheeled his swivel chair around. With his eyes focused on the tip of his cigar, Time Inc.'s vice president for magazines pronounced judgment:

"This is the most boring goddamned résumé I've ever seen!"

"It is like hell!" Dunn shot back, astonished that the words had even leaped from his mouth. Perhaps it was in that instant that something clicked. For here was a corporate executive who had climbed so far so fast that he had not had much time—or maybe even inclination—to reexamine where he had come from. And now there stood before him the living embodiment of his own outspoken drives and desires of sixteen years earlier.

From this meeting came a job for Jeff Dunn as a management trainee in Time Inc.'s Corporate Circulation Department —the very department that Sutton himself had created several years earlier. This was an excellent opportunity for the young Harvard man, and he behaved accordingly. Dunn was quick-witted and self-confident, and it did not take long before others in the department recognized his abilities. He was said to be able to size up a situation rapidly, reduce complex problems to their essentials, and take action. He was, as one Corporate Circulation colleague later put it, "a diamond in the rough. We all knew Jeff would go far, we just did not know *how* far—or imagine how fast!"

One Corporate Circulation executive spotted Dunn's abilities immediately—a young Dartmouth man named Stephen C. Meigher. A member of Dartmouth's Theta Delta Chi sports fraternity, class of 1968, Meigher prided himself on being a dedicated "team player" as well as a fierce competitor both on the playing field and off.

Competition and discipline were qualities instilled in Meigher from his earliest years. At Albany Academy, a military school where he pursued secondary studies, he was quarterback and a three letter man in varsity football, swimming, and baseball. At Dartmouth, he abandoned two of the three sports, but continued with swimming as his father, also a Dartmouth alumnus, had done.

Meigher's self-possession and drive were accentuated by a trim physique, a movie star profile, and a preference for being referred to not as Stephen C. Meigher but as S. Christopher Meigher—the same mannerism affected by another of Time Inc.'s most rapidly rising top executives, Video Group Vice President John R. Munro, who chose to be known by the stylized inversion, J. Richard Munro.

As with many other Time Inc. executives, Meigher had joined the corporation directly out of college, and in the succeeding years had advanced through a number of increasingly

important posts that normally went to older men. Thus, it
hardly went unnoticed when Meigher began to take an interest
in Dunn, involving the department's new trainee in many of
Corporate Circulation's most challenging and coveted assignments. This is wonderful, thought Dunn; he had been hired into
the corporation by Sutton himself, and now his emerging mentor within Corporate Circulation was Sutton's own protégé,
Meigher.

Yet as time passed, Dunn felt troubled by something—it
was not so much *what* he knew as *who* he knew that was
bringing him advantage. What if Sutton should suddenly get
run over by a truck? What if Meigher should emerge not as a
mentor but a rival? Where would Dunn be then?

Dunn began to feel the need to establish credentials of his
own in the corporation, not just advance in the shadow of someone higher up. But to acquire individual clout, he needed a solid
grounding in the intricasies of business and finance. What he
needed, he decided, was an M.B.A.

A master's degree in business administration had not always been seen as the way for bright young college graduates
to start making their way in the world. In 1965, less than 8,000
M.B.A. degrees were granted by universities and graduate
schools around the country, as compared to nearly six times as
many advanced degrees in technical fields like engineering and
electronics. Yet by 1979, the change in what employers valued
in young job seekers had become apparent: though the number
of advanced technical degrees awarded had less than doubled,
the number of M.B.A.s conferred had grown by nearly 600
percent.

In part, this shift reflected the growing size and complexity
of business and the need for professional managers to help
administer the bureaucracies. But other more subtle pressures
than size also spurred demand for M.B.A.s. Key among these
was inflation, which from the mid-1960s onward began consuming America's economic strength, forcing one company after

another to turn to financial gamesmanship and numbers juggling for the illusion of growth when the reality of it eluded them.

Though the nature of their people, products, and marketing problems may vary widely, one thing all companies have in common is a need for profitability, the most immediate measure of which are not production rated on the assembly line or product innovation in the research lab, but cash flow on the income statement. In a world of inflation, this bottom-line perspective made the M.B.A. a valued employee; here was an expert schooled not in any one business alone but in the financial abstractions of all business—in high finance and strategic planning, in structural decision making and computer modeling. Here was a person at ease with corporate earnings reports, who understood the world of Eurodollars and floating exchange rates, who knew how to set up a currency swap or a bond arbitrage.

Even as an undergraduate, Dunn had intended eventually to pursue an M.B.A., and now after eighteen months in the corporate world, the time seemed right. He had already been granted deferred admissions status at the Harvard Business School, and in the summer of 1979 he tendered his resignation from Time Inc. to return to his alma mater—now not as an undergraduate but as one of 780 entering students in the oldest and most prestigious graduate business school in the nation.

Keep in touch, Dunn's boss, Meigher, advised him on the day of his depature, this is not an ordinary company; at Time Inc., bright individuals can go far. Two years later, in the late summer of 1981, Dunn would return to Time Inc. and heed that advice, but with consequences far different from what either he or Meigher, or even Meigher's boss, Sutton, might have guessed at the time. For with his head filled with notions of "strategic plans" and "decision trees," of "internal rates of return" and "discounted cash-flow analyses," Dunn would find himself teamed with another young Harvard M.B.A. named

Sarah Brauns. The resulting thinking of these two executives would set in motion forces that no one could control, least of all them.

Much has been written about the troubles that can befall a company when it loses a sense of purpose beyond financially driven growth, and the business history of the 1970s offers many examples: oil companies that feared for their future in an energy-scarce world and diversified into retailing (Mobil) or manufacturing (Exxon) or mining (Arco) only to lose billions of dollars in the process; technology companies like Xerox and RCA that drifted into insurance and finance and suffered badly; conglomerates like LTV and ITT, which bought up everything from bakeries to steel mills and became little more than corporate kitchen sinks.

At the start of the 1980s, Time Inc. as well was headed down the path of conglomerate growth. Having begun life more than a half-century earlier as a magazine publisher, the company since the mid-1960s had been drifting off into fields about which it knew little—from forays into Hollywood movie-making, to schemes for the distribution of "educational services," to confused churning about as it bought and sold newspapers and broadcast TV stations, even buying, selling, then buying back again parts of the same cable TV system.

What emerged was a $2.8 billion collection of only vaguely related businesses: the company's magazine operations, gathered together under "Magazine Group"; some unrelated book publishing and distribution operations; a "Forest Products Group" that consisted of an Indiana box company and a Texas paper mill; and "Video Group," which consisted of its own growing collection of activities.

Scattered around the country under "Other" could be found supermarket inventory monitoring services, a network of racquetball clubs, the *Washington Star* newspaper, a string of suburban Illinois weeklies, a construction company, a real estate firm, and a weekly magazine that not even many Time Inc.

employees had heard of, called *Q*, targeted at upscale readers outside Chicago.

To investment analysts on Wall Street, the whole arrangement seemed confused and poorly organized, the result not of sound planning so much as of haphazard growth. The company's employees also felt confused. Was Time Inc. destined to be swept along by yet more mergers and acquisitions (the company had itself been the target of several recent takeover overtures), or was Time Inc. in some groping way moving from print media to the world of electronic high-tech? The company's officials seemed set upon asserting the latter, yet spoke in such vague terms as "maga-tronics" and "informa-zines" that people remained puzzled as to what the company would do or buy next.

Though the rank and file of Time Inc. did not know it, nowhere did the future seem less certain—more subject to redefinition by the fuzzy thinking of non-words—than in the paneled and white-carpeted thirty-fourth floor offices of Time Inc.'s top executives, where a struggle had already begun over corporate resources. On one side were the officers and executives in charge of the company's traditional business lines of magazine and book publishing, and lining up against them, their counterparts who headed a group of newer, more profitable activities that clustered around communications satellites, movies, and cable TV.

The print side of the struggle was on the defensive. For while Magazine Group earnings continued to rise year after year, the gains came largely from the company's established weekly magazines—*Time, Sports Illustrated,* and *People*—and not the newer, struggling monthlies.

In contrast to the uncertain prospects for many of Time Inc.'s magazine and book operations, the company felt able to look forward to steadily rising revenues and profits from its growing Video Group enterprises. In half a decade, the group had jumped from no income at all to become the largest single profit-maker in the company, contributing nearly 50 percent of all Time Inc. earnings, as well as providing a steady stream of talent for top jobs on the thirty-fourth floor.

Three men had benefited most: J. Richard Munro, who by the start of the 1980s had advanced from Video Group head to become Time Inc.'s new president and CEO, and his two top advisers. These were a mustacheoed former Wall Street lawyer named Gerald M. Levin, and a diminutive financial expert who bore an unforgettable hiccup of a name: Nicholas J. Nicholas, Jr. Because he had served as Munro's direct deputy during the early explosive growth of Video Group, many outsiders believed Levin would eventually succeed Munro to Time Inc.'s presidency. Insiders were less certain. When a colleague asked Munro who his own best bet would be for a successor to the presidency, Munro offered this answer: "If I were you, I would keep my eye on Nick Nicholas."

The son of a naval officer, Nicholas had been graduated from Princeton in 1962 with a degree in economics, received an M.B.A. from Harvard two years later, then joined Time Inc. as a staff assistant in the Office of the Controller. By 1971 he had climbed to the position of assistant treasurer, and three years later had been appointed head of the company's fledgling cable television operation, HBO, reporting to Munro. Not long after Munro was chosen president of the corporation in 1980 he designated Nicholas his chief "strategic thinker," from which position Nicholas soon began advising his boss to divest the company of its Forest Products group and invest more heavily in cable and entertainment.

Munro acted nearly as impressed with the abilities of Video Group's current head, Levin, the man most often credited as the principal architect of Video Group's success. Accustomed to managing projects on a grand scale, Levin at one point in his career had headed a hydroelectric development program for the Shah of Iran, before joining Time Inc.'s cable operations as vice president for programming in 1972. Like Sutton, Levin was less concerned with numbers than with concepts. He liked to "blue-sky" ideas to judge their potential, and would often let his mind wander to grand extremes as he ruminated on various growth options for Video Group's businesses.

In addition to these individuals, the thirty-fourth floor had begun filling with numerous second- and third-ranked executives, all with Video Group credentials and experience and now aspiring hopefuls on the carousel of opportunity. Not one person who knew how to make a movie, operate a cable television system, write a magazine article, or sell an ad, rode that carousel—just accountants, lawyers, and M.B.A.s. Said Munro of his career: "I never had to sit before a typewriter and type a story. I got here by the good grace of the Lord."

As Levin as well was ready to admit, Video Group's success began with a bit of luck: a decision by the company in 1970 to dispose of its ownership of five broadcast television stations. Having no firm idea what to do with the proceeds, the company began looking for investments, eventually settling on a local New York cable television operation in which it already held a minority interest, Sterling Manhattan Cable. By the fall of 1973 the company had acquired 79 percent ownership of the cable firm, along with a Sterling Manhattan pay-TV service called Home Box Office. Known at first as the "Green Channel," HBO had been set up to cablecast sports events from Madison Square Garden to the company's subscribers.

Where others saw only a fluke acquisition, Levin saw an opportunity, and set about turning Home Box Office into a national distribution system, not just for sports programming but for first-run Hollywood movies as well. Levin's idea: to transmit the programming to local cable companies around the U.S. by satellite. The cable operators picked up the signals using so-called earth station dishes, then distributed the signals through their local cable wires to subscribers, who paid a monthly premium charge that was split with HBO.

The scheme became the nation's first successful approach to "pay TV," and as costs declined, more and more cable operators began offering the HBO service as a way to boost cable viewing in their communities. In the process, HBO's revenues rose dramatically, launching Video-spawned projects in all directions. In 1978, Time Inc. moved back into a field it had earlier abandoned, outright ownership of cable systems, by buying the American Television and Communications Corporation, which owned much of a cable-TV distribution system Time Inc. had previously disposed of. In the interim, ATC had grown to become the second-largest MSO ("Multiple System Operator") in the country, with 2.1 million subscribers in 400 town and cities in 33 states. Now Time Inc. not only owned the biggest pay service in the industry but a leading customer of that service as well.

Next, to the surprise of Wall Street and the consternation of Hollywood, the company moved back into the motion picture business from which it had also earlier retreated after heavy losses. Now the plan was for Time to get a share of the profits that came from financing the programming that HBO and ATC distributed. One after another the deals began rolling in, as Time Inc. films such as *On Golden Pond* and *Fort Apache, The Bronx*, screened first in the nation's movie houses then headed for cable play week after week on HBO.

In little more than five years, Time Inc.'s aggressively expanding cable- and film-related enterprises had shaken up the entire American entertainment industry. Broadcast television executives found that smash movies—up to now surefire hits with viewers when they aired on the networks—were losing their allure because they had already been shown repeatedly on cable. Nor were Hollywood studios happy about the encroachments of Time Inc., and West Coast executives warned of dire consequences for moviemakers if a New York magazine publishing house wound up dominating the distribution system for all of moviemaking.

The feuding made good press copy, but it also tended to obscure the subtler, though equally dramatic, change going on within Time Inc. itself, as Video Group more and more eclipsed Magazine Group as a center of growth and opportunity within the company—upending a fifty-year balance of corporate power. Unlike other media companies such as CBS and ABC, which had begun in broadcasting and only later broadened into publishing, here was a corporation that had begun in publishing and was now leaning through conglomerate growth more and more toward broadcasting's latest high-tech innovation: cable TV. Though much has been written over the years about the marketplace struggle between "print versus TV," Time Inc. was one company—in fact, the *only* company—that was destined to undergo such a struggle internally.

Besides conglomerate growth, the men of Time Inc.'s thirty-fourth floor also thought much about Wall Street and the price of the company's stock. Time Inc. had become a dominant presence in three of the growth industries of the 1970s—magazine publishing, cable television, and forest products—and the company's executives worried continuously that sagging stock prices might encourage a takeover bid from a conglomerate raider such as Seagrams, Mobil, or American Express.

These were concerns unknown to Time Inc.'s founder, Henry Luce. Like many entrepreneurs, he was far more concerned with the quality of his products than the opinions of Wall Street, and made it a point to ignore the market price of the company's stock when Time Inc.'s shares began trading on the New York Stock Exchange in 1964.

Fifteen years later, Luce's successors seemed to think and talk about little else. Eager to overcome his own limited grounding in high finance, Munro received regular updates and briefings on Wall Street from the company's new vice president for investor relations, J. Winston Fowlkes, as well as from Nicholas and Levin. Moreover, all paid regular calls on the investment community to brief analysts on new plans and projects for the corporation.

Mostly, the executives enthused over the promising prospects for the company's video enterprises. Since 1975, the surging growth of HBO had pushed the value of Time Inc.'s stock to more than 14 times earnings, the highest annualized multi-

ple in a decade, and Munro, Levin, and Nicholas were anxious
that the trend continue.

Though they did not discuss the matter publicly, the Time
officials had reason for worry. Like a high-tech equivalent of
McDonalds, which wound up saturating virtually every geo-
graphical market in the U.S. with fast food restaurants, HBO by
1981 was available on nearly every cable system in the country.
In the same way that McDonalds, having reached the outer
limits of its physical growth, began trying to squeeze more
profits out of existing outlets (by, say, adding "breakfast" as a
fast food concept), so too did Video Group need to get more out
of its existing markets. More customers had to be persuaded to
buy HBO than the 50 to 60 percent of each cable system's
viewers who were presently signing up.

One of the biggest problems in this regard concerned what
Video men called "churn." Industry statistics showed that in
any given month, anywhere from 2 to 5 percent of cable subscribers would cancel the service. Some would sell their homes
and move away, and resubscribe in a new community later on.
But a significant number of others would grow disenchanted
and drop cable altogether. Group officials were already waking
up to the implications of churn, for it meant that Time Inc.
might eventually find its cable and video markets filled with the
toughest prospects of all: disenchanted ex-customers.

One reason for churn was the repetitive nature of cable
programming on HBO, as the same movies kept playing day
after day throughout the month. After a week of watching,
HBO subscribers had seen all there was to see for the rest of the
month. But as competition within the industry began to inten-
sify, a new problem emerged: the proliferation of program offerings. For a basic monthly fee of $6 to $15 to a cable operator,
a viewer in 1981 could receive all three broadcast networks,
public television, up to eight local independent stations, and
perhaps as many as twenty different basic- and pay-cable stations. Yet no newspaper or magazine in the United States in
1981 was publishing comprehensive cable listings for viewers.

Subscribers simply could not find out what show was on and on what channel. After a month or so of frustration, many customers would throw up their hands and cancel cable altogether, adding to the churn problem.

Somehow Time Inc. needed to overcome churn. If the problem continued indefinitely, Time's stock price might stop rising, and in the end the company might be devoured on Wall Street.

TWO

A Visit to the Sink Hole

WHAT EVENTUALLY became the most elaborate and costly development project in Time Inc.'s history began with a task force of two individuals: a business executive and an editor, one reporting to the group vice president for magazines, Kelso Sutton, and the other reporting to Time Inc.'s editor in chief, Henry Grunwald.

Sutton, who by now had been elevated to the position of Group Vice President, had been enthusiastic about the idea of a cable listings magazine from its inception. In that spirit he had selected as his representative on the task force Richard Durrell, an executive who enjoyed a reputation throughout Magazine Group as an effective, assertive, and detail-oriented executive. Late in middle age, Durrell had been the founding publisher of *People* Magazine and relished immersing himself in the most intimate details of everything from advertising campaigns to printing and production techniques. Stories abounded of seeing Dick Durrell stop at neighborhood newsstands, or at an airport kiosk, and rearrange a magazine display rack to make sure that copies of *People* were prominently positioned for passers-by. "God is in the details," he liked to tell colleagues, echoing the architect, Mies van der Rohe. "The little things add up."

In contrast to Sutton, Editor in Chief Grunwald chose for the task force a man who seemed Durrell's polar opposite, a bashful and unassertive *People* Magazine editor named Richard Burgheim. In his late 40s, and given to mumbling mannerisms and diffidence, Burgheim seemed about the last person on earth to entrust with the management of anything, and his appointment to the task force by Grunwald was quickly read as evidence of Grunwald's lack of interest in the project.

That perception was reinforced by an aura of global preoccupations that seemed inseparable from the man himself. Born during the interwar years in Austria, the son of a Viennese playwright and librettist of some repute, Time Inc.'s editor in chief basked in a reputation of intellectual brilliance and erudition. Beginning as a *Time* Magazine copy boy in 1945, he had risen to become the highest editorial official in the corporation, along the way authoring a number of books, including *Churchill, The Life Triumphant* (1965) and *The Age of Elegance* (1966). Now approaching 60 years of age and recently widowed, Grunwald was at that point in a man's life when one's thoughts turn increasingly to questions of summing up, destiny, and even life itself—not the merits of a television listings magazine.

Grunwald's appointee to the task force may have seemed casual to many, but Dick Burgheim did in fact know a great deal about cable television and programming. During the 1960s Burgheim had worked for a period as editor of *Time* Magazine's television section, then during the early 1970s had worked as well for Munro on cable programming strategies for the company's newly formed Video Group.

Yet the manner in which he learned of the task force and that he might wind up being offered a job on it, surprised Burgheim. As an editor, Burgheim was answerable through a chain of command that led ultimately to Editor in Chief Grunwald on the thirty-fourth floor, and not to any of the company's

business officials, no matter how senior their rank. By a long and
venerable corporate tradition, Time Inc.'s editor in chief would
no more think of offering his advice on the selection of a particular publisher or advertising director than the company's chairman or president would intervene in the appointment of a
managing editor or one of his top deputies. At Time Inc., the
editing and publishing of magazines were viewed as two different worlds—the worlds of "church" and "state"—and over the
years a powerful corporate culture had evolved to preserve that
view.

Burgheim was thus understandably surprised when one
day in late spring of 1981, Munro's new financial strategist, Nick
Nicholas, a man whom Burgheim knew only vaguely at best,
telephoned the editor and invited him to lunch at a midtown
restaurant. Not knowing what to expect, Burgheim was even
more surprised when, as the meal progressed, Nicholas began
pointedly probing him for his thoughts on whether Time Inc.
should get into the listings guide business. Some sort of task
force was apparently being formed, and in his way, Nicholas
seemed to be sizing Burgheim up for a slot on it.

Burgheim's first reaction was that he did not particularly
like the idea of a Time Inc. listings guide, and he said so; he
wondered whether a market for a cable TV magazine really
existed, whether *TV Guide* would prove easy prey if Time Inc.
entered its turf, whether the TV pages of local newspapers
might not begin to improve as cable itself spread.

Yet though he remained skeptical, in the following days
Burgheim began to sense in the project the seeds of opportunity. In recent years, his career had not gone as well as he might
have hoped, and though he now held the rank of second in
command among *People*'s editors, he expected to be passed
over when it came time to choose a new managing editor for
the publication. Thus the notion that Time Inc. might be planning to develop a magazine devoted to cable television suggested possibilities. If Time Inc. should indeed venture into
such a business, Burgheim felt that he was the man to develop

the editorial product. The more he mulled over the matter, the more it seemed that this was a real opportunity—the chance to manage the development and editing of a Time Inc. television magazine.

In the world of magazine journalism, the job of managing editor is the ultimate challenge—as Grunwald himself would sometimes observe, not unlike that of an orchestra conductor ("a kind of Toscanini or Solti of the press"). But being an editor means more than just shaping words and meanings—though that is vital.

Being an editor also means pursuing a plastic, living art—interpreting and shaping events, understanding readers, perceiving patterns in the random events of experience. Being an editor means doing that not just once, like a motion picture director perhaps, but week after week, month after month, year after year. It is arguably the toughest, most demanding job in all of journalism, and it now began to seem to Burgheim that the opportunity was within his reach, to tap the resources and financial might of Time Inc. in pursuit of a new magazine that he very well might wind up heading.

Yet as he pondered the situation, one person troubled him: Grunwald. Ten years Burgheim's senior, Grunwald was already a *Time* Magazine senior editor when Burgheim joined the magazine in 1960 as a trainee writer five years out of Harvard. Bashful and inarticulate, Burgheim soon felt himself overshadowed and even intimidated by Grunwald, who had a habit at corporate social functions of entering into conversation with colleagues, then abruptly wandering off if someone more interesting passed by.

New to the world of Time Inc., and lacking a corporate mentor, Burgheim soon found himself typecast as a "back of the book" writer for *Time* Magazine sections such as "Television" and "Modern Living," even as Grunwald kept advancing steadily higher on the magazine, from foreign editor in 1961 to assistant managing editor in 1966 to the top job of managing editor in 1968.

From time to time Burgheim's career seemed to gather momentum; during the early 1960s he served for a period as an editor of *Time* Magazine's Canadian edition, based in Montreal, and not long afterward was loaned to Video Group to help develop a cable programming strategy for Munro. But it was not until 1974, when corporate higher ups assigned him to help in the launch of *People* Magazine, that his talents found a home. As clever with a typewriter as he was awkward verbally, Burgheim quickly demonstrated a flair for anticipating pop culture trends, and was soon recognized among the staff as the source of much of the magazine's editorial personality and zip.

Meanwhile, *People* had begun to emerge as the publishing phenomenon of the decade—a magazine that not only gave legitimacy to the journalism of gossip, but bolstered Time Inc.'s reputation for leadership in the development and marketing of general-interest weekly magazines. Burgheim felt justly proud of his contribution to *People*'s success, and in his own private way he was more than a little hurt by the ill-disguised attitude of Grunwald, who somehow seemed to feel that the magazine just wasn't a "Time Inc. quality" publication.

In the weeks following his luncheon with Nicholas, Burgheim thought back often to those early days with Grunwald. It seemed to Burgheim that if Time Inc. really were serious about a listings magazine, its best chance for success with readers lay in infusing the publication with a frothy, almost superficial tone —something with about the same intellectual depth viewers demanded of TV itself—in short, exactly the sort of magazine that Grunwald had turned up his nose at once already. Would he do it again?

One day in mid-July an answer began to appear, but in a way that gave Burgheim encouragement. Grunwald called him to his office and briefed him on the project. "I want you to get involved," he said. "You'll be writing on a blank slate. I want you to look at every option. See what you think."

Though neither Sutton nor Grunwald gave their subordinates more than a cursory briefing on the matter, Time Inc.'s brass had in fact been quietly trying for years to develop a cable television listings guide. But one after another the efforts came to nothing. The first traced as far back as the winter of 1974–75, and was terminated, it turned out, when the company failed to secure favorable postal mailing rates for the publication—an obvious disappointment to one young executive involved in the effort, Sutton himself.

In 1980, the company convened a special task force to explore the idea all over again, but this one proved equally disappointing. Instead of problems with postal authorities, the group now ran into what seemed an insurmountable technological obstacle: how to make the guide's listings accurate for each cable system. The United States currently has more than 4,000 such systems, some with as few as 100 subscribers, others with as many as 100,000 or more. They are scattered across different time zones, not all offer the same menus of programming, and, as often as not, the actual channels on which the programs are available differ from one system to the next.

In 1980, no computer system in publishing could organize such a vast body of data efficiently.

There was another problem as well: producing small press runs of "system-specific" guides would undercut the economies of scale on which magazine publishing is based. Said one official involved in the study, "The technology was just not available. The undertaking would have been too huge and complex." Instead, the group recommended publishing a kind of TV gossip magazine, filled with personality features and without listings.

This was not what the thirty-fourth floor brass wanted to hear, and no sooner had the task force disbanded in the spring of 1980 than Time Inc.'s top officials started privately mulling the idea all over again.

One of these men was a tall and balding one-time Dallas banker named Clifford Grum. He had joined the corporation several years earlier as part of a conglomerate merger deal, and had since risen to the number-two slot in the company, executive vice president. Though he knew little of either publishing or cable television, Grum nonetheless believed Time Inc. should publish a cable listings guide of some sort, and during a gathering of top corporate officials in Bal Harbor, Florida he let his feelings be known. When the subject of the recently disbanded task force came up during a conversation at the bar, Grum paused in thought and then declared to a colleague; "Well, so far as I am concerned, we are going to push ahead with the idea anyway. It's a good idea and we're going to do it."

Based on what little they had been told of the earlier task forces, Durrell and Burgheim expected their immediate problem to be the fragmentation of the market. In Manhattan alone, one cable company served residents north of East 86th Street and West 79th Street, while another served residents on the south side of those streets. Producing system-specific guides for the two neighborhoods meant supplying newsstands on one side of the street with one version of the publication, and newsstands on the other side of the street with an alternative edition.

Such anomalies existed in towns and cities all across the country, so to familiarize themselves with the industry the two men embarked on a whirlwind tour of many of the nation's largest cable systems. They wanted to meet the key players, find out how cable companies operated, see what sort of guide would most appeal to subscribers. Their first discovery was that a fragmented industry was not their only problem. It seemed that cable operators had some views of their own regarding what a listings magazine should contain, and these views did not always coincide with those of Burgheim or Durrell.

Problems surfaced during their first visit to a cable company, Orange County Cablevision in Orlando, Florida, the second largest cable system in ATC. The visit had been recommended by Video Group officials as a good starting point to get an overview of the industry. But the introduction proved unsettling, as disagreements developed immediately over editorial policy. Burgheim felt readers would benefit most by a guide that contained comprehensive and complete listings of *everything* on their cable sets, but video officials wondered whether it would be wise to include broadcast listings. Cable operators made much of their money from commissions on the sale of pay channel services like HBO, and the video people argued that including broadcast listings in a guide might upset them.

More tension arose over what sorts of feature articles the publication might offer. The cable officials wanted articles that promoted blockbuster movies premiering on the pay services, while Burgheim felt that doing so would turn the magazine into little more than a promotional tool for HBO. As the cable officials saw things, the men from New York were supposed to be learning how to produce a guide that would help solve the churn problems of the cable industry. But as Burgheim saw things, he was there to develop a consumer magazine for readers, not cable operators, and he did not welcome what he took to be their encroachments on his prerogatives as editor.

After more discussions and a tour of the Cablevision premises, the group headed off for a visit to some of Orlando's local attractions, the most memorable of which proved not to be Disney World, but a geological "sink hole" that had opened up in a local neighborhood, swallowing more than 700 feet of ATC cable wire and a local Porsche dealership in the process.

Once at the site, Durrell and Burgheim bought sink-hole T-shirts from a young man who had set up a stand, then lapsed into more discussion with their hosts about the magazine project and the industry. Yet when the subject of editorial content came up again, Burgheim flushed in anger and thought to himself, Who's the editor of this thing anyway, them or me?; and he wondered how his own boss, Grunwald, a man who spoke often and eloquently on the importance of editorial independence, would take to cable industry businessmen trying to tell *him* how to edit a magazine. Durrell as well had fallen silent, and when the group turned to leave, he remained motionless, hand in pockets, staring into the sink hole at his feet.

A week or so later Burgheim attended a meeting with cable officials throughout the Midwest. The gathering took place in Overland Park, Kansas, just outside Kansas City, and similar themes came up again. The cable people agreed that readers would welcome comprehensive listings, but they wanted to make sure that no magazine available to *their* subscribers contained information about programming services not already offered on the system.

This was especially true for many new high-tech innovations such as home security and electronic banking that were now being introduced on only the most advanced cable systems in the country. The cable people feared that subscribers would begin demanding that these services be added to their own systems, which could mean millions of dollars in new investment. Yet if they did not make the investment, the cable men worried that their subscribers might complain to their local city councils, and that their franchise licenses might be revoked. One cable official summed up the prevailing sentiment nicely: "The most dangerous subscriber is the one who knows what's going on down the road, if you get my meaning, Mr. Burgheim. We have to be careful about these sorts of things."

Not long after that meeting came a dinner with industry officials in Boston, after which even the normally ebullient Durrell grew despondent over the problems of editorial control. He had begun seeing sink holes for the project wherever he looked. Now he blurted out his fears to Burgheim. The two had settled into seats aboard the Boston–New York shuttle, and as the plane shuddered skyward and the lights of Logan Airport grew dim below, Durrell turned to his colleague and declared; "As far as I am concerned, we simply cannot do a publication in conjunction with these people. It's that simple." Then he turned to the window and stared into the dark.

Whatever their private feelings toward Durrell and Burgheim, the ATC officials remained eager to help when it came to the use of a consumer sampling technique that soon became the research bedrock of the project: so-called "focus group sessions." At the beginning of the 1970s, focus group research was only beginning to be used in consumer marketing, and facilities were practically nonexistent. A decade later they had become the rage of Madison Avenue, with dozens of different laboratories and centers having sprung up to serve market researchers around the country. Many of these facilities had begun appearing just over the Hudson River in New Jersey, where research analysts believed suburbanite shoppers more closely reflected true consumer tastes and preferences than those to be found in Manhattan.

Market researchers liked to use focus group sessions as a way to judge consumer attitudes toward specific products and marketing campaigns, and then use the resulting insights to develop more rigorous market tests of actual products. In these sessions, six to ten consumers would sit in a room equipped with one-way mirrors and be led through semi-structured discussions designed to reveal their likes, dislikes, and other more subtle feelings toward a product.

Though focus group research is by its nature impressionistic and "soft," such research is doubly suspect when no product can actually be given to the group's participants to handle and examine. But that was the problem faced by Durrell and Burgheim, who for over twenty such sessions arranged by Video Group colleagues, stood behind one-way mirrors in cities around the country and watched as members of focus group after focus group talked about the one TV listings magazine they knew anything about: *TV Guide*.

Burgheim was aware of the limitations of focus group research, but what he saw through the one-way mirrors confirmed his belief that what readers really wanted in a TV magazine was an all-inclusive listings guide—something that eliminated the need to flip back and forth from *TV Guide* to their local newspapers and pay TV handouts to find out what was on. Back in New York, Burgheim summed up his observations this way: "People wanted a guide that they could pick up just seconds before the hour, flip through, and find a program before the damned thing was half over. But there wasn't any such magazine—one that was complete, easy to use, with everything about what came out of your TV all in one place."

As the summer of 1981 drew to a close, one could not have imagined a seemingly more ill-suited man than Dick Burgheim for the work that now awaited him. Disorganized in his professional habits and uncommunicative by nature, he neither looked the part of a leader nor seemed concerned about behaving like one. Disshevelment said it all, from the thinning ashen hair and wispy mustache, to the sentences that trailed off into nothing as they approached completion.

Yet anyone who only read Burgheim's surface qualities missed the man's whole point. Behind the facade lurked an editor of fierce intensity, with an adder-like wit, the drive of a workaholic, and now as it happened, a focus for his energies. For as the summer had progressed, Burgheim had grown more and more convinced not only that system specificity was the way to go with the project, but that no matter how many different editions of the new magazine Time Inc. wound up publishing, be they ten or ten thousand, each one had to be held to the same high standards of editorial independence, literacy, and factual accuracy to be found in Time Inc.'s other magazines—in short, a "quality" product in every way. Burgheim wanted a magazine with engaging and colorfully written feature articles; with carefully designed and laid out listings pages; a publication in which every sentence, every phrase, indeed every word would be up to Time Inc. standards.

Burgheim's first shock came when he discovered that his right to insist on these things had been usurped by business-side executives before he had even been appointed to the task force. Executives in the company's manufacturing division had already designed and tested a editorial/production system for the magazine based on work done for the thirty-fourth floor the year before, and now proclaimed it to be the system Burgheim would have to use.

The man in charge of this effort was Richard Labich, a top official in Time Inc.'s Corporate Manufacturing and Distribution department. Widely seen by the corporation's writers and editors as a kind of Dark Force ranged against them, CM&D was charged with running the company's printing, production, and distribution operations, much of which was directed from a factory loft on Pine Street, on Manhattan's Lower West Side. Over the years, feuding between Pine Street and the Time & Life Building had become almost routine, as CM&D would complain about editors who missed deadlines and drove up printing costs at the plants, and editors who would retort that the delays were all at CM&D's end.

Presiding over much of this action was Labich. Hulking in appearance, the number two boss-man of CM&D was more important to the smooth running of Time Inc.'s magazine businesses than any combination of the company's top twenty editors; *they* could be replaced, but only Labich knew how the magazines really got made—only *he* had managed to master the labyrinthine twists and turns of CM&D. They were Labich's presses, Labich's contracts, Labich's computers. Designing a magazine was one thing, but if one wanted to get it printed, it was a good idea to involve Dick Labich.

That notwithstanding, from the moment he learned of Labich's involvement in the project, Burgheim viewed the CM&D executive with suspicion, seeing him as an interloper whose computers and printing presses threatened his prerogatives as editor. From these beginnings, relations between Burgheim and Labich went quickly downhill, as Labich would roll his eyes at the mention of Burgheim's name, even as Burgheim would sneer at CM&D as standing for "Corporate Mediocrity and Dinosaurism."

Of the many things Burgheim disliked about Labich's computer system, the one he felt most strongly about concerned collecting and editing the actual program listings—the heart of the magazine. The raw data (what program would be on what channel and at what time) was, it seemed, not to be gathered by Time Inc. employees at all but purchased from a company called TV Data, an upstate New York subsidiary of the Scripps Howard newspaper chain. TV Data was already supplying "plain-vanilla" listings to nearly 2,000 different newspapers and Sunday supplements around the country, and the plan was for Time Inc. to become, in effect, another customer.

Ambivalent about this arrangement from the start, Burgheim grew more apprehensive after visiting TV Data's headquarters, located in a shopping mall in the Adirondacks village of Glens Falls. There he discovered not the efficiently humming data-processing operation he had expected, but several dozen workers eating pizzas slices and tapping away at computer keyboards as they transcribed program schedules and press releases mailed in from TV stations and broadcast networks.

The specter of building a business on listings supplied by what he termed TV Data's "laid-back, low-motivation, high-turnover team" rattled Burgheim no end. What if the listings were full of errors, had misspelled names, had gross grammatical mistakes? Who would buy a TV listings magazine filled with boners and blind leads?

But there was more to it than that. What if subscribers started noticing that the magazine's "plain-vanilla" listings were identical to the listings appearing in their local newspapers—right down to the misspellings and mistakes! Wouldn't people start putting two and two together—realize, in effect, that they were being ripped off, that they'd been paying Time Inc. for the same information they were getting for free in their daily newspapers?

Though Burgheim quickly concluded that the only sensible course for Time Inc. was to "get into the listings business" for itself, Labich was less certain. With over 1,000 different broadcast channels alone to contend with, as well as thousands more in cable outlets that would have to be included, such an undertaking seemed an organizational and administrative horror. Be-

sides, the prospect of actually having to sit at a computer terminal for eight hours a day and "edit" TV listings evoked visions
of such sorrowful tedium that no self-respecting editor or writer
would be willing to do it in the first place.

To Labich, Burgheim's worries were, in a sense, beside the
point anyway, since the production system being proposed contained a customizing feature that allowed Time Inc. to "edit"
the TV Data plain-vanilla listings before publishing them. But
how Labich's system would actually operate baffled Burgheim,
and the more he heard Labich talk about it, the less he liked it.
For his part, Durrell did not appear to care much one way or
another any longer, but spent more and more of his time on
chores back at *People,* seeming to Burgheim at least to distance
himself as much as possible from this confusing undertaking.

THREE

A "Me Too" Addendum

MORE THAN PERSONALITIES, the task force faced a bigger problem in its organizational underpinnings. With responsibility split between Burgheim and a now retreating Durrell, and with no one on the thirty-fourth floor assuming direct sponsorship, the project effectively had no leader and was vulnerable to conflicting pressures from many directions.

When such situations arise in corporations, it is usually not long before the dynamics of bureaucratic growth take over, and individuals having widely varying expectations and objectives become attached to the project. In the case of the task force, the first such individual was none other than Jeffrey Dunn. Two years had passed since Dunn had departed to pursue an M.B.A. at Harvard. Now it was September of 1981, Dunn was back, and by a fluke of circumstance the young M.B.A. was about to begin work for Durrell on the task force.

Upon his return from Harvard several weeks earlier, Dunn had been assigned by Sutton to a department called Magazine

Development, where it first had seemed as if he might have leaped onto the fast track all over again. Magazine Development was where the company's new and most promising publishing ideas took shape, from *Money* (1972), to *People* (1974), to *Discover* (1980). Yet the impression created by his new boss, a man named Lawrence Crutcher, recently named vice president for finance and development, raised doubts in Dunn's mind about how fast the track really was.

To Dunn, Crutcher seemed uninspired in his new job, and Dunn wondered whether it might be a mistake in career terms to grab hold of what could prove to be some exceedingly short coattails. Crutcher seemed to lack the drive and energy of Dunn's old boss in Corporate Circulation, Meigher, and appeared to have a habit of automatically pushing many of his own chores off on his underlings, a quality that a friend later recalled joking with Dunn about as Larry's "sloped desk" syndrome ("Whatever lands on his desk immediately slides off onto mine!").

Chafing for opportunity, Dunn came to work one morning early in September to find it staring him in the face. The occasion was a gathering of over one hundred Magazine Group employees, from top managers down to secretaries, in a forty-seventh floor conference room where President Munro was to brief them on corporate plans for the year ahead.

A Marine Corps veteran with two Purple Hearts from the Korean conflict, Munro had risen through the Magazine Group ranks before making what came in time to be viewed as the Big Jump to Video, where he now stood out as what might be termed the New Time Inc.'er, a man with credentials that ranged the full spectrum of corporate possibilities, from the world of print journalism and magazines to high technology in the cable age.

Soft-spoken and engaging, Munro had been president less than a year and had already won the respect of employees throughout the corporation. They admired his candor and openness, and thought of him (as he thought of himself) as an approachable man of simple tastes and pleasures. When an editor from *Fortune* Magazine asked his thoughts on the subject of executive lifestyles, Munro had a ready answer: "You won't find any limousines waiting at the door for me"—an unmistakable dig at thirty-fourth floor colleagues like Editor in Chief Grunwald, who had become known for his fondness for corporate jets and limousines.

Though he felt uncomfortable issuing orders and edicts, and preferred to lead by example, Munro did feel the need to speak out often on questions concerning the direction he planned for Time Inc. Through his experience in Video Group, Munro had grown increasingly intrigued by the promise of high technology, from satellite transponders to electronic data banks and information retrieval services.

Guided in his enthusiasms by Levin and Nicholas, he now yearned to give his vision more concrete form as a foundation for the new Time Inc. and had authorized the development of two promising-sounding high-tech projects already—a cable-distributed electronic information service called teletext, and a technologically complex concept called subscription television, in which pay TV programming would be distributed over the air.

Standing before the assembled staff of Magazine Group, flanked by Sutton, Levin, and other top corporate officials, Munro now began his *tour d'horizon* for the year ahead. The employees listened closely. Big things were shaping up for Time Inc., he told them, opportunities in subscription television, the teletext project, and of course the further exciting growth of HBO.

Yet when it came time for Sutton to speak, the group vice president for magazines offered what seemed almost a "me too" addendum—as if to say, Hey, guess what, Video is not the only fast track in this company. Sutton's announcement: before the year was out Magazine Group would test market a new television magazine in which everyone saw enormous potential.

Sitting in the audience, Jeff Dunn hunched forward. The market testing of magazines was a responsibility that belonged to Magazine Development, his own department, but here was a magazine project in which Sutton apparently seemed quite interested but that Dunn had never heard of. He wondered if Crutcher had heard of it.

After the meeting broke up, Dunn went to Crutcher's office to ask if Crutcher had heard of this "TV magazine." Crutcher apparently knew of the project's existence, but professed surprise to learn that Sutton had said there would soon be a market test. Crutcher said he would look into the matter.

Several days later Crutcher held a meeting in his office with Durrell and Labich. At the meeting Labich produced some charts of boxes and arrows showing how his computer system would process listings. It was all to work automatically, explained Labich as the presentation progressed; it would be untouched by human hands.

As the meeting ended, Crutcher turned to Durrell with what seemed an innocent request—that he keep Dunn updated on the task force's progress. Crutcher naturally assumed, as did Dunn, that once Durrell had developed a dummy sample of the publication it would be time for Magazine Development to conduct a market test. But Durrell, who had no staff of his own, took Crutcher's request as an invitation to enlist the services of Dunn on the project, and in the days that followed he began urging Crutcher's assistant to become a kind of ad hoc financial aide.

This put Dunn in an awkward position, for he was already burdened with work from Crutcher. If he accepted more from Durrell he might wind up producing work that satisfied neither man. Even so, the task force intrigued Dunn. Here he was back from business school for little more than a month and suddenly a fascinating situation had opened up before him—unstructured, promising, an opportunity to operate outside the normal chain of command and perhaps even wind up dealing directly with Magazine Group's highest official, Sutton, the very man who had hired him in the first place.

Dunn decided to try to have it both ways—see if he could serve Crutcher *and* Durrell. It was a mistake. Seemingly resentful of Durrell's claims on his assistant, Crutcher tilted the slope of his desk more steeply and let more work slide off. But Dunn now discovered that Durrell also had a sloped desk. Soon the young Harvard man was disappearing from view altogether, as the two older executives burdened him with more and more chores they did not want.

Finally Dunn went to Crutcher. "Larry, I've got to have some help on this thing. There's too much to do. I need somebody from Corporate Circ, who's got access to a computer. Isn't there some way we can get another body around here?"

Dunn did not know it, but Corporate Circulation contained a person who had been hoping for weeks for such an invitation —a bright young Harvard M.B.A. much like himself. Her name was Sarah Slater Brauns, a wholesome-looking blonde woman of 29, whom Dunn vaguely knew from his pre-M.B.A. days under Meigher.

The daughter of a McGraw-Hill publishing executive, Sarah Slater had dreamed as a child of becoming a writer. But by the time she was graduated from college (Cornell, class of 1973) the notion had begun to lose its allure, and she was turning instead to visions of a career in business. Like Jeff Dunn, she too realized the value of an M.B.A., and in September of 1976 was fortunate enough to be admitted to the Harvard Business School to get one.

At Harvard, Sarah married Robert Brauns, a student one year ahead of her in school, and when the couple moved to New York after graduation their future looked bright—his in investment banking and hers as an executive-level assistant in the circulation department of Time Inc.'s Magazine Group.

Unfortunately, Sarah Brauns had made a mistake that was destined to get her off to a rocky start from her first day on the job. Subsequent to being hired by Time Inc. but several weeks before actually reporting for work, she had granted an interview to a *New York Times* reporter who wanted to write profiles of three "typical" graduates of the Harvard Business School's class of 1978.

The resulting profiles seemed harmless enough, if rather stereotyped. One involved a 25-year-old black who was pictured as having risen far from his early years as the son of a bus driver. The second revealed a young man seeking to break into the executive ranks of business in the midwest. And the third (Brauns) suggested a young woman who had apparently spent a somewhat spoiled youth shuttling through private boarding schools, and now sought through a degree from the Harvard Business School to be taken seriously in a man's world. Among other things, the article quoted Brauns as saying of her degree: "It shows that you do seriously intend to have a career. [At Harvard] they teach you in a year a whole new way of thinking that changes you for the rest of your life."

Whatever effect the article may have had on the careers of the two men, it did Braun's new career no good at all. She was about to begin work in the highly competitive—and almost totally male dominated—world of Time Inc.'s Corporate Circulation Department, and her imminent arrival had now received front-page advance billing in the Business Section of the *New York Times*.

Worse, in Braun's case at least, the article was misleading regarding two matters that are enormously important in corporate hierarchies: salary and title. By sloppy editing, the article incorrectly implied that Brauns would be receiving a starting salary approaching $30,000 yearly—substantially higher than what many veterans in the department were receiving in the spring of 1978. Moreover, the article went on to report, again incorrectly, that she was scheduled to begin work as a "corporate circulation manager"—a rank several steps higher in the hierarchy than was customary for new young executives entering the department.

On the day Sarah Brauns reported for work, she was already widely known and gossiped about within the department. Who was this M.B.A. superwoman who had leapfrogged the normal career path and was being paid more than some of her superiors? From her first day on the job, Brauns found herself the focus of both curiosity and even resentment, and it did not help that among those she seemed to rub the wrong way was the fastest rising executive in the department: Chris Meigher.

Now it was three years later, the autumn of 1981, and nothing much had changed. She needed a lift, a new opportunity, and when she learned of the Durrell/Burgheim task force she approached Meigher, by now head of the department, and asked to be assigned to it.

One day in mid-autumn Meigher called Brauns to his office and told her that he was granting her request, that the opportunity was a good one, and that she would be working for Durrell. Brauns was ecstatic, and spread the news to her friends around the department. This could be the opportunity she had been waiting for.

Swept up in the excitement of the moment, Brauns did not realize—because Meigher did not tell her—that he harbored doubts about the project. Sensitive to the shifting balance of the corporation, Meigher recognized the opportunities that the task force had to offer. But he was also in a sense troubled by it, and would sometimes share his concerns with colleagues.

In fact, at about the time he assigned Brauns to the task force, Meigher wound up in conversation with a Time Inc. executive named Don Elliman, head of Time Distribution Services, and stated: "That project's a loser. Anyone in it is going over a waterfall in a barrel."

Elliman also had views on the project. Unbeknown to the task force, Elliman had more than a year earlier privately approached Meigher's own boss, Sutton, and proposed that a task force be formed to develop precisely the magazine Durrell and Burgheim were now studying. Though Elliman had wanted

Sutton to let him head up the team, a full year had passed and now Sutton had given the job to Durrell.

Fifty miles north of Manhattan, in the unlikely setting of a converted factory warehouse in Norwalk, Connecticut, a pudgy-faced young man named Peter Funt was already busy publishing several editions of a magazine not unlike the one the Time Inc. task force was only now beginning to study. Funt, the 32-year-old son of TV personality Alan Funt (host of "Candid Camera"), had long believed that a market existed for system-specific listings guides for cable viewers. Yet unlike Burgheim, who wanted to include listings information on *all* programming in each system, Funt chose to limit his listings to basic and pay cable, and only some cursory details of broadcast network programming. This allowed one press run of the listings to be useful to cable viewers in many systems.

Not shackled by a large corporate bureaucracy, Funt had avoided task forces and focus groups. In June of 1980 he had formed a partnership with two backers, and four months later had begun market testing a monthly listings guide called *On Cable.*

Normally, publishers market their magazines in a variety of ways, from direct-mail promotional efforts to newsstand sales. But as Funt had realized from the start, the easiest and most efficient way to reach cable viewers was via cable operators, and he had gone into business in effect as a wholesaler to individual cable systems. Cable operators would buy his magazines in bulk quantities, then either resell them at a mark-up to viewers or just give them away as a monthly bonus that came with cable service itself.

By now, Funt had been in business for nearly a year, operating on a limited budget that, to Burgheim at least, made the magazine look amateurish and cheap. "It's a merde of a magazine," said Burgheim of Funt's effort as he thumbed a copy one day in the office, "a publishing rip-off."

Sitting behind the desk in his converted factory office, Funt knew little of Time Inc.'s emerging interest in the listings guide business—or its view of his product. But as he stroked the Siamese cat that lounged by his telephone, Funt had reason to be hopeful for what the future might hold. In the last year his circulation had risen from ten thousand to more than half a million, and every week brought new expressions of interest from cable operators eager to learn more about *On Cable.*

Though he did not yet realize its full dimensions, Funt had also scored an unexpected coup against Time Inc. itself—a coup made possible by the very hugeness of Time's internal bureaucracy. For in March of 1981, while the brass on the thirty-fourth floor were still worrying over how to develop a magazine like the one Funt was now producing, the young Connecticut publisher had managed to slip in and sign an exclusive long-term deal with Time Inc.'s own flagship cable company, Sterling Manhattan Cable—a deal that now blocked the Time cable company from having anything to do with the listings guide that Time Inc.'s own task force was trying to develop.

Dunn and Brauns knew little of Peter Funt or his maneuvers, but they were impressed by the idea of co-marketing a publication in cooperation with cable operators. Other publishers had also adopted the co-marketing approach, and with similarly encouraging results. A company called TVSM was now in the market, along with a firm called Metro Home Theater. Both were producing monthly guides and marketing them to cable companies in the same way that Funt was doing.

The more they studied the matter the more convinced they became: a Funt-like arrangement with cable operators was the best and most efficient way to market a listings guide. Each cable system was, in effect, an individual market all its own, and the cable operator had the name and address of every potential subscriber in it. Whether Time Inc. chose to wholesale the guides directly to the operators or set up some form of joint marketing arrangement, it seemed clear enough that the cable operator ought to be included in the marketing effort somehow.

One day in the office Brauns summarized her thoughts on the matter. "There are two ways to sell a magazine in this market," she said to Dunn. "There's the traditional one that we know all about. But this is not really a traditional market. It's highly fragmented, and besides, there's *TV Guide*. The second one's better—selling directly to the cable operators. We can give them marketing support, and they can then turn around and sell the guides to their own subscribers. That one's the winner, don't you think?"

Dunn agreed, but then thought for a moment and offered a word of caution: "The cable operators are going to have to work together with us on this. We can't be rivals for power. So long as we understand each others' needs, this approach will work. But if we don't cooperate, the odds are against us."

However the magazine was marketed, both knew the most important question was how many people would buy it; in short, what size "market penetration" would the magazine get? To earn a profit on the venture, Time Inc. would have to do business with only the biggest cable companies in the country, and would have to get very high market penetration in each such system.

How high?

Neither one knew, so they started experimenting with various penetration assumptions. At 3 percent penetration in any given cable system (roughly what *Time* Magazine enjoyed in its own markets), losses for a system-specific weekly magazine ran far into the millions annually without letup. But what if one raised the penetration assumption to 8 percent? Still a loss. Try 10 percent. Still in the red. Go for 15 percent. No deal. Try 20 percent.

At 60 percent penetration, the numbers at last showed a profit: $94 million on cumulative annual sales of $403 million over eight years. Suddenly, the concept of system-specificity seemed less frightening. For as it happened, 60 percent market penetration, while admittedly a level unheard of in mass magazine marketing, equaled almost exactly the level of penetration enjoyed by HBO in its own cable markets. Seeing that, the players reasoned thus: if HBO can get such penetration, then why not a listings guide that tells viewers what HBO is showing? The thinking was logical, the mathematics impeccable.

But the conclusion was totally out of touch with reality. For no mass market magazine had ever gotten more than one-fifth the market penetration their project now seemed to require to show a profit.

But Dunn and Brauns knew their assumptions were un-precedented and questionable—and they had reason to believe Time Inc. would test them in the marketplace before going into production with a real magazine. The market testing of new products is, after all, a fundamental prerequisite of consumer product marketing itself, as they both had been taught at the Harvard Business School.

FOUR

B-School Training Takes Over

A S BUSINESSMEN OFTEN STRESS, it is a truism of corporate life that the higher one moves up the executive ladder, the greater grow the time pressures and the briefer become the opportunities to analyze a problem or weigh a decision. Yet some problems cannot be compacted to the neat dimensions of an executive memo no matter how hard one tries.

That was the task force's dilemma as November of 1981 became December and the players were told by Sutton to be ready for a major corporate-level briefing on their work sometime soon. As Sutton explained it, the briefing would include not just President Munro, a sobering enough prospect, but more than two dozen of his top aides and corporate colleagues, from Chairman of the Board Ralph Davidson, to Executive Vice President Clifford Grum, to the company's five group vice presidents, to more than a dozen of their senior lieutenants. The briefing would even include Editor in Chief Grunwald and his deputy, Ralph Graves.

This was Time Inc.'s so-called "COO" Group (Corporate

Operating Officers), the highest ranked, most powerful individuals in the corporation, and the thought of appearing before them gave pause to everyone. It seemed incredible that everything had gone so far, so fast. Only three months ago there had been no real task force at all, just transcripts of a summer's worth of focus group sessions and some talk from Burgheim about system-specific weekly publication concepts. Then Dunn and Brauns had come aboard and begun developing the idea of co-marketing with cable operators, and the next thing anyone knew, the team was being brought before Time Inc.'s COO Group for a presentation of its work.

Burgheim did not like the marketing plan. Instead of keeping the cable operators at bay, the plan seemed to get them even more involved in the magazine. "They're bullies," he would explain. "The next thing you know, they'll be wanting to read page proofs."

Whether they were from Time Inc.'s own ATC or other cable companies made no difference; as far as Burgheim was concerned cable operators all seemed to want the same thing: any listings guide going to *their* subscribers was going to contain the information *they* wanted, not what the editor wanted.

The attitude disturbed Burgheim greatly, for it seemed to place the interests of readers last, not first, inverting the publishing equation. This was supposed to be a Time Inc. consumer magazine, not a promotional guide for the cable industry, and he was already coming to regard it with an almost proprietary interest. Throughout the autumn he had worked hard to design a graphically pleasing, easy-to-read magazine, and the resulting dummy prototype showed real promise. A damn fine little magazine, he said to himself, people will like it.

The dummy consisted of two parts, 64 pages of yellow-tinted newsstock that would form the system-specific listings for individual cable companies and, wrapped around it, 24 pages of four-color feature articles that would appear in every edition. Since no one on the task force knew for certain whether the COO Group preferred a weekly or a monthly publication,

Burgheim had prepared versions of both, yet his heart was with the weekly. It was well laid out, easy to read, and because it was a weekly, it would provide readers with up-to-date listings information that would be unavailable if the magazine were to be published on a monthly cycle.

Dunn and Brauns also liked the weekly frequency. "A monthly won't make any money," said Dunn at one point. "Sarah and I did the numbers on it six ways to Sunday, and the only way we're going to make a profit on this thing is with a weekly."

Now the group needed to find an organizing concept for the presentation, something the busy executives of the COO Group could grasp and understand—and they needed to find it fast. What was the point of talking about "system-specific" listings guides, or "innovative marketing concepts" if no one in the audience understood the industry?

Yet as they sifted their numbers and research, the players kept returning to a single, hard fact: this was not a homogeneous industry or market they had been examining, but a broad range of different publishing ventures: big guides, little guides, ones produced and distributed by independent publishers, by newspapers, by cable companies. The market seemed as baffling and dense as the cable business itself.

Week after week the players read and reread their research looking for an organizing concept. Brauns began to grow worried, as did Dunn, Durrell, and even Labich. Time was running out, and no one seemed able to agree on how to explain what they had been doing. It was all so confusing, so vague.

Periodically the group would be summoned to Sutton's office to brief him on their progress, and this only added to the pressure. There was so much ground to cover: the technology, the marketing, the questions of editorial control. Work on the project seemed hardly to have begun and already it was evolving into something of enormous complexity. Sutton would listen to the group's discussions of these matters, but from time to time one got the sense that his attention was wandering; the group needed crisp analyses, a cogent and to-the-point presentation of what this magazine would be all about.

One day in Sutton's office the group turned to plans for a market test. With the help of a cable executive on temporary loan from Video Group, they had already begun selecting potential sites for a test, and making calculations of the potential costs involved. The group vice president listened as his subordinates explained their reasoning, but after they had finished he frowned:

"What's the point of a market test?" Sutton asked, looking around the room. "What's the point of spending millions for a market test if *TV Guide* can discount its copies and foul up our results? If I were *TV Guide*, I'd hire some guy to sabotage everything we did, then where would we be!"

Dunn and Brauns exchanged glances. Both had assumed from the start that their magazine idea would be subjected to a thorough test before gearing up for full production; so had Durrell. If the idea proved unworkable, the company had better find out beforehand.

Traditionally, magazine publishers do not perform "live tests" of new magazine ideas, since doing so can cost almost 50 percent as much as actual production. Instead, publishers normally "dry test" their ideas by various forms of direct-mail advertising that describes the magazine and invites people to become charter subscribers.

Families by the millions receive such appeals in the mail from publishers every week, for they are an economical and accurate means of sampling market demand and normally cost no more than a few hundred thousand dollars. But the co-marketing approach being developed by Dunn and Brauns required the new publication, in effect, to be sold *first* to cable operators, and by them in turn to subscribers. The arrangement made a "dry test" meaningless since much of the marketing effort would depend not on the appeal of the magazine to readers, but on the cooperation of the cable operator middlemen.

The task force members saw a full-scale "wet test" as cru-

cial. It was not enough to know that readers wanted the magazine; for the concept to work cable operators also had to be
willing and able to sell it. This, it was already clear, was no
ordinary magazine but an "information product" that needed
to be market tested in the same rigorous manner required of
any new consumer product: by actually making it, marketing it
on a limited scale for an extended period, and seeing if anyone
bought it, before going into mass production.

Now the group was being told by Sutton that he personally
saw little point in a market test at all. Dunn was baffled. Sutton
apparently either did not understand the risks involved, or
wanted to press ahead in spite of them. Why then had he stood
at Munro's side four months earlier and declared before the
whole of Magazine Group that the publication *would* be market tested? Had there been a change of plans?

That afternoon Durrell and his two young assistants talked
about how they would handle the situation.

"We've got to get on the record as calling for a test," said
Dunn. "We've got to make it clear to the COO Group that a wet
test is essential."

"I know," said Brauns. "I agree with you. We've got to call
for a market test somehow." Durrell agreed; a market test was
vital.

The project's editorial head, Burgheim, had not become
involved in the market-test questions that had begun to concern Dunn and Brauns. Instead, he remained immersed in his
own responsibilities, examining layouts, moving around pictures on artists' grid sheets. Sometimes he would read industry
trade publications about the cable television industry, or study
Neilsen viewer ratings of programs on the broadcast networks,
or just put his feet on the desk and stare out the window,
thinking up possible feature stories for the national wrap.

Occasionally Dunn or Brauns would wander past and wonder why Burgheim seemed to have so little to do while they
were so busy, but neither said anything and soon were en-

veloped again in their own more urgent concerns involving the upcoming presentation.

Though headquarters for the task force remained the fortieth floor of the Time & Life Building, the group had begun to sequester itself from time to time in the *People* Magazine suite in the Dorset Hotel, four blocks north at Avenue of the Americas and Fifty-fourth Street, where there was freedom from the ringing phones and distractions of the Time & Life Building.

There were five business-side players by now: Durrell the publisher, Labich the production man, Dunn the financial expert, Brauns the circulation expert, and a new arrival: a young M.B.A. from New York University named Michael Dukemejian.

One day in late December Durrell went from office to office rounding up his staff. "Jeffrey," he said, ". . . Sarah . . . Michael . . . let's go over to the hotel and get some work done."

The room was much as they had left it. Computer printouts sat piled on tables, and here and there could be seen the doodlings and notes of earlier brainstorming sessions.

From the beginning Durrell had functioned as a father figure to the young M.B.A.s, but as time passed, Dunn's quick intelligence and take-charge nature had begun to single him out as the group's dominant personality. Now, as the group sat ringed around a rectangular table in the suite's dining room, scratch pads in front of them, Dunn felt more than ever the frustration of recent weeks.

"Look," he said at last, "we've got to organize this stuff somehow. Why don't we play this game we used to play at the B-School—*If You Could Tell Them Just One Thing?*"

As Dunn explained it, the game was designed to reduce complex problems to their essentials, to find the conceptual core of an issue by addressing the "one thing" from which all other "things" were derived.

If you could tell them just one thing. . . .

Dunn went first. If you could tell them just one thing about how to finance a cable magazine, what would it be?

Then it was Labich's turn. If you could tell them just one

thing about how to produce a cable magazine, what would it be?

Over to Brauns. If you could tell them just one thing about how to market a cable guide, what would it be?

But Brauns did not answer, and for a moment the players fell silent. Even to this day, no one is quite sure who the vision came to first, or even the source of its inspiration. But somehow, perched on the edge of exhaustion, their minds quivering with anger at the confusion about them, the players got a glimpse of . . . The Big Picture.

In the same way that Picasso took handlebars and a bicycle seat and made a bull's head that now hangs in the Louvre, one of the group—Brauns or Dunn or Dukemejian or Durrell or Labich, no one quite remembers who—reached for a pencil, drew two lines on a sheet of scratch pad paper, and set in motion a deal worth $100 million. First, a vertical line, then bisecting it a horizontal line, and out of months of confusion came insight and clarity—a scheme for representing the market itself. It looked like this:

To the right of the vertical line was the "free market," in which magazines reached the reader by traditional means, such as newsstand sales and checkout counter racks. To the left was the market for magazines co-marketed with cable operators. Above the horizontal line were the weeklies, below were the monthlies.

It was so simple, so neat. Best of all, it seemed to clear up so much. Said Dunn later; "Everyone looked at that thing and we all had the same reaction. It was as if B-School training just took over, and we started filling in the blanks."

In Quadrant 1, the free-market weeklies, one would put *TV Guide* and the Sunday newspapers. To go up against that kind of competition would cost millions. Foolhardy even to try. Draw a big X through Quadrant 1 and move on.

Quadrant 2 was where the free-market monthlies would go. Not many of them around anyway—and for good reason. Who wanted a once-a-month TV magazine in the first place? The way the stations shuffled their program lineups, half the listings would be out of date by the time the publication reached the reader. Call Quadrant 2 the Bermuda Triangle and steer clear of it.

In Quadrant 3, the co-marketed monthlies, one would find Burgheim's *"merde"* of a magazine, *On Cable,* and its upstart look-alikes. Sure, this little sketch explained everything.

Then of course at long last one came to Quadrant 4, the co-marketed weeklies—with no competitors in there at all. A whole empty quadrant for the taking.

A day or so later the group showed the grid to Sutton. At first, he appeared puzzled. But as Dunn explained the meaning of each quadrant, a smile broke across the group vice president's face, as if he were beginning to share in the revelation that had earlier been visited upon the players—as if, in a way, he had been presented with the ultimate executive memo: a document with no words at all, just two crossed lines on a piece of paper.

Several weeks later, on January 29, 1982, these two crossed lines formed the centerpiece of a morning-long presentation to the COO Group, each member of which received in preparation for the meeting an "executive briefing kit." The kit contained, among other relevant documents, two different "dummy" samples—one a weekly, the other a monthly, and both bearing the make-do title of *TV-Cable* Magazine, an invention that everyone agreed would have to suffice until something better came along.

It was easily the most auspicious day of their professional

lives, and the players had worked hard to ensure that no detail was overlooked, even down to the seating arrangements for the gathering, which took place in the same eleventh floor conference room in which *Time* Magazine four times each year played host to its much-quoted "Board of Economists." Gone now was the long felt-covered table around which the economists would sit, and in its place were neatly aligned rows of chairs and tables facing a lecture stage. It was from there that the task force members rose one after another to speak, creating in the process a tutorial-type environment that left the conference's high-powered audience both impressed and even a bit intimidated.

As host of the meeting, Sutton welcomed the guests, then turned the proceedings over to Durrell, who presented an overview of the group's work. But the center of attraction were the two young Harvard M.B.A.s, Dunn and Brauns, who presented the group's financial and marketing findings. Underscoring the seemingly indivisible nature of their joint effort, the two rose as one and walked to flanking podia at either end of the stage, where they turned and faced the audience. From Video had come Group Vice President Levin and two of his top aides, James Heyworth and Tony Cox. From Denver came ATC Vice President for Marketing Gary Bryson. Nearby sat Munro, and not far away, Sutton. Also in the audience were several inside directors on the board, including Executive Vice President Grum, Editor in Chief Grunwald, his top assistant, Editorial Director Graves, and Corporate Secretary Charles Bear.

It was as dazzling a gathering of corporate brass as the eleventh floor conference room had seen in some time. Yet as their presentation progressed, and a steady succession of slides and charts flashed past on the screen behind them, it soon became clear that it was the two young M.B.A.s, and not the executives, who were in control.

Dunn spoke first. Flashing a confident smile he began: "Dick Durrell has given you a brief overview of the cable industry and its characteristics. Now Sarah and I would like to explain to you how the industry's publishing business is structured, who the key players are, and what the future is likely to hold for them." He took a breath and continued. "As we studied the cable industry and attempted to develop a successful publishing formula for Time Inc., we realized over time that the business of providing television listings to consumers is evolving along two major lines. The first of these is an editorial issue—the amount of listings information the publication contains, and the second concerns marketing—the specificity with which the publication defines its audience."

In a projection booth against the far wall an assistant squeezed a remote control unit and a screen behind Dunn lighted up. It displayed the four-quadrant diagram of the market. Dunn continued.

"Speaking broadly, the upper half of this matrix represents weekly publications that have higher risks and higher rewards, than those on the lower half, which are monthlies."

He signaled the projection booth and a second slide slotted into place. It showed the same quadrant matrix, this time neatly labeled "High Risk/High Reward" above the horizontal axis, and "Low Risk/Low Reward" below it.

"What we would now like to do," said Dunn, "is take you on a brief, though we hope complete, guided tour of each of these business segments, using it as a backdrop against which we will examine Time Inc.'s opportunities."

There was a settling in the chairs, a slight shifting for more comfortable positions, and an almost palpable sense among the audience that it was in capable hands. These kids had done their homework.

Indeed they had. With an aura of thorough-going preparation that left even the Video Group executives a bit awed, the two moved with effortless logic through an industry that eight weeks earlier no one in the room could even define. From Quadrant 1 ("a business segment most familiar to you as the home of *TV Guide*) to Quadrant 2 ("we have affectionately named it 'The Bermuda Triangle' ") to Quadrant 3 ("moving in

here is like crossing the Continental Divide") to Quadrant 4
("entering this market is akin to opening up China"), there was
little doubt that the two knew what they were talking about.

Nor were they above some carefully crafted stage business
to heighten the interest level, keep the audience awake and
attentive. First Dunn would speak, one to three minutes or so,
no more, then Brauns would take her cue. Dunn would address
the market as presently construed, Brauns would speak of its
future potential; Dunn would set forth the major competitors,
Brauns would sketch out the economic environments in which
they competed. Back and forth, back and forth, the eleventh
floor conference room had never seen anything like it before.
It was theater—business world theater—and the audience ate
it up.

Though Brauns and Dunn did not know it, the executives
before them were more than willing to be convinced of the
project's viability. To Levin and his colleagues of Video Group,
here was a product that promised salvation from the looming
problems of churn and disconnects. To their counterparts in
Magazine Group, here was a coherent rationale for a new
weekly magazine—a concept that had eluded the corporation
since the creation of *People* eight years earlier. To Munro, here
was a high-tech publishing concept that brought together
magazines and video in an important new undertaking that
would impress Wall Street and the investment community.

Because they were unaware of these dovetailing agendas,
the two young M.B.A.s did not realize that what Dunn was now
about to say would be ignored. Though Dunn and Brauns had
already been told by Sutton that he could see little point to a
market test, the two had labored under Durrell's direction to
prepare a test-market proposal to include in their presentation
anyway. They were determined to have their feelings displayed
on the record, and Durrell had encouraged them to do so.

The two had edited and re-edited the passage many times.
They wanted it to be firm, forceful, and above all unambiguous.
If the publication were to be brought to market without a mar-

ket test, they wanted the record to show that it was the COO Group's responsibility, not theirs. Now they had come to the nub of the matter, and Dunn began his plea:

"Gentlemen, I am now going to give you the publishing world's equivalent to the surgeon general's warning. Caution! The following numbers may be hazardous to your financial health. These profit-and-loss projections are based on some assumptions for which there are no precedents in this building, and for some, no precedents anywhere. It is important to be honest with you up front; many of these numbers are our reasonable guesses for new businesses never tried before.

"To make a decision to launch this publication on a large scale, you need to gauge the accuracy of our assumptions, from market penetration to the feasibility of the production technology, to advertising sales levels. In short, we are going to have to produce this publication in a limited number of test markets, for a not inconsiderable length of time. It's not unlike General Motors taking a prototype for a drive around a test track. We need to find out if it works."

Dunn began to spell out how to conduct the test—from the four specific cities that he and Brauns had identified as being typical of the sorts of cable markets in which the group wanted to do business (Orlando, Albany, Seattle, and Tulsa), to the amount of time the test would take (six months), to how much of a budget to provide ($9 million), to which areas of uncertainty to examine. These included such concerns as whether cable operators would cooperate in marketing the magazine, whether consumers wanted such a publication in the first place, whether 60 percent of the cable viewers in a market could be counted on to buy it, and whether the production technology proposed could actually handle the huge volumes of data required.

It was, in sum, a full listing of every pitfall and unknown in the project, and just before he sat down Dunn offered "one parting thought." Summoning up the image of the New Frontier, he scanned the corporate chieftains before him and said:

"Exactly twenty years ago this month, John Kennedy told a joint session of Congress that they were not 'rivals for power but partners for progress.' It is an apt statement to describe the future relationship between the magazine and cable industries.

"The publication we envision requires both of these groups to work toward a common goal. So long as each can understand the other's needs and work together, there is reason to believe that a new, successful, all-inclusive listings source can be launched.

"But if we do not cooperate with each other, for whatever the reasons, the odds are long against what we have called 'a new magazine for a new medium.' "

After Dunn came Labich. All autumn he and Burgheim had quarreled over technology, as Burgheim kept insisting that Labich's system for customizing TV Data's plain-vanilla listings was too complicated for any editor to master, and Labich kept replying that it was the soul of simplicity. Further arguments had erupted over whether Labich would ever be able to keep track of the thousands of individual pages of press film that would flood into printing plants each week for the individual listings pages. Labich said it would be easy, Burgheim said it would be impossible.

Now Labich chose, in effect, to plant his flag before the COO Group, and moving to the lectern, he placed a script before him and began to read: "In essence, our system will provide pages that are untouched by human hands. During the task-force study, we have developed a method to produce a national magazine that would require as many as 250 separate editions for a single issue. Although our current specifications are for fewer editions, the new technology will allow us to handle 250 editions in 16 hours." Sitting in the audience, Burgheim gritted his teeth, for he doubted Labich's computers could process 250 editions in 16 *days*.

Last to speak was the editor himself. But by now the audience was so mesmerized by the business side's "numbers" that they hardly seemed interested in the editorial product at all.

"Well," said Burgheim, clearing his throat, "it looks like we've reached the last act of the only show this season seemingly longer and potentially more costly than *Nicholas Nickleby.*"

A twitter rippled through the audience, but before many minutes had passed, amusement had given way to impatience, as people began shifting in their seats and glancing at watches. They had heard what they had come to hear, and now they wanted the meeting to be over.

At 12:30 P.M. Burgheim concluded, and Sutton rose to thank Durrell for the presentation as well as to invite the group to adjourn to one of the company's private, upstairs dining salons for luncheon. Yet scarcely had he finished than Munro, his face beaming, pronounced his own judgment on the morning-long proceedings, saying: "Now that was one of the finest presentations I've ever had the privilege of attending in this company!" Grunwald was more circumspect. Standing nearby, he offered a noncommittal grunt and walked out the door.

FIVE

The Right Stuff

L ATE THAT AFTERNOON Sutton summoned his task
force to his office to inform them of the COO
Group's decision. Sutton seemed to enjoy possessing information that others did not have,
and he would sometimes make guessing games out of such
situations, inviting subordinates to speculate on the actions of
their superiors.

When the group arrived they found Durrell already in the
room. Sutton gestured to various chairs, and once the new arrivals were seated, the group vice president spoke:

"Well, what do you think? What do you think was decided?"

There was a moment's pause as the subordinates pondered
the possibilities. Brauns spoke first: "That they're not going to
do it? That they didn't like the presentation?"

Sutton smiled and shook his head no, then looked to Dunn.

"I know," said Dunn. "They decided to test it. They're
going to go with a test."

"Nope," said Sutton, relishing the situation. "We're not

going to test it. Clifford wants us to go back and do more numbers." He was referring to his own boss, Clifford Grum.

For several moments no one said anything, as the implications of Sutton's disclosure sank in. It had been only a couple of hours since the task force had spelled out the dangers of the project to the COO Group and urged a six-month market test. Now, here was Sutton telling them that his own direct superior, Grum, the second-ranked executive in the corporation, apparently wanted to let numbers and financial modeling do the work of a market test.

The speed with which the decision had been reached seemed astonishing. It had taken the task force four months, from September to January, to analyze the market and develop a set of proposals—nearly two weeks of which had been devoted to preparing a four-city market test plan. But it had taken the COO Group less than a single afternoon to decide that it knew better. Did Time's brass really understand what it was getting into?

One executive sensed trouble ahead. Two thousand miles away, in the Denver suburb of Englewood, Colorado, the senior marketing official of Time Inc.'s cable system subsidiary, ATC, sat at his desk preparing a confidential memorandum for his Video Group superiors. The executive, a former Bell & Howell official named Gary Bryson, had recently been appointed ATC's vice president for marketing, and had attended the Friday presentation in New York as a stand-in for his boss.

Like Dunn and Brauns, Bryson also thought a market test was needed, and he had left the meeting believing the COO Group would approve one as a matter of course. But over the weekend, as he mulled the presentation, Bryson wondered whether cable operators would prove all that enthusiastic about a publication of the sort Time Inc. seemed interested in producing. The rhythm of the cable industry operated on a monthly cycle, from the scheduling of pay channel movies to the billing of customers. Cable operators might object to a weekly because

it would automatically cost more than a monthly, siphoning off
revenues that viewers might otherwise spend on pay channels
for which the cable operators received hefty commissions.

The more Bryson considered the matter the more basic the
issue seemed to get: did cable viewers really need—and did
cable operators really *want*— a high-cost high-quality weekly
listings guide, or might a lower quality monthly publication be
a better bet?

Bryson appreciated the sensitivity of sending confidential
memos to corporate higher-ups in a company that he had only
recently joined, so he reread his words several times, making
sure that they said precisely what he intended—no more and
no less—that a weekly publishing frequency might be wrong for
the industry; that to find out, the task force's proposed publication really did need to be test marketed; that as "good corporate
citizens" ATC would stand ready to help with the test.

Satisfied at last that his memo communicated what he
wished, Bryson dispatched it to his boss, ATC president Joseph
Collins, with confidential drop-copies to both Collins's boss,
ATC chairman Trygve Myrhen, and even *Myhren's* boss, Video
Group Vice President Levin. If Time Inc. were going to develop a system-specific weekly listings guide, Bryson wanted
the record to show that he, as the Time Inc. marketing executive most closely in touch with actual cable TV viewers, had
warned his superiors that it might not be such a good idea.

Bryson was not the only Time Inc. executive to leave the
Friday COO Group meeting harboring doubts. In contrast to
the ATC marketing official, who had been with the organization
only a few months, Editorial Director Ralph Graves, 58, had
been a Time Inc. employee his entire adult life. A man of polished mannerisms and grace, Graves was very much at home in
the world of Time's brass. Yet whereas most of his colleagues
had responded with overwhelming approval of the task force's
presentation, Graves, like Bryson, was skeptical. He too wondered whether the publishing plan that had been outlined at

the meeting made much sense. Would cable operators help market such a magazine? Could it be economically produced with existing technology? The whole approach seemed fraught with risks and unknowns, and he wondered whether publishing such a magazine might turn out to be little more than Russian roulette.

Unlike Bryson, whose brief tenure and middle-ranked position in the organization almost automatically reduced the importance of his counsel among his COO Group superiors, the opinions of Graves carried weight. Highly regarded among his colleagues as a man of reasoned and careful judgments, Graves was, along with Grunwald, one of only two editors in the company to occupy seats on Time Inc.'s board of directors. In that sense he stood very high in the company's hierarchy, outranking Sutton, Levin, Nicholas, and nearly all other COO Group members—most of whom did not have seats on the board.

There was another thing one sensed about Graves and his views: they came not just from the mind but from the heart. Alone among the corporate brass, Graves had experienced in a direct and painful way what it meant to preside over a major national failure. Whereas the careers of both Grunwald and Munro had benefited from being in the right place at the right time—from Grunwald's rise through *Time* Magazine to Munro's lucky association with Video Group—Graves had been less fortunate: he had made his mark at a doomed magazine, *Life*, which had been shut down in 1972 with Graves as its managing editor, after years of deepening losses.

Graves had little to do with *Life*'s woes, which were largely the result of the magazine's inability to compete for advertising dollars with television. But it had been his fate to preside over the failure anyway, experiencing first-hand the trauma of having to let go his entire staff. Graves had worked hard to find his people positions elsewhere within Time Inc. and by and large had succeeded. But the anguish of the ordeal had stayed with him, for he knew as did none of his colleagues the toll that failure could exact.

Now here was his company preparing to venture into a
strange new publishing project that had danger written all over
it. During the week following the meeting Graves pondered
the matter. Should he keep his opinions to himself or should he
lodge them on the record? As a member of Time Inc.'s board,
what was the proper thing to do? At last Graves decided he
would write Sutton a memo spelling out his fears: the project
as outlined had too many risks and pitfalls. He had little doubt
that a memo of that sort, coming as it would from a member of
the company's board, would have an effect, and at the beginning of the following week he had it delivered to the group vice
president.

The memos from Bryson and Graves may or may not have
given pause to either Levin or Sutton. But their contents would
unquestionably have been helpful to the task force. Yet neither
of the two group vice presidents chose to enlighten the task
force that such documents existed. Left in the dark, the task
force simply pushed ahead with its financial modeling for Sutton and Grum—oblivious to the accumulating record of doubt
and dissent.

In the weeks that followed, the numbers poured out, one
projection after another, until there were dozens of them—
huge printouts on fan-fold computer paper that stretched
across desks and onto the floor. Brauns prepared the circulation
and marketing numbers, winnowing down the nation's more
than 4,000 cable companies to the 100 or so largest ones that
seemed promising sales prospects. Dukemejian put together
"production financials," developing manufacturing costs at various numbers of editions per week. Dunn assembled the compo-
nents into overall profit-and-loss projections.

Traditionally in Magazine Group, profit and loss forecasts
were limited to five-year time frames. But as the group already
knew, at the fifth year they were still losing money. To see how
long it would take to get back their investment, they needed
not a five-year plan, but a *ten*-year plan—a computer model so

elaborate that the task force eventually had to hire an outside consultant to devise one, since no one in Time Inc. could handle its complexities.

Yet once they got it working, the ten-year forecasting model showed something quite amazing: assuming one could make the required penetration levels, and assuming renewals were satisfactory, and assuming cable operators kept signing on to distribute the magazine, then all one had to do was to pour $100 million into the product over a five-year time frame, and in the sixth year the money started flowing back in broad rivers of profit.

To Dunn, the notion suggested a publishing-world version of *The Right Stuff*. Time Inc. needed the fortitude to keep pumping tens of millions of dollars a year into the project to get the whole thing up to speed. So what if everything started to shake and tremble like one of those early test jets approaching mach I? The company had to hang tough, keep leaning on the throttle until the project went crashing through the $100 million barrier into the smooth sailing beyond.

If there was something disquieting about all this, there was also something exhilarating. Here they were—Dunn, Brauns, and now Dukemejian—still in their twenties and barely out of business school, yet suddenly they were developing multi-million dollar financial business strategies for the highest officials of the industry's leading magazine and cable television conglomerate.

Of the three, Dukemejian felt the most unsure of himself on this super-fast track, and perhaps for that reason tended to over compensate by trying to involve himself in one task after another. A rugged- featured young man with dark eyes and black curly hair, Dukemejian had seen in the Durrell/Burgheim task force the same opportunity spotted by Dunn and Brauns. For the better part of a year, he had worked as a low-level staff assistant in Labich's old department, CM&D, while attending New York University's M.B.A. program part-time in the evenings and hoping for a way to escape the drudgery of

Pine Street's blue-collar world. He had already told Labich that he was eager for a challenging opportunity beyond Pine Street, and when the CM&D executive called him to his office before Christmas and invited him to join the task force as his assistant, Dukemejian jumped at the chance.

Since then, Dukemejian had been yearning to slip free of Labich and involve himself in what he took to be the more glamorous activities of his two Harvard M.B.A. colleagues, Dunn and Brauns. They were where the action was, and seemed always to be heading to thirty-fourth floor meetings with Sutton and other top executives while all he got to do was trail along behind Labich, making telephone calls to printers and computer vendors.

But try as he might, Dukemejian simply could not seem to get himself accepted as an equal to Dunn and Brauns or be brought into the inner world of their decisions and debates. Whenever he had an idea or proposal, it seemed that Jeff and Sarah had already thought of it. Sometimes they would dismiss his ideas out of hand, as if to say they did not have time to be bothered with such things—that they had more important problems to concern themselves with.

Nothing he tried seemed to work. He tried sprinkling his conversation with phrases from his M.B.A. classes—words like "targeted marketing" and "unit volume output"—but Dunn and Brauns seemed to understand the concepts better than he did. He tried dressing like an executive, with trim-fitting suits and Windsor-knotted ties, but somehow the effect came off overdone and rigid.

After work, Dukemejian would go home to his Greenwich Village apartment, get out his rowing machine, and sweat out his frustrations on the living-room floor. He wondered what it would take to break through, to be recognized as a real executive, and stop being dismissed as a Pine Street shopworker in a suit and tie. Being treated that way by Dunn was bad enough, but being made to feel small by Brauns, a woman scarcely older than he was, was even worse.

With Durrell eager to return to *People* Magazine, Sutton had been casting about for a replacement—someone he could count on to manage and push forward the project without a lot of second-guessing and doubts—and at last he settled on a choice: Daniel Zucchi, a hard-charging and earthy advertising sales director for *Money* Magazine.

Zucchi seemed just the man. A person of almost radioactive drive and determination, he conveyed a no-nonsense attitude in his every move, from his rock-solid frame, to his black wavy hair, to his habit of punctuating his remarks by thrusting his shoulders forward and barking, "Get it?" to drive home a point. On Madison Avenue, he had been said to bear down so hard in sales presentations as virtually to scare clients into placing ads in *Money* Magazine.

Zucchi entered in a blur of energy that stunned everyone, not least of all Burgheim. Cautious, quiet, and an extraordinarily attentive listener in meetings with cable operators and Video Group executives, Burgheim was far ahead of Zucchi in his grasp of the cable industry. Yet when Zucchi would attempt to sum up Burgheim's remarks by slapping his hands together and snapping, "Okay, so what's the deal?", the editor would fall silent, as if unsure whether Zucchi would even listen if he responded.

Every meeting of the two men seemed to begin the same way. Zucchi would surge in, shirtsleeves rolled to the elbow, with Labich wheezing along behind. "Well, this is it," Zucchi would boom. "The pressure's on now. We gotta make some decisions, no more fartin' around, gotta get this fucker out the door, know what I mean?" Then he would jut his face forward and grin hugely at everyone.

There would be a moment's pause, followed by a rustling of papers and tugging of neckties, after which would come the inevitable question:

"Where's Dick?"

"He's on the phone," someone would answer. "He'll be here in a minute."

More time would pass, and just when no one could stand it any longer, in would slip Burgheim. He would be wearing an Oxford button-down shirt a size-and-a-half too big, with cuffs that hung to his knuckles, and in his hand he would clutch a Masonite clipboard of the sort that every Time Inc. writer seemed to acquire the day he turned editor. All in all, he would look more like a bureaucrat from the Motor Vehicle Department than a middle-aged editorial executive of Time Inc., and before too long the conversation would be swirling over, under, around, and right past him—or seemed to.

No sooner did Zucchi arrive than the staff began to swell. Zucchi brought his secretary; soon a computer consultant arrived. Before long the project's offices could not contain everybody.

"We gotta do something," said Zucchi as he surveyed the bodies. "Gotta get some more room!"

Zucchi told Dunn to speak to Crutcher, his old boss in Magazine Development. Among his duties, Crutcher was responsible for allocating magazine office space within the building, and Zucchi wanted Dunn to have Crutcher get them larger quarters. But neither Zucchi nor Dunn knew that Crutcher apparently still nursed resentments at the manner in which Dunn had slipped free of him six months earlier, and when his former subordinate now came to him with Zucchi's request Crutcher dragged his feet.

So Zucchi turned in frustration to Labich, who offered an idea: he would speak to *his* former boss, a man named McCluskey, the official in charge of all CM&D. Maybe McCluskey could think of a way to get them more space.

The intervention of McCluskey apparently had an effect, because not long afterward Sutton telephoned Crutcher to ask what the holdup was with space for the project. Later that day a Crutcher assistant phoned Dunn to ask that Zucchi provide some information on the project for Crutcher's approval. Dunn was surprised because, although Crutcher still carried the title of vice president for magazine development, he did not possess direct responsibility for the project, but was at best a sidelines kibitzer. Was Crutcher trying to pull rank on Zucchi?

"Sorry," said Dunn, "but Kelso approves Dan's decisions." Hanging up the telephone, the young M.B.A. wondered what would happen next.

Shortly before six o'clock he found out. Slipping on his overcoat, Dunn picked up his briefcase and headed toward the elevator bank, at which moment Crutcher unexpectedly emerged from a doorway, spotted Dunn, and began bellowing in the hallway: "Everyone is going behind my back! You've got to crawl before you can walk! This magazine isn't born yet! I hope the fucking thing dies!"

Three weeks later, Zucchi had more space, but Crutcher had what looked to Dunn at least to be the last laugh. The task force's new offices turned out to be not in the Time & Life Building at all, but across the street in a vacant seventh-floor suite of offices in the Amax Building, until recently the corporate headquarters of a mining concern that had fallen on hard times and moved to the suburbs.

Zucchi could care less where Crutcher put the project, but Burgheim was livid. In contrast to the growing numbers of business-side players, Burgheim had a staff of just one person, an all-around helper named Ed Adler. In recent weeks Burgheim had been drawing up lists of edit-side people he might begin recruiting for the project from elsewhere within the organization. But moving the task force out of the building and across the street made the project look like a kind of corporate urchin. Who would want to sign aboard now?

Dark thoughts began to enter Burgheim's mind. For months he had been hearing scuttlebutt that Sutton planned to use the cable magazine for some mysterious "union-busting" purpose, and now he began to wonder whether the move to Amax might be the opening gambit. Would Sutton next try to move the project to low-rent quarters out of New York altogether, then force him to staff the magazine with underpaid, non-union employees?

In the weeks that followed, Burgheim began to talk of somehow getting back into what a staff secretary took to calling "the Big House." He brought it up with Zucchi, with Dunn, once or twice even with Grunwald and Graves. Yet no one seemed to pay him any mind, and like mold in a root cellar, distrust and suspicion began to grow silently within him, unnoticed by his colleagues.

With Zucchi and Burgheim barely able to communicate with each other, let alone cooperate on matters of controversy or importance, it was already possible to catch glimmerings of the confusion that would soon spread throughout Amax-7. There was, for example, the case of the *TV Guide* microfilm.

It all began, it seemed, around the time of the COO Group presentation, when someone on the business side (no one could remember who) was seized with the notion that nothing could go forward until the task force had its own in-house archive of past *TV Guide* issues. Exactly what would be done with the treasure remained unclear, but someone in Marketing later recalled talk of using it to study how *TV Guide* structured its regional, demographic advertising editions. But how to get one's hands on such an archive without tipping off *TV Guide* in the process? That was the question.

Into the breach went Burgheim's helper, Ed Adler. Did he have someone in his family who might telephone *TV Guide* and sort of innocently order up copies of all their back issues? This way, no one would know that Time Inc. was behind it. The issues could be shipped to Adler's apartment, say, then put in his car and brought to the building.

Adler swallowed hard at the proposal, then allowed that his brother might oblige. Six weeks later, 225 microfilm rolls of back *TV Guide* issues arrived by truck from Radnor, Pennsylvania, along with an invoice for $5,871.00, which Adler paid and promptly vouchered on his expense account. But by that time no one could remember why the copies had been ordered in the first place, so Adler just stacked them in a corner of his office where they began to gather dust.

The hiring of the project's next employee, a middle-aged copy-processing expert named Anne Davis, seemed the result of similar confusion. With a background in electronic typesetting and pagination, Davis had risen through *Time* Magazine's copy-processing department to become its deputy director of operations, only to find herself suddenly detached by corporate higher-ups in early April and assigned to Amax-7 as what appeared to be a *de facto* computer adviser to Burgheim.

Davis felt baffled by the assignment, for no sooner did she arrive than she found that Burgheim in the interim had hired an aloof, middle-aged Hungarian named Gedeon Demargitay, who thought that *he* was the project's computer expert. So competitive and suspicious did Demargitay grow of Davis that as time passed he took to writing memos to himself *in Hungarian* in the project's computers—ultimately even learning how to encrypt his secret store of knowledge so that not even another Hungarian could read it, let alone Davis.

Eventually, observing Demargitay became a diversionary pastime among the staff. Late one evening, two junior members watched in fascination as Demargitay emerged from his office, glanced at his watch, and announced in a gutteral, Hungarian accent to no one in particular: "Eeet ees ghetting late! I must deeparrt by meed-night!" From that moment onward, Demargitay was known as "the Count," underscoring the project's increasing balkanization.

SIX

An Industry at Floodtide

ONCE THE PLAYERS MOVED INTO Amax-7 the pace began to speed up. Every time Zucchi came back across the street from the Time & Life Building he brought more news of the pressure to launch. "Gotta be ready," he would say to Dunn and Brauns. "We've got a window of opportunity for this thing, and Kelso wants to be sure we can get through it while it's still open. No more playing around, we gotta be ready to roll."

This was Zucchi's big chance, and he seemed positively driven to get the magazine to market.

Here he was, Dan Zucchi, a man who lacked the smooth polish, finesse, and credentials for success on the fast track at Time Inc.; who had been graduated not from an Ivy League college but from the University of Connecticut; who lived in a middle-class family neighborhood in Westchester, with two kids, a wife, and in the driveway a decade-old station car (aka the "Zukemobile"), with tools on the front floorboard, rips in the seats, and plenty of crumpled newspapers in the back to wipe off the windshield on frosty mornings.

Now Zucchi's prospects had abrubtly brightened. Sutton had put him on the task force, told him to do whatever was necessary to get the magazine to market, and the next thing he knew, he was pulling together what looked more and more like a colossal new Time Inc. mega-project, a venture in which people talked not of millions, or tens of millions, but of one hundred million dollars! This was not just an opportunity, this was as if Kelso Sutton had decided in his wisdom to upend the cornucopia of Time Inc. and shower the contents on Zucchi.

With all that before him, Zucchi was not about to let himself prove wanting. If he was, indeed, a super-salesman, now was the time to prove it.

While Dunn and Brauns worked on their numbers, Zucchi criss-crossed the country. He met with cable operators one minute, industry consultants the next. Then it was back to New York for meetings with executives on Madison Avenue.

The advertising community was Zucchi's home turf, the world he knew best, and he worked it with a frenzy. Cable TV viewers were the "hot button" of the 1980s, he would tell the ad men, and Time Inc.'s new magazine was how they could "reach out and touch it." This was going to be "the new magazine for the new television," the way to reach the "upmarket, affluent, involved" consumer. By 1990, cable TV would be in 60 million homes, and *TV-Cable* would be right there with them. "Cable subscribers will be the new consumers of the late 1980s and 90s," Zucchi would declare, "and we're going to be how to reach them in print!"

Sometimes Dukemejian would try to catch Zucchi for a few words, give him an update on the "production financials," but Zucchi could not spare the time. There were too many people to see, too many places to be at once. So excited did Zucchi grow that he became literally Johnsonian in his determination to make the most of every minute, and soon began taking the contents of his in-basket with him into the Amax-7 men's room—a facility that became known as "the Zuke's other office."

One important reason for Zucchi's eagerness to push ahead was the contagious excitement of the cable industry, which by the spring of 1982 seemed to grow hotter by the week—thanks in no small part to Time Inc. In addition to its ownership of HBO and ATC, the company had lately launched an all-movie pay channel called Cinemax, as well as acquired a one-third interest in a basic cable sports and entertainment programming service, the U.S.A. Network. To finance these activities, Video Group executives had begun developing tax-advantaged investment partnerships to be sold by Wall Street brokerage firms.

All this growth took place against the backdrop of an industry that was itself rapidly expanding. Situated at the corner of Fiftieth Street and Sixth Avenue, Time Inc.'s forty-eight-story world headquarters seemed almost like an East Coast version of Hollywood and Vine—only instead of studio chieftains and aspiring starlets the cast featured business executives in Brooks Brothers suits. These were the individuals who were bringing ideas and money to the world of cable TV programming, and by the mysterious chemistry of the industry, they all seemed to work within a five-minute walk from the glass-and-aluminum headquarters of Time Inc.

Across Sixth Avenue in the RCA Building, executives of the Rockefeller Corporation and RCA worked to develop a pay service to be called The Entertainment Channel. The group's founder and head, Arthur Taylor, a one-time broadcast chief at CBS, spoke of quickly reaching upwards of two million culture-hungry cable viewers around the country with TEC's blend of British sitcoms, Broadway blockbusters, and feature films.

Two blocks south, a joint venture called Warner Amex Satellite Entertainment Company, a creature of Warner Communications Inc. and American Express, generated a steady stream of new programming ideas, from "Nickelodeon," a children's service (1979), to The Movie Channel (1980), to MTV, a contemporary music outlet for young people (1981).

In the same building could be found CBS's foray into advertiser-supported "high-brow" cable programming, CBS Cable, as well as an advertiser-supported programming service known as the Cable Health Network.

Around the corner on Broadway, Viacom Inc., a leading cable system operator, had set up its own pay channel service, Showtime.

Several blocks south at 1440 Broadway, executives of WOR TV, a local broadcast station, had followed the lead of an Atlanta entrepreneur, Ted Turner, and turned WOR into a cable "superstation" by beaming its signal to cable companies around the country via satellite, using much the same technology as was employed by HBO.

A quarter-mile east at Fifth Avenue and Forty-sixth Street an advertiser-supported "women's programming" venture known as Daytime had begun to take shape, while on another floor of the same building was the headquarters for a joint venture cultural outlet between Hearst and ABC known as ARTS (Alpha Repertory Theater).

The preferred gathering spot for executives in this deal-a-minute industry was the smokey, oak-paneled bar of 21, the fashionable midtown restaurant. Long a favored watering hole for show-business celebrities and broadcasting executives, the bar now became a hot house that nurtured gossip on the industry's burgeoning new opportunities. Addressable converter boxes, rooftop satellite dishes, consumer databases, electronic banking; around the bar at 21, these were the widgets that would unleash the marketing wonders of the 1980s.

But the men who gathered at the bar at 21 were not the market for Time Inc.'s new magazine. Those people, known derisively to media executives as "pole climbers," were to be found instead in places like Mahanoy City, Pennsylvania, and Astoria, Oregon; and Zucchi had some fairly specific ideas about how to deal with them. "We gotta hang tough with these guys," Zucchi would say. "Drive a hard bargain." For months, he and Brauns had been meeting with different cable officials—"testing the waters," as Zucchi put it—and the results seemed en-

couraging. "They like the idea," he would inform Dunn back in
New York. "They're not ready to sign a deal just yet, but when
they are, we'd better be there with the product. Otherwise,
they'll go elsewhere."

In fact, though they said little of the matter to Zucchi and
Brauns, the cable operators were growing ever warier of Time's
effort. Some felt troubled by the editorial control issues that had
been raised by Time Inc.'s own ATC from the project's inception the previous summer. Others were disturbed by the sheer
size of Time Inc. within the industry and their own vulnerabil-
ity to the company should they become dependent on yet another Time Inc. product.

Burgheim felt a certain foreboding. He didn't like Zucchi's
style of "management by frenzy," and he wondered if the publisher in his rush to move the project forward might be blinding
himself to the difficulties inherent in dealing with these people.
He and Durrell had experienced trouble from the cable operators since day one on the project; now through the marketing
approach of Dunn and Brauns, the magazine had become more
entangled with them than ever. Did Zucchi really understand
where this whole thing might lead?

But Zucchi remained a fountainhead of optimism, and nowhere was his excitement more contagious than in Las Vegas
early that May, as cable people from around the country gathered for the 31st annual National Cable Television Association
convention. The NCTA convention is the annual high point for
the U.S. cable industry, attracting executives by the thousands.

As befitting their company's dominant presence within the
industry, representatives from Time Inc. turned out in abundance. In addition to Zucchi, Burgheim, and the cable listings
task force, the entourage included everyone from Munro and
his lieutenants Levin, Nicholas, and Sutton, to numerous executives from HBO and ATC.

This was Sutton's first visit to Las Vegas, and excitement
danced in his eyes. He had come to meet cable operators, promote his magazine project, and establish the contacts that

would help cement his reputation as Magazine Group's cable-savvy new leader.

Two limousines sat waiting on the tarmac as the Time Inc. corporate jet taxied to a halt. As the executives climbed in, Sutton paused to scan the far horizon. This was his hour, the unveiling of a magazine that would dazzle the industry.

At the entrance to the Dunes Hotel the limousines pulled to a halt and the executives stepped into the midday glare. Though the convention was being held at the Las Vegas Hilton, the group had been booked into rooms at the Dunes, having been advised by someone in Time Inc.'s travel department that it was a short walk between the two. Porters began lifting luggage from the trunks, and followed behind as the group entered the building.

The entourage was halfway to the registration desk when Sutton, his hand massaging a silver dollar in his pocket, spotted a bank of slot machines against the far wall. Without missing a beat, the group vice president wheeled from his colleagues, strode across the lobby, and in a single, smooth movement placed the coin in the slot, pulled the lever, and waited.

Clunk, a lemon . . . clunk, another lemon . . . clunk, a third lemon. Jackpot!

Standing in the check-in line, Zucchi's jaw dropped. He had never seen anything like it. Kelso Sutton had not been in Las Vegas for thirty minutes—the first trip in his life—and with his very first bet he had money pouring at his feet.

The next morning the group assembled at 8:30 in the Time Inc. hospitality suite. Waiting for them was a breakfast buffet of coffee, tea, and pastries. Get-together appointments had been scheduled beginning at 9:00 for cable industry executives from each of the leading systems: Viacom, TCI, Warner-Amex, Cox, Daniels & Company, and several others. The meetings were to be devoted entirely to presentations of the magazine by Zucchi, Dunn, and Brauns. The higher ranked executives had come to observe, to see the reaction of the pole climbers.

At 9:00 the executives straightened their ties, positioned themselves about the room, and waited.

But no pole climbers.

At about 9:05, Sutton glanced at his watch, then shot his cuffs and began staring at the wall. It was the group vice president's way of saying, Okay, what happened?

Zucchi broke a piece of pastry from the buffet, popped it in his mouth, and said:

"They must be late."

At about 9:10 Nicholas spoke:

"This is nothing. At HBO, people are late all the time."

Sutton offered a look that said, Well this isn't HBO, Nick, and lighted a cigar.

By 9:30, Sutton was on his second cigar, and smoke was filling the room.

What was happening just was not done. Here stood the president and three top executives of the nation's leading communications conglomerate. They had flown 2,500 miles to *be* in this room. They had come to unfurl a magazine concept that they believed would revolutionize the cable industry, and who should know better? These executives headed the biggest magazine publishing house in the country, they controlled the largest pay service in the industry and its second-largest cable system. When it came to magazines and cable, these executives were some of the most important men on earth. But where were the pole climbers who were supposed to appreciate that fact?

A few minutes later an elevator door opened down the hall, and muffled voices could be heard heading their way. The pole climbers at last. Sutton put down his cigar, everyone positioned himself . . . and the voices faded past.

By 9:45 the Time Inc. executives were visibly distraught. Sutton was puffing like a locomotive as he darted glances at Zucchi; Dunn and Brauns had begun making nervous jokes to each other; Nicholas had exhausted his entire repertoire of excuses to be late.

And then suddenly there they were, standing in the doorway, four of them. They wore cowboy string ties with steer's head slip knots, one had on a hat, and all wore boots.

"Well, shoot," said the big one, "you must be the boys from Time/Life! What're you fellas doin' all the hellangone way out here in the Dunes? It takes half the dang mornin' t' git here from the Hilton!"

Zucchi thought, Oh Christ, how did this happen! He turned to Dunn. "I thought the Hilton was next door. What happened?"

"So did I," said Dunn, and he thought, boy are we going to get it now!

The introductions were barely finished when Munro had to leave. He was scheduled for an 11 A.M. speech on the main convention floor, and he dashed off with Nicholas and Levin, leaving Sutton, Zucchi, and the others to make their presentations.

Considering the rocky start, the presentations seemed to go quite well. Zucchi would run through his prepared remarks —that whether they knew it yet or not, the cable operators had a "guide problem"; that Time Inc. could solve that problem; turn the chore of providing a guide from a "cost center" to a "profit center"; provide a magazine that would stop "disconnects" and "pay channel churn." Yes, said the pole climbers, we like that idea, it's timely, just what we need, go ahead and do it, we're very enthusiastic.

After the last of the presentations was finished, Sutton turned to Zucchi. "Let's move to the Hilton. Today. I don't want to stay in this place another night."

As Burgheim mused later, the 31st convention of the National Cable Television Association was probably the highwater mark for the entire cable industry. Every company of significance in the country had set up a booth or exhibit, and in many cases the offerings seemed bent on nothing less than outdoing each other in sheer gaudiness and extravagance.

At the soon-to-be-launched Playboy Channel the theme was girls with high-on-the-hip bunny suits and cotton tails; across the way at the Disney Channel one could get a picture taken with Mickey Mouse; over at the booth for the Nashville Network attendants gave out straw farmer's hats to all comers; further along at the ESPN sports network passers-by could take away free coffee-table books. To carry everything around, one needed only stop by the Entertainment Channel and pick up a free tote bag. Nearby stood the CBS Cable exhibit, raised magnificently on a platform as if the entire creation were a kind of Le Corbusier memorial sculpture.

The effect was dazzling, even hyper, and presiding over it all, setting the tone of endless bounty: Time Inc. Befitting such stature, Munro had agreed to act as an opening-day speaker in the main convention hall, and having now arrived from the Dunes, he proceeded to the grand ballroom, where he was scheduled to participate in ceremonies at 11:00. Rising to the podium, he surveyed the throng, then cleared his throat and held forth on a theme he knew well, enthusing over the "social and economic trends" affecting the industry.

One trend Munro did not need to spell out for anyone concerned both his and the industry's fascination with the promise of high-tech. For even as he spoke there loomed above him on the dias, in Oz-like enormity, a billboard-sized television screen that displayed for the crowd an electronically disembodied image of his own talking head. Unfortunately, when Munro turned to look at it, both he and the audience beheld instead his billboard-sized bald spot.

On the morning of the second day in Las Vegas, a man with a graying beard walked up to Dick Burgheim on the convention floor and introduced himself. His name was William Marsano, 41, the editor of *TV Guide Canada*, and meeting Burgheim had been the principal reason for his trip. A rumor had reached him in Toronto that Time Inc. was preparing to enter the cable TV listings business, and Marsano sensed an opportunity; working for *TV Guide Canada* was respectable enough, but to Marsano a job at Time Inc. had always seemed like a final step up for any magazine journalist.

Through a contact at *People* Marsano had learned that Burgheim had been chosen the project's editorial head, and that he would be in Las Vegas for the convention. "Sound him out," said the *People* source. "You'll spot him right away, he's a strange little man with a mustache."

By the spring of 1982, Burgheim had already accumulated a fairly thick folder of job applicant letters and résumés, but it was obvious as his conversation with Marsano progressed not only that the man wanted a job but that hiring him away from *TV Guide* would be a coup.

That afternoon the two men met and talked more, not so much about the industry as about gathering and publishing actual TV listings (the area of Marsano's expertise) or, as it was known in the evolving argot of Amax-7, as "the editing of the plain vanilla." It was a subject that drove Burgheim to distraction, as it would any balanced mind. But the project's editor believed that the measure of value in a TV listings magazine was the completeness and accuracy of its listings, and he was determined that any magazine he edited would have perceived value to readers. If not, why would they subscribe?

Moreover, the more he examined the plain-vanilla listings supplied by TV Data the less he liked them. A sports fan, he particularly cringed at howlers that mixed up teams, events, even cities, and he had taken to mulling how many of his readers would subscribe to a listings magazine that referred to, say, the Cleveland Yankees. Somehow, everything TV Data provided for his magazine was going to have to be rechecked for accuracy and completeness, all the way back if necessary to the original networks and station programming departments that had supplied the information to TV Data in the first place.

Burgheim wondered why the business-side people seemed so determined to use TV Data at all, especially since he now intended to recheck everything TV Data supplied. He wondered whether Zucchi and Dunn were just being obstinate, or whether Labich and his CM&D friends merely wanted to buy more and more computer equipment.

Perhaps he could find a role for Marsano in all this. Yes, thought Burgheim, here was someone he was not about to let get away, and by the time the conversation concluded, the two men had agreed to meet that evening for dinner, one purpose of which would be for Marsano to have a look at a document that his colleagues at *TV Guide* would have paid dearly to examine: a complete and unabridged version of the *TV-Cable* dummy.

SEVEN

A Bombastic Epiphany

TIME INC. was not the only company vying for attention in Las Vegas. More than three hundred different firms had set up booths and exhibits, by far the most extravagant of which belonged to CBS, the wealthiest company in broadcast television.

CBS had been late getting into cable TV, but once they entered the field in 1981, the network's executives launched themselves on a spending spree that astonished everyone, at various times renting forums as diverse as the New York Public Library and a Mississippi riverboat side-wheeler simply to have parties.

Now CBS was about to outdo even itself. For as Burgheim and Marsano stood firming up their dinner arrangements, conventioneers by the hundreds were descending upon a fleet of buses waiting in the parking lot. The buses were there to take them to what was already being referred to up and down the convention floor as the greatest, most spectacular exhibit in the history of entertainment—a project so gargantuan and sprawling that there was not enough room for it in all of downtown Las Vegas.

What precisely was this too-big-to-be-believed extravaganza? Just this: somewhere in the vastness of the Nevada desert—beyond where Wayne Newton lives with his private planes and Arabian horses, where cowpokes sing to their dogies and the sky stretches on forever—CBS Cable's public relations executives had erected nothing less than an entire Arabian tent village, even going so far as to create a man-made lake, and all to stress the theme of CBS Cable being an "oasis" in the desert of broadcast TV. Cost of the one-day event: $250,000.

Nobody could believe it. You swung off the highway just beyond the city limits, continued down a dirt road, and eventually you arrived at a huge parking area filled with cars. And off in the distance, like the bivouwak of a Saudi prince, you saw tents—dozens of them—and people wandering around in burnooses and veils, and you saw smoke curling from charcoal braziers, and you smelled roasting meat and couscous, and you thought, My God, the only thing they forgot was to throw in the goats. And then you saw them—the goats—wandering among the rocks and stubble, their bells tinkling lightly in the gathering evening. And after that came the camels, and the horses, and the pigs, and the chickens. And looking at all this, at the tents and the animals and the people wandering around dressed up like Arabs, you began to feel like a comic-strip character so befuddled and baffled that you had question marks and exclamation points and stars and asterisks popping out of your head all at once, like this: ! * ? *.

If the 31st convention of the National Cable Television Association was the industry's high-water mark, then CBS Cable's Arabian village was its bombastic epiphany. Yet had there been among the throng a reader of goat entrails, he might have found omenlike two seemingly trivial details that CBS Cable's executives had overlooked.

In Nevada, night comes quickly. And in the desert there are no street lights.

As a result, by early evening what had started as a kind of cable-industry nose-thumbing at *Lawrence of Arabia* had turned into a spectacle of people groping their away among tents and animals as they stumbled through the dark toward the safety of the buses.

The next evening found Marsano and Burgheim continuing their discussion of the U.S. cable industry over dinner in a quiet wood-paneled restaurant a short walk from the Hilton. For Burgheim it had been a meeting to look forward to, since he had brought along a copy of the dummy for his guest to critique. The dummy represented the culmination of six months' work and refinement, and he was very proud of the result. Now the dummy contained not only a more elaborately laid out national wrap, but additional listings features for the yellow pages as well. These included day-by-day grid spreads of program offerings, selected program highlights for each day, and several pages of crisply written pay-channel movie reviews —all system-specific for each cable system, or as Zucchi like to tell the ad men, "the whole TV scene in one magazine."

It was an impressive piece of work, and Marsano recognized its value immediately. But when the discussion moved to the computer technology that was going to produce this product, Burgheim snorted strangely and let his thoughts trail off in mid-sentence. Marsano said nothing, but chalked it up to a man under pressure.

Back at the hotel, Zucchi, Dunn, and Brauns were shaping up their own plans for the evening—a night on the Strip—and Kelso Sutton was not included. Zucchi had arranged everything, beginning with dinner and a Diana Ross concert at Caesar's Palace, and ending with a midnight topless show at the Tropicana.

Dunn had a good enough idea what this was going to be like, and he was looking forward to it. But Brauns had been uncomfortable in the city from the moment she had arrived. She did not like the glitter, the flash, the floor shows, the gambling. She had brought her jogging suit and Nikes to run before breakfast, but one look at the 24-hour-a-day street scene had cured her of that ambition immediately. Now all she wanted to do was stay in her room.

But uncomfortable as she knew she would feel being out on the town with Dunn and Zucchi, she knew it would be far worse to be alone in her hotel room while the two of them were out together without her. She looked at the two:

"Okay, let's go."

Looking back on it later, Sarah's strongest memory of the evening was the fantastic grinning expression on Zucchi's face as the night wore on and the floorshows got progressively raunchier.

They began at Caesar's Palace, where HBO had booked nearly every table in the house for Diana Ross's evening show. The room was enormous and smoke-filled. Columns rose to the ceiling, and lights from mirror balls danced on the walls. Cocktail waitresses in miniskirt togas moved between the tables, and up on the stage, wrapped in sequins and a boa, Diana Ross sang. Zucchi was in heaven.

Sarah fanned at the smoke, then turned to say something to Jeff about the marketing plan, but one look told her to forget it. He too was entranced—not by Diana Ross but by a nearby coctail waitress who wore a toga so small it could have fit in a Dixie cup.

Diana completed her set and the backup band took over. The lights came up slightly, more drinks were ordered, and Zucchi began to light a cigar. Then he stopped and stared across the room. Dunn looked at him.

"Dan?"

Zucchi just stared.

"What is it?" and Dunn twisted in his seat.

"It's Kelso!" said Zucchi. "He's here with Nicholas!"

Sure enough, the group vice president had entered the room, accompanied by Nick Nicholas, and the two were headed their way.

Sutton had come with Nicholas in hopes of meeting HBO and cable industry people in the audience. But the two men were not halfway into the room when Nicholas, seeing some people he knew at a far table, headed off to greet them leaving Sutton standing alone in bewilderment.

Then he spotted the players. But as Sutton could see, their table was filled. So for that matter was every other table in the house. What to do? Should he approach his subordinates and wait for someone to offer him a seat, or should he wave graciously and look for a friend elsewhere?

His subordinates were having similar anxieties, for their boss was in an obviously difficult situation. Yet no one wanted to take the initiative to help. Dunn did not rise, nor did Brauns, nor for that matter did Zucchi. For a long awkward moment they simply stared back and forth at each other, then across the room at Sutton.

At last the house lights dimmed for the next set of numbers, and when next anyone looked, the group vice president had disappeared into the crowd.

After the show, the group headed off for some gambling, winding up eventually at a blackjack table. Dunn and Brauns did not enjoy gambling, but Zucchi did, and did not seem to mind in the slightest as a series of winning bets became an abrupt string of losses. Steeper and steeper grew his losses, as his chip pile dwindled until at last Zucchi had but one $5 chip remaining.

Then abruptly his luck changed again, and by continuously doubling up, he ran his holdings to $20, $80, and finally nearly $200. "Quit while you're ahead," counseled Dunn, pulling at his collar as the chip pile grew higher. But Zucchi doubled up again, and in a flash it was all gone—even his first $5. At this, Zucchi looked at his two assistants in silence, then his face erupted in a grin, and the man who would become publisher of *TV-Cable Week* declared in a booming laugh, "Well hell, if you don't take the ride you'll wonder forever how far you could have gone!"

EIGHT

The Whole Thing
Is Jury-Rigged

W ELL-MANAGED CORPORATIONS work hard
to inspire employee loyalty, but mere
longevity of service is no measure of
success.
Scholars of American corporate culture recognize that dynamic, successful companies to a large extent result from clear
and compelling values and work ethics that are shared and
understood by employees at every level. In such firms, employee loyalty runs to the corporation as a whole, not to individual bosses and power seekers. Shrewd companies like IBM,
General Electric, and Proctor & Gamble prevent cronyism
from taking root by coupling regular staff reassignments with
strongly paternalistic employee policies. Unless accompanied
by an overriding sense of shared values, paternalism can do
great damage, for it almost inevitably means that the price of
security ceases to be performance; instead of doing the job one's
aim becomes little more than keeping the job.

By the beginning of the 1980s, that was how many Time
Inc.'ers had come to regard their own corporation. The com-

pany's drift into conglomerate growth had so eroded Time's corporate identity that virtually all that remained for most employees was a sense of belonging to an amorphous, protective, and not terribly demanding bureaucracy.

One staff survey stunned management. The survey showed that while 84 percent of employees thought Time Inc. had a "good to very good" benefits package, only 46 percent thought top management was "good to very good." Worse, only 38 percent thought the company was "good to very good" at applying policies and rules fairly to everyone, while a mere 30 percent thought they were fairly paid in relation to others. Only 26 percent thought pay increases were awarded on the basis of performance.

What did most Time Inc.'ers believe to be the key to advancement? Sixty-seven percent of those surveyed, the largest single group, regarded "having the right image" or "having gone to the right schools" as the secret to winning promotion.

These revelations shocked Time Inc.'s brass, but they merely reflected a set of attitudes and perceptions created by the brass itself.

When they looked to their bosses, many Time Inc.'ers saw only image-conscious executives more concerned with their own futures than with the future of the company that employed them. Preoccupations ranged from where to eat lunch and who to be seen with, to concerns about whether a degree from Harvard, Yale, or Princeton could still be counted on—as had traditionally been the case—to help the young and ambitious keep moving ahead.

Though Munro (a graduate of Colgate, 1956) insisted that Time Inc. was no longer the Ivy League ghetto it once was, staffers saw contrary evidence wherever they looked. Sutton's own protégé, Chris Meigher, a Dartmouth man, headed a department (Corporate Circulation) so filled with Ivy Leaguers that it was known throughout Magazine Group as "the Yacht Club." In Video Group, nearly every top official had Ivy League credentials. Two executives, Robert Bedell and John Redpath, had been catcher and starting pitcher on the same Princeton baseball team. Eventually, they became *TV-Cable Week*'s director of marketing and HBO's general counsel. Of the 42 management-level employees on the staff of *TV-Cable Week*, 12 had Harvard credentials, 3 had Yale degrees, and 2 had degrees from Columbia.

Patterning one's behavior on the style set by the boss is common in business; at Time Inc. it was no different, as corporate climbers mimicked the behavior of Munro to a degree that seemed almost obsessive. No sooner did word spread that the company's new president ate breakfast early most mornings at the Dorset Hotel on West Fifty-fourth Street than numerous subordinates began doing the same. It was there, one hot September morning in 1982 that Munro, having breakfast, stood up and removed his suit jacket to be more comfortable; all around the room Time Inc. executives promptly rose and did the same. When a Munro-watcher subsequently observed that the boss did not wear a belt with his trousers, subordinates stopped wearing belts also. And when Munro took to carrying a red bandana with a corner flapping loosely from his hip pocket, the corridors of the Big House were soon ablaze with red bandanas waving jauntily from the hip pockets of hopeful executives.

Because he had worked hard to cultivate staff loyalty, Munro alone among Time Inc.'s thirty-fourth floor figures enjoyed a strong and positive image with the company's rank and file. Eager to please and be liked, Munro prided himself on "management by persuasion," and was said to make a point of avoiding giving direct orders whenever possible.

Yet the members of the cable listings task force, having been lifted by their project to ongoing contact with the company's highest officials, soon began to see the dark side of life in a corporation headed by a nice-guy chief executive. For Munro's easy-going demeanor had let power pass increasingly into the hands of his group vice presidents, one of whom (Levin) now no longer seemed to involve himself in the work of the task force in any way, while the other (Sutton) seemed anxious to push the project forward faster and faster.

The man ostensibly in charge of coordinating the inter-group work of these two men was Munro's second-in-command, Clifford Grum. But Grum seemed most concerned to gather more and more "numbers" from Zucchi and his aides. A banker by training, Grum had joined the corporation in 1973 as part of a conglomerate merger deal when his employer, Temple Industries Inc., a Texas logging concern, had been merged into Time Inc. The merger had been arranged by the firm's owner, a buffalo-sized lumberman named Arthur Temple, who acquired 15 percent of Time Inc.'s stock as well as a seat on its board of directors in the process.

As part of the arrangement, Temple had relocated Grum to New York to keep watch on the investment. Though Grum had no particular experience in publishing beyond that of advertising manager for his high school yearbook in San Antonio, Texas, he was soon appointed publisher of *Fortune* Magazine. In 1980 he was elevated to executive vice president, the number-two slot in the company. On the corporate flow chart he appeared sandwiched between the group vice presidents below him and Munro above him, but many in the organization wondered whether he might not enjoy an invisible dotted line that looped around Munro and went to Temple, his patron.

After the decision had been made to move the task force to Amax-7, Burgheim too began to wonder about Grum. He wondered whether the relocation idea had originated with Sutton, with Grum, or perhaps with Temple himself. Not knowing the source of the decision, or the reasons behind it, made Burgheim apprehensive. Who was in charge of this project anyway, and what was going to happen next?

Sutton also had Grum on his mind, but for a different reason. Before the cable magazine could be launched, the project would have to be presented for approval by Time Inc.'s board of directors. And as a member of the board, Grum could provide valuable insight in how to present the proposal to the other board members, Temple included, once the work of the task force was completed.

One day Grum came to Sutton's office to discuss the matter. "Clifford!" said Sutton, as he rose from behind his desk and offered Grum a chair.

"Thank you, Kelso," said Grum, stretching out his lanky frame. "You know, the important thing is to sound positive before the board. We're going to want to be upbeat and positive."

Sutton listened earnestly as Grum continued with his advice: keep the presentation simple, emphasize the up-side, and above all do not dwell on the complexities and uncertainties— the very risks the task force had highlighted in the January presentation.

While Sutton and Grum pondered how to deal with Time Inc.'s board, the members of the task force were becoming embroiled in increasingly nasty disputes over Labich's technology. The first casualty of these fights was a 32-year-old computer expert from the the *New York Daily News* named Carmen Siringo. A mere splinter of a man, Siringo made up in enthusiasm for what he lacked in stature, and he soon found himself entangled in quarrels that every day seemed to grow bigger and angrier and involve more people.

Siringo had joined Time Inc. after answering an advertisement in the Sunday *New York Times* for a job described as "director of editorial systems." The man who interviewed him was the head of the department, a gangling, sandy-haired executive named Robert McGoff. McGoff told him nothing about the cable listings task force across the street but said only that Siringo's job would involve a number of important projects in McGoff's own department, Information Systems Group.

Ignorant of the task force, Siringo also did not know the politics of the situation. The responsibilities of McGoff's department, ISG, overlapped those of Labich's old group, CM&D, and the two officials had clashed repeatedly over control of the project's technology.

Now Siringo found himself dragged into the fight. His first assignment, presented by McGoff within days of reporting for work, was to evaluate the computer plan for the proposed publication. As Siringo understood it, the project's editorial executive, a man named Burgheim, had been complaining that the computers being developed by a man named Labich were never going to work, and wasn't there something Siringo could do to help straighten it out?

"Be careful," warned McGoff. "I have grave concerns about that project. The technology's a mess."

Several days later, Siringo reported back to his boss.

"You're right, Bob, what an abortion! There's some foreign guy over there who's got a drawing with little boxes on it that he says is the system. I don't get it!" Siringo was referring to Burgheim's Hungarian computer adviser, Demargitay, "the Count".

McGoff rubbed his chin, then offered some advice: go see Larry Crutcher, who was thought to have a copy of the business plan. With it, Siringo could figure out exactly how many computers were really needed.

But neither man knew Crutcher's true feelings toward the project, and Siringo was understandably startled when the Sutton subordinate looked up from his desk and announced, "The plan's confidential. You can't have it. Go see Chuck Martin."

That person proved to be no help either. Though virtually everyone on the task force believed that Martin, a recently arrived ex-editor from the *Washington Star*, had been designated by Grunwald to consult with Burgheim on the project's technology needs, Martin insisted that he really had nothing to do with the project at all. When Siringo approached him, Martin pushed the plea over to a Grunwald aide named McManus who had worked on a cable listings task force more than two years earlier. McManus in turn referred the request to one of the company's five group vice presidents, Charles Bear, the thirty-fourth floor official in charge of Siringo's boss, McGoff, thereby closing the loop and sending Siringo in effect around in a circle.

Thus Siringo, a lower-middle-management employee on Time Inc.'s staff for all of six weeks, one day found himself and McGoff sitting side by side at a long mahogany table in a thirty-fourth floor chamber known as "the Chart Room." Over the years, the room had been the scene of meetings and interviews involving a long list of public figures and dignitaries, from congressmen to show business celebrities. Now the room contained Siringo and McGoff, and opposite them, Bear, Zucchi, Labich, and several others, all waiting to hear what Siringo thought to be so "inappropriate" about Labich's computers.

As a strategy, McGoff and Siringo had agreed to keep focusing the discussion on long-term questions—the perils of getting into the market and then finding that the technology could not deliver the required numbers of magazine editions. But the meeting quickly degenerated into a shouting match between Labich and McGoff—"the technology is absurd." "No, you just don't understand it." When he could take it no longer, Bear cut the two off and turned to Zucchi for his opinion of the situation. Was it really necessary to launch in September, as now seemed the plan, or could the project be put on hold for a year to get this computer mess straightened out?

No way, said Zucchi, with his eyes locked on Siringo. The cable operators were eager, and if Time Inc. didn't give them the product they'd go elsewhere. The market was hot, no time for delay. September was Time Inc.'s "window of opportunity," and later would be too late.

No sooner had the Chart Room gathering ended than Zucchi called his own "big meeting." Its purpose: to get to the bottom of the computer problem once and for all. As Zucchi said to his aides, he'd had it up to here with Burgheim and his computer complaints.

Mostly, Burgheim seemed to feel that Labich's plain-vanilla editing system was too complex for writers or editors to master. But Zucchi thought the editing of listings was a job for minimum-wage data keypunch operators, not magazine editors. Yet every time he said so, Burgheim countered that that was what was wrong with Labich's plan to begin with—the plain-vanilla listings supplied by TV Data were being gathered by data input people who knew little about TV programming and kept inserting errors. Burgheim wanted skilled people, "Time Inc. quality" people. But, Zucchi would retort, what Time Inc. editor or writer would do *that?* Arguing with Burgheim was like shouting at fog.

Meanwhile, Zucchi fumed, someone (probably that little pain-in-the-neck Siringo) had gotten a computer consultant from the outside involved, and now all Zucchi heard was talk about a "wall" beyond which Labich's system could not go. Zucchi did not want to hear problems, he wanted solutions— don't tell him what Labich's system could not do, tell him what it could do. How could he make it better, faster, cheaper—that was what Zucchi wanted to know.

Finally Zucchi could take the negativism no longer and had called the big meeting. They were going to get to the bottom of this "wall" business once and for all—find out what the problems were get everybody squared away. "Hell," Zucchi would say, "we gotta quit fucking around, make some decisions, know what I mean?"

To the meeting Zucchi had invited everyone who had anything to do with computers, and he meant everybody. Burgheim, Labich, Dunn, Davis, Siringo, McGoff, even Martin. The Zuke was going to get this bunch together and start cracking some heads.

As Zucchi saw it, the process was simple: they would hear the man out, get to the bottom of the "wall" problem, then go back to work and get on with the project. Hell, Zucchi thought, he had ads to sell, he couldn't be fucking around with "walls."

The consultant turned out to be a contemplative computer engineer named Jonathan Seybold, Jr., a member of the Seybold Group Inc., the industry's leading authority on computerized graphics and editing. After everyone had settled into chairs, Seybold shuffled the papers in front of him and began to speak, quite apparently uneasy at the burden of his remarks. "I am sure I only state the obvious when I say that this is a very different product from anything Time Inc. has produced before. Basically, my feeling is that it may indeed be possible to produce the magazine with the proposed techniques, but it will be expensive, labor-intensive, and draining. I don't know exactly how many editions can be produced using these techniques, but my feeling is that there is a limit, a wall, beyond which you cannot go, that will prevent the publication from ever reaching break-even."

When Seybold next suggested that considering the general state of confusion it would be unwise to attempt a launch in less than a year, Zucchi interrupted.

"We gotta do it sooner than that," Zucchi said. "September and we're out the door. That's where the rubber meets the road. No way around it, folks."

Burgheim looked up. September and they were "out the door"? It was nearly June, and Zucchi had not yet signed a deal with a single cable operator. Moreover, none of the computers worked, no editorial staff existed, and Grunwald would not let Burgheim start recruiting one until the board of directors had approved the project, which could not happen until August at the earliest. Burgheim looked at Zucchi and thought, Seybold's right, a September launch is absurd, all this frenzy is just another Zucchi-ism.

Meanwhile, Labich had spread some proofsheets of actual TV listings across the table. They were from a test he had begun running with CM&D pagination equipment on Pine Street. "See," he said, "it works fine. We can do 250 editions. Definitely."

Anne Davis examined the proofs, then turned to Labich. "These are all just plain vanilla. This test proves nothing!"

"Right," chimed in Burgheim. He shifted in his seat and

now brought up another complaint: that Labich's system made the project dependent on TV Data, and what if that company decided at some future date to stop supplying listings?

Labich rolled his eyes; he had been waiting for that from Burgheim. "Don't worry," he said, leaning forward in his chair and dropping his voice. "We've set up Project Mustang!"

As Labich explained it, the project was so secret that few in the room were supposed to know of its existence. Project Mustang, it seemed, was a clandestine software development project involving the Curtiss-Wright Aerospace Corporation; its purpose was to prepare a fall-back computer system as an emergency alternative to TV Data. "We've got to be very quiet about this," Labich stressed. "We don't want TV Data getting wind of Mustang in any way!"

Davis was unimpressed. She didn't trust Labich, and she didn't trust his Project Mustang. What was a high-tech aerospace firm doing in the TV listings business anyway? The whole thing smelled fishy. Besides, as Davis judged the situation, there were many more immediate problems they should be focusing on, and now she started to tick them off: no copy-processing department could possibly produce the volumes of pages required; Labich's computer scheme was absurd; besides copy processing they needed an entire makeup system that no one had yet focused on.

"No one is tracking this project," she declared. "Taken separately, each of these problems might be solvable, but taken together they guarantee a low probability of success. The whole thing is jury-rigged."

Oh brother, thought McGoff as he listened to the quarrels continue, this is never going to work. His concern only intensified when a memo from Zucchi turned up in his in-basket the following Tuesday. Addressed to each of the six who had attended the earlier gathering, it began: "Let me summarize very briefly the results of our meeting. (1) The consultant's report did not indicate major problems with the system we now have planned for editing and producing *TV-Cable* . . ."

McGoff was stunned. Had Zucchi willfully not heard what had been said? McGoff decided to get his own view of the matter firmly planted on the record, and sent Zucchi a memo in response: "In recent meetings I've expressed a number of concerns regarding the potential startup of the TV-Cable magazine either in September or early '83. In past project meetings, all or most of these issues had been raised individually, yet it was not until the detailed task review last week that the totality of the problems became apparent. In hopes of avoiding any future confusion as to what my position is on our current approach, I'll state again that I believe the current strategy is *fundamentally wrong*. We are evolving a system that merely makes use of some existing equipment capabilities and avoids investing in a long-term strategy."

NINE

Zucchi's Can-Do Guy

IN THE WEEKS that followed, the computer fights grew worse, as the project's executives clashed in meeting after meeting: how many editions could Labich's system really produce; how many people would be needed to operate it; how highly trained would they have to be? As the quarrels continued, it occurred to Dunn that Burgheim did not understand the implications of his position—that his insistence on being able to edit every word of every edition was not only unnecessary but impossible. Dunn wondered why Burgheim seemed so fixated on the subject, and he began to grow fearful that the price of "perfect information" would turn out to be beyond the reach of even Time Inc.

At about this time, Labich decided to make Project Mustang Dukemejian's responsibility, and one day Labich called the young M.B.A. to his office to tell him so. It runs itself, Labich explained; Dukemejian did not have to do anything, just sign the checks. Dukemejian felt proud, and began convening meetings of his own on the matter. When Burgheim learned of Dukemejian's new responsibility, he laughed out loud, "Little

Mikey, the prince of ambition!" then headed off to see what Anne Davis thought of this development.

Meanwhile, the pressure on Zucchi to get the magazine to market continued to build. Competitors like *On Cable* kept signing deals with more and more systems, the market was growing hotter by the week. Zucchi wanted to be part of the action, not arguing with Burgheim while opportunity passed them by.

Zucchi felt most galled of all by the success of Peter Funt. Manhattan is the advertising and media capital of the world, the home of the country's major advertising agencies, the headquarters of the three broadcast networks, the nation's leading book and magazine publishing houses, and now the cable industry as well. But because Funt's *On Cable* had already signed a long-term deal the year before with Time Inc.'s own flagship cable company, Sterling Manhattan, Zucchi had no Manhattan outlet, even via Time Inc.

The thought of it drove Zucchi wild. Here he was heading up the most closely watched magazine development effort in his company's history—a magazine to serve an industry that was literally outside the front door of the Amax Building—yet Funt had managed to block him from marketing the magazine in the very capital of the industry.

"Goddamit," he growled to Dunn one day on his way to "the Zuke's other office." "We gotta do something about that guy, buy him or something. Here, take care of these" and he handed Dunn a fistfull of memos and reports.

Zucchi's drive and determination simply added to the pressure-cooker atmosphere of Amax-7, where the feeling had begun to take hold that the project had acquired a life of its own. Instead of guiding the evolution of the magazine, the players now felt themselves being swept along by the momentum of the thing.

Sometimes Brauns would think back to her request to Meigher the year before to work for Durrell on the task force. Now Durrell was gone, but she was still here, her life more and more consumed by the project. She wondered if some day she would look back on the experience as having been exciting and challenging, or as something less pleasant to remember.

Sometimes she would ruminate on the pressures behind the project, the political rumblings they all could hear going on high above them in the corporation. The rumors made her uneasy. Some said the magazine was a grandstand gesture by Sutton, an attempt to position himself for the presidency in a company in transition from magazines to cable. Others said the situation was more complex, that a real war had broken out between Magazine Group and Video Group and that the project had become the battleground. The rumors sent a chill through Brauns, and she would push them from her mind.

Dunn as well felt a gathering unease, and repeatedly the same image would come to him. He would close his eyes and see himself floating in a broad and lazily flowing river, just drifting with the current under the shade of overhanging branches. Then a breeze would ripple the water, he'd open his eyes, and notice that suddenly the current was not flowing so lazily anymore. He'd begin to stroke for shore, but now he'd find that he could not make headway because the current was getting stronger and stronger—until suddenly he and Brauns and Zucchi and Burgheim were all hurtling down a rapids towards who knew what.

Much of the tension derived from the incredible pressure to keep moving the project forward. Instead of luncheon conferences at midtown restaurants, the team would now send out for pizza and deli and never leave the Amax-7 conference room, as they agonized over their untested and unprecedented numbers, assumptions, and hypotheses: what was a reasonable penetration assumption, what was a reasonable pricing assumption, how many cable operators could one reasonably assume would sign distribution deals? Often it would be 2 A.M. before the meetings adjourned and the executives departed for the various midtown hotels that had become their homes-away-from-home for weeks at a time.

Eight-thirty the next morning would find the group reconvening all over again. Day after day, week after week—the same faces, the same issues, sometimes even crusts from the same cold pizza left over from the night before. On and on it would go—what was the smallest cable system at which "minimum reasonable assumed penetration" would yield a profit; how could one guarantee maximum immediate penetration in every cable system selected as a market; what was the most that one could charge for the magazine without discouraging sales in the process; how big a support staff would be needed for the project and how rapidly would it expand as the magazine grew?

Answers to some of these questions had by now begun to emerge. The previous autumn it seemed possible that as many as 250 different cable systems might sign up for the magazine, producing a total circulation that could approach eight million. But by now the number had dropped to 90, as Brauns and Zucchi had more rigorously examined the potential markets. Some cable systems turned out already to be publishing guides of their own. Others had signed contracts with competitors like *On Cable.* Still others either did not want to involve themselves with Time Inc. or were too small to be worth the trouble.

A price for the magazine had also been set: $.69 per copy. This was higher than the $.50 per copy charged by *TV Guide,* but was made necessary by the higher production costs resulting from system-specific publication of many small editions per week. People would pay it, the group reasoned, because of the perceived added value the magazine provided cable viewers. It would, after all, be the only publication in America to provide detailed listings of *everything* available on a particular cable system, identifying not only the time it was on but also the local cable channel that carried it.

Advertising revenues had also come into focus. In January, advertising income from a weekly system-specific magazine seemed likely to reach about $130 million by the eighth year of publication. Now the figure looked to be higher. One reason was Zucchi's salesmanship on Madison Avenue. Though no cable operator had yet signed a deal, Zucchi was already getting a warm response from advertisers for everything from cars and cigarettes to wines, liquors, and consumer electronics products. "The boat's gonna sail," Zucchi would tell them, "and you don't want to be left on the dock."

The two big unknowns remained circulation and marketing. The past autumn Dunn and Brauns had settled on a circulation target of 60 percent market penetration in the individual systems. But Brauns had lately begun to wonder whether 40 percent might be a safer target. Moreover, she now began to argue that even if initial sales were lower than that, it still would be possible through aggressive marketing to "grow" the figure to 40% over time.

Dunn thought the prospect of "growing" the figure unlikely, and they debated the matter often, particularly in light of what was beginning to take shape as a kind of go-for-broke marketing strategy dictated by Grum and Sutton. Anxious that every potential subscriber be able to read and examine the actual magazine before determining whether to subscribe, the two men had decided early on that whenever Zucchi signed up a cable system and began publishing magazines for it, each cable subscriber on the system would get the first four issues free of charge. Only after a month of free magazines would he be asked to subscribe.

Both Dunn and Brauns agreed that the four-issue-giveaway was a good idea, but Dunn worried about what could be done as a circulation booster if even *giving* the magazine away did not bring in the required minimum number of subscriptions.

It was Saturday morning at the end of a tiring week when the two young M.B.A.s found themselves debating the matter in the conference room all over again. The room showed evidence of countless such sessions. There were stacks of computer printouts and acetate slides, and even a box of molding breadcrusts and mustard tubes from a long-forgotten luncheon. Suddenly Dunn rounded on his colleague: "Lookit Sarah, if you actually give away four free issues of the thing, and you still don't make your minimum, what's the topper? What else is there to do? I'm telling you, we can only go to the well once on this deal. We either make the nut in the first four weeks, or we're dead, understand?"

Brauns disagreed. At the January COO Group presentation the task force had envisioned what Dunn termed "essentially a wholesale relationship" in which Time Inc. would publish the magazines and sell them to cable operators at a discount. The cable operators would then resell them at a markup to their subscribers. But since then, she and Zucchi had refined the notion into a "marketing partnership" concept. Time Inc. would now offer to handle subscription fulfillment and distribution. In return, cable operators would use their own door-to-door salesmen to solicit subscriptions, bolstered in their efforts by a campaign of local newspaper ads, and radio and TV spots, all paid for by Time Inc.

Brauns stared at her colleague. "You don't understand, Jeff, we *can* grow it. There's lots of ways—ads, promotionals, everything." As far as she was concerned, they could just crank up the heat.

Burgheim had not become involved in the marketing debates. Distrustful of the cable operators, yet doubtful of Zucchi's willingness to listen to his opinions on anything, Burgheim had confined himself to filing away story ideas as well as preparing mental lists of writers and editors he might recruit once Grunwald gave him authorization.

Grunwald's attitude toward the project baffled Burgheim. From the beginning, Burgheim had worried that the editor in chief might try to impose a tone of high-mindedness and even pomposity on the magazine, but his fear had been misplaced. Grunwald had shown no interest in the project whatsoever.

Burgheim welcomed the non-involvement, for it gave him a sense of freedom and independence he had not expected. Yet now Burgheim began to worry about the dark side of this benign neglect. Neither Zucchi nor Sutton seemed to grasp the peril in rushing the magazine to market in its present state of disarray, but every time Burgheim complained to Grunwald, the editor in chief would listen impassively and do nothing.

Burgheim would often mull over these matters far into the night, until he was the last person remaining in Amax-7. Some adventure this was turning out to be. Now there was even talk about Sutton planning to move the project to cheap rental quarters in the suburbs. Great, thought Burgheim, the industry at his doorstep and they want to move him out of town. Did anyone care about this project except him?

One night as Dunn departed he saw Burgheim sitting in his office, his back to the door, staring out the window into the dark. A typewriter was at his side and old newspaper clippings littered his desk. Dunn went downstairs, said goodnight to the security guard, then walked into the cool spring night. Halfway up the block he turned and looked back, and saw the light still burning in Burgheim's window. Seeing it, the thought came to Dunn that perhaps Burgheim was not really working at all, just staying late to show the business-side people that he too had responsibilities to attend to.

A week or so later, Dunn entered Zucchi's office holding a piece of paper in his hand.

"Dan," he said. "I don't know what we're going to do about Burgheim, but we've got to do something. Did you see this?" Dunn placed the paper on Zucchi's desk. It was a memo that Burgheim had distributed that morning proposing a "radical eleventh-hour solution" to the computer wars: Delay the launch of a weekly version of the magazine for a year, and in the meantime publish a low-cost monthly that would be less technologically demanding.

Zucchi had seen the memo and he was boiling. For the last six months he had worked nonstop to get the project up to speed, and now here came Burgheim—a man who so far as he could tell had done nothing from the beginning except bleat about plain vanilla and drag his feet—demanding to delay everything for another year more.

"What a pisser," said Zucchi, "a fucking monthly magazine!"

"I know," said Dunn, "we looked at monthlies back with Durrell. You can't make any money with them."

Fifty miles away in Norwalk, Connecticut, Peter Funt was having no trouble at all making money with a monthly magazine. But he soon learned that Time Inc. was likely to. The revelation came when Dunn's old boss, Larry Crutcher, told a trade reporter for *Multichannel News* that Time Inc. planned to launch a TV listings magazine that would probably be not unlike *On Cable*.

Reading the article that followed, Funt got a devilish idea and ran a quarter-page ad in the *New York Times* thanking Crutcher for the flattery. At 10:00 the next morning, Funt's phone rang; it was Crutcher threatening to sue him. Said Funt as his face broke into a grin: "Larry, let me answer you this way. If there is anything that I could do—any possible steps that I could take—to ensure that you *would* sue me, please tell me what they are and I will do them immediately. The publicity of such a suit would be absolutely invaluable to *On Cable*." The remark was a conversation-stopper.

Not long after that, two magazine consultants telephoned Funt. They informed him they were on retainer to Time Inc., and inquired if *On Cable* might be for sale. Funt was amazed. After all, Crutcher had just told *Multichannel News* that Time Inc. planned to publish its own magazine. Why would they now want to buy his? Could Time Inc. be running into trouble? That would be wonderful, Funt thought, anything Time Inc. did could not help but benefit *On Cable*. I'm sorry, Funt told the two, but his magazine was definitely not for sale.

Of all the project's troubles, the one that Zucchi understood the least, and felt most frustrated by, involved the computers. In desperation he turned to Siringo, who officially did not work for the project at all, but still reported to McGoff and worked across the street in the Time & Life Building. Every morning Siringo would come to work and find his desk littered with telephone message slips from Zucchi: he wanted terminals hooked up, multiplex transmission modems wired in, printers connected—everything up and running and all of it done yesterday.

Whenever possible, Siringo would do what he thought McGoff wanted him to do: drag his feet. Day after day it went on; the same pleas, the same demands—do this, do that, get it done now—and Siringo would drag his feet.

One day the telephone on his desk rang, and on the other end was Zucchi. Siringo looked at the blizzard of telephone messages covering his desk already that day and thought, Here we go.

He was right. There was an edge to Zucchi's voice, low and sharp and mean-sounding; so when Zucchi said would Carmen stop whatever it was that he was doing and come across the street, Carmen figured, Okay, you got it, I'll be right over.

Ten minutes later Siringo stood at the door of Zucchi's corner office in Amax-7 and rapped gently to enter. Zucchi rose from behind his desk and smiled—a big bear-like smile like you'd see from a linebacker ready to blitz. "Hey, Carmen," said Zucchi, opening his arms wide, "come on in."

To get the full flavor of what happened next, one needs to have some appreciation of the disparity in size between the two men. It was not that Zucchi towered over Siringo; he did not. At 5 feet, 9 inches, the publisher had only one and a half inches in height on the man. The difference involved the mass, the sheer bulk. A junior welterweight at 130 pounds, Siringo could have held his own against your average ninth-grade bully, but after that the smart move would have been to start talking fast and backing out of the schoolyard. But one look at Zucchi and you knew right away: at the age of fifteen Zucchi was already eating guys like Siringo for breakfast.

So there the two stood, Siringo smiling bravely and saying, "Hi, Dan," in a voice that suddenly sounded a touch too squeaky, and Zucchi looking at him with a leering grin that seemed to say, "Never mind the 'Hi' shit, gimme your lunch money."

Zucchi thereupon moved next to him, extended his arm around Siringo's back, and clamped a hand the size of a catcher's mitt on Siringo's bony, twitching shoulder. And never letting the grin fade from his face, Zucchi began pulling him close in a great snuggling bear-hug. And when he had the man virtually jammed into his armpit, the publisher of what would eventually become *TV-Cable Week* said to the man destined to become its director of editorial systems:

"Hey, paisanno, I wancha to do me this favor, huh?"

Siringo's jaw dropped. He did not think it was funny, he did not think it was cute; for an instant he actually thought he had turned up in the maw of someone who belonged to what Italian Americans like to call "the other church."

What Zucchi wanted, it seemed, was for Siringo to stop the stonewalling crap and get a computer hooked up and running to TV Data in Glens Falls. Zucchi didn't understand the details of the problem, and didn't want to know, either. All he knew was that they needed some multiplexer thing up there, and if they didn't get it they couldn't transmit listings for one of Labich's plain-vanilla tests. Without the test, there wouldn't be any production system. Without the production system there wouldn't be any magazine. And without the magazine, Zucchi was going to get angry. Got it?

"You betcha," said Siringo; he got it all right.

By car it is approximately 185 miles from midtown Manhattan to the Adirondacks village of Glens Falls, and in the following two days Siringo made two complete round trips to sort out the problems.

Late in the afternoon on the second day he returned to New York feeling tired and anxious, but decided he could not possibly sleep that night without seeing if the multiplexer hookup he had installed actually worked. So he activated the system, then called Glens Falls for a test transmission. To his relief, the connection worked perfectly.

Zucchi was about to head off for the day when he looked up to see Siringo standing in his doorway.

"It's all set, Dan," said Siringo. "Ready to go."

Zucchi rose from his desk and a huge, excited smile broke across his face. "Atta boy," said the publisher clapping him on the back several times in a row. "I finally got me a can-do guy!"

Feeling, as he put it later, "pretty damn good" at about that point, Siringo went back across the street to call his wife and leave for home. But his feelings of accomplishment lasted for as long as it took to cross Sixth Avenue, get in an elevator, and travel to the sixth floor of the Time & Life Building. For no sooner had he entered his office than there came surging in behind him, red-faced and furious, his 6 foot, 2 inch boss, McGoff.

With the veins on his temples pulsing wildly and his eyes bulging out in a rage, McGoff began screaming in his face:

"Never do that again! Never! Don't you understand? You're a manager in a $3 billion corporation. You don't *do* things like that!"

Thirty minutes later, Siringo climbed into his car and with a trembling hand started the ignition. As he did so, the thought came to him that he had fallen into a den of big business lunatics. On one side of the street he faced a man who sounded like he wanted to stuff him in a car trunk in the Bronx; on the other side, someone who seemed ready to start throwing him around like a rag doll! What kind of a situation was this? Caught in a technology free-fire zone, Siringo was learning the hard way that when it came to computers and Time Inc.'s cable listings magazine, there was nothing he could do that would not enrage someone.

TEN

Marsano's Favorite Show

IN TORONTO, CANADA, William Marsano knew nothing of the project's woes. Rather, the Time Inc. cable magazine remained in his mind an alluring opportunity, just as Burgheim had assured him in Las Vegas.

Marsano had thought back often to their night together at the NCTA convention and to the rumors that were already swirling through *TV Guide* at the time. Time Inc. was apparently going to spend millions on its new magazine—$20 million, $30 million, maybe even $50 million. The rumors drew credibility from the very company to which they were attached—Time Inc.—with its reputation for sticking with ventures for years if need be, to make them profitable.

Marsano wanted to be part of it. His career at *TV Guide* had lately stagnated, and he yearned for new horizons. The Time Inc. cable magazine could be just what he was looking for.

With his mind all but made up, Marsano had decided nonetheless to take Burgheim up on an offer he had made in Las

Vegas, and visit Time & Life before finally deciding. "Come on down," Burgheim had said. "See what it's all about."

During his two-day visit, Marsano met a long list of people, from Zúcchi and his multiplying assistants, to Burgheim's own much smaller staff of Adler, Davis, and Demargitay. The more he saw, the more he liked. The project was big, the backers were rich, the opportunity was unique.

Yet there was something about the project that troubled Marsano. He could not quite put his finger on it—a kind of loose, unbuttoned feel, as if the enterprise somehow lacked direction. One problem involved understanding Burgheim, whose verbal obliqueness often left Marsano puzzled as to exactly what the man was driving at, what role he envisioned for him on the project. "There are so many things to do, Bill," Burgheim had said, "thousands of them, really."

Though Marsano did not know it, Burgheim had already received permission from Grunwald to hire the *TV Guide Canada* editor as his second-in-command. But before extending a formal offer Burgheim felt it only proper to arrange courtesy visits for Marsano to both Grunwald and his deputy, Graves— meetings that Burgheim had expected would involve no more than a few minutes of pleasantries.

Yet Burgheim had failed to make the purpose of the meetings clear to Marsano, who now assumed that the two officials were in fact going to interview him themselves. The more he thought about the interviews the more nervous he got. If both the editor in chief and his top deputy were going to interview him for the job of assisting Burgheim, it seemed plain to Marsano that they must be attaching great importance to the project.

That night Marsano rehearsed his repertoire of television expertise. Working for *TV Guide* was fine as far as it went, but this was Time Inc.—another league altogether—and he wanted to be ready for anything.

Early the next day Marsano presented himself at the office of Editorial Director Graves, and when he emerged, he was sure he had made a favorable impression. They had discussed the listings business, cable operators, satellite technology, the motion-picture industry—in short, the entire lavish world of cable television.

Back in his office at Amax-7, Burgheim was staggered. "Wow," he said, "you were penciled in for ten minutes and you were in there for over an hour. That's great, that's great!"

Now Marsano was to have an audience with Grunwald, and the change in Burgheim was remarkable, as his demeanor swung from one of enthusiasm to intense apprehension. The meeting was to take place in the editor in chief's spacious thirty-fourth floor office, facing west across the vast expanse of New Jersey and the Hudson River piers. As Marsano and Burgheim walked the long, silent north wall corridor toward it, Burgheim began to bite his lip and glance back and forth from his watch to a clipboard full of notes in his hand.

In his office, Grunwald waited. He did not particularly want to meet Marsano, or to have to deal with Burgheim. Every time Burgheim got in his office he would bring up the same thing—plain vanilla—and for all Grunwald knew, he might be planning to do it again. Grunwald had bigger issues to contend with than Burgheim's plain vanilla—though in a way, plain vanilla was an annoying reminder of them all.

Though he was widely thought to be the single most influential individual in the company, Grunwald knew the truth was less grand. In the Time Inc. of the 1980s, he had emerged among his thirty-fourth floor peers as little more than an intellectual figurehead—largely, he had to admit, as a result of his own self-absorption in *Time* Magazine as the only publication in the corporation that truly seemed to interest him.

Wherever he was and whatever he was doing—be it meeting with political dignitaries at No. 10 Downing Street in London or enjoying the salt breezes at his weekend home on Martha's Vineyard—Grunwald could always make time to read galley proofs of articles on world and national affairs in *Time*

Magazine. The magazine's editors thus lived in constant dread of being second-guessed by their editor in chief. Yet the editors of Time Inc.'s other magazines had no such worry, for Grunwald rarely read their articles, leaving that task to deputies like Graves.

For the most part, Grunwald's accomplishments as editor in chief had been modest. He had been responsible for the launch of a science monthly, *Discover*, which had been poorly positioned among advertisers and had already accumulated losses that approached $30 million. A year later he presided over a six-magazine special project called "American Renewal," in which all the company's magazines had simultaneously addressed the theme of national rebirth. The company's public relations apparatus had promoted the project heavily but few critics had praised the result. The series itself had not done well as a money-maker.

Grunwald's diminishing influence was quickened by the conglomerate growth of Time Inc., which had reduced journalism to but one of many corporate enterprises, while elevating "business" to the principal preoccupation of the thirty-fourth floor. During the 1970s, as managing editor of *Time* Magazine, Grunwald had shown little interest in his publication's business and economics reportage. But when he ascended to the thirty-fourth floor as editor in chief in 1979, his attitude suddenly changed and he began speaking of "my friends in business," cultivating his new easy access to bankers like Walter Wriston, the chairman of Citicorp, and Felix Rohatyn, a Viennese-born partner in the investment firm of Lazard Freres, whom Grunwald would address chumily at corporate cocktail parties as "Fearless Felix."

Now the TV cable listings magazine somehow seemed to embody all his problems at once. Here was a subject, television, in which he had no real interest, a subject that lacked intellectual depth or even celebrities. Worse, the magazine not only represented the further expansion of Video Group's power and influence in corporate affairs, but that expansion was coming at the direct cost of further erosion of Magazine Group's independence and autonomy. Most distressing of all, the funds to develop the listings magazine looked to be potentially so enormous as to preempt for years to come the launching of any new magazine that Grunwald himself might want brought to market.

As Grunwald pondered these matters they seemed threatening in every way. Somehow, in some way, he needed to preserve his independence, and after much thought he had reached a decision. He would go to Munro, indicate his concerns, and come to an agreement. He would support the further development of the TV cable project, but only if Munro agreed to find the needed resources for a new Magazine Group publication that Grunwald himself wanted (if, in fact, Grunwald could decide on one.)

Even that course of action was not without difficulties. For although Grunwald occupied a special and exalted slot at the top of the mastheads of each of Time Inc.'s magazines, and had the opportunity each year to pronounce on matters of importance in Time Inc.'s annual report, he realized that his power and prestige was not equal to his predecessors': their corporate counterweights had been Time Inc.'s chairman of the board; for all practical purposes his was now merely Sutton, a group vice president.

William Marsano knew none of this, however, as he and Burgheim now entered the outer, secretarial antechamber to the editor in chief's office, a suite of rooms decorated in beige and wheat tones, and equipped with its own private bathroom. After several moments, the secretary opened the door to the editor in chief's inner office, and glancing in Marsano beheld, standing at the window, his back to the door, rocking gently on his heels as he gazed across the cityscape of Manhattan's West Side, Grunwald himself—short and pear-shaped, with wiry gray hair.

"Come in," said the editor in chief in a deep, gutteral voice, as he turned from the window. "Welcome to New York." He was hoping to make some brief small talk, be civil, then get the two men out of his office.

But Marsano had been preparing for the meeting all day, and he now tingled with anticipation, as ready as he had been earlier in the day with Graves to answer any TV question no matter how esoteric or unexpected.

What thus transpired was for Marsano without question one of the most bizarre conversations of his life. For as the three men faced each other—Burgheim having retreated to something like a crouch in a corner chair, and Marsano having seated himself nervously at Grunwald's elbow—Time Inc.'s editor in chief did not ask him his views of the American cable television industry; did not ask him his thoughts about gathering, editing, and publishing TV listings; did not ask him his opinions regarding the cable operators who would have to market this complex new product. Instead, Grunwald dispensed with the small talk and cut right to the heart of the matter. Leveling a penetrating stare at the man he was sizing up to take on the number-two editorial job in what was shaping up as the biggest, costliest project the company had going, Grunwald fired off a single, blunt question:

"What's your favorite TV show?"

Marsano turned to stone. Was this some idea of a joke? Out of the corner of his eye he spotted Burgheim; the blood had drained from his face and he sat in ashen stillness. No, thought Marsano, this was no joke at all; there was apparently an actual "right" answer! His mind raced wildly, what could it be—"The McNeil/Lehrer Report," "60 Minutes"? He needed something with class, quality, respectability, but not too much—kind of middle-brow TV, a sort of *Time* Magazine of the air, but what? At last he spoke:

" 'The Mary Tyler Moore Show'?"

In the summer of 1982 more than 40,000 different network and syndicated series program offerings played on American television—the total of nearly three decades' worth of commercial entertainment—and the astounding thing was, out of all of them he had apparently picked precisely the right one. By the fortune of the Gods, Marsano had come up with Grunwald's favorite show! In front of him, the editor in chief broke into a smile, while across the room he could hear Burgheim breathe a sigh of relief.

What followed thereafter Marsano could not recall, save that everything had ended as abruptly and discordantly as it had started. Grunwald rose, extended his hand, and the next thing Marsano knew he was heading back down the corridor, past oil portraits of previous corporate chieftains, past framed photographs by great Time Inc. practitioners of the craft: Alfred Eisenstadt, Margaret Bourke White, and others. Then it was back down the elevator, out the door, and across the street to Amax-7.

Jesus, thought Marsano, big powerful company, big powerful men at the top, but did they really have hold of this thing? That afternoon Burgheim officially offered him a job, and though Marsano promptly accepted, that night he too began to wonder what the future would hold.

ELEVEN

Meigher Meets the Sector Slides

O
NE DAY in early June Dunn showed up for work with his jaw set and went from office to office, conducting a poll. "Okay, Anne, what do you think Dick should name the magazine?" Next he went to Demargitay. "How about it, Gida, what name do *you* like for the magazine?"

Dunn was upset because he and Zucchi could not get Burgheim to make up his mind on almost anything about the magazine—not even a name for it. In the tradition of Time Inc., selecting a name for a magazine is an editorial prerogative, just as is choosing which articles to publish, what pictures to run, or how to lay out a spread of artwork on a page. But as far as Zucchi and Dunn could tell, Burgheim had been dallying over a name for the publication since January, and the more he and Dunn urged him to make a decision, the more difficult and evasive he seemed to get. Zucchi hated Burgheim's endless mulling over issues, and he wondered how the magazine would ever get published if its editor had such trouble making decisions.

Down the hall, Burgheim had learned of Dunn's poll and

he was fuming. Not only was it an affront to him personally, but it revealed how little grasp Dunn and Zucchi had of his own problems in the matter. He was as anxious as they were to get the title question resolved, but the decision was out of his hands and rested with Grunwald, the ultimate authority on all magazine titles for the corporation. Unknown to his business-side colleagues, Burgheim had been sending Grunwald proposals all spring, but the editor in chief had not responded or acted on any of them. Now here were Zucchi and Dunn pillorying him for the delay when the real culprit was Grunwald.

Back in his office, Dunn tallied up the results of his poll. It consisted of eight choices, all cleared by Time Inc.'s legal department as being free of copyright infringement with other publishers. First place went to the title *All TV*, followed by *Viewer*, and *Choice*. Next to last on the list came a clumsy-sounding title that made Dunn think of industrial equipment every time he heard it: *TV-Cable Week*. It seemed wrong in every way—wordy, dull, completely without zip—and he was glad the staff agreed. A name like that could turn out to be a disaster. He could see himself as a typical American television viewer, sitting in front of the television, and turning to his wife and saying, "Hey hon, what else is on? Will you pass me the whatchamacallit?"

Across the street in the Time & Life Building, Kelso Sutton also faced a problem. In two weeks time his task force was scheduled to present a second, and what he hoped would be final, briefing on their work to Munro and the COO Group. After that they would have to go before the board of directors for formal authorization to take the product to market—a product that had not been market tested in any way, and was dependent for distribution upon a radically new and untried marketing plan.

Sutton had already told his subordinates to prepare a "bailout plan" to include in the presentation in case the magazine proved to be a failure. Yet unknown to his subordinates, Sutton now had more reason than ever to doubt the project's success.

For his own protégé, Chris Meigher, head of Corporate Circulation, had begun privately warning him that the circulation assumptions of his two former aides, Dunn and Brauns, were untested, unprecedented, and improbable.

This put Sutton in an extraordinarily difficult position. Meigher was more than just his protégé, Meigher was also the leading circulation expert in the corporation. Jeff Dunn and Sarah Brauns had already said to the COO Group that the project's circulation assumptions were unprecedented and risky; now Meigher was saying the same thing.

What if they all were right? Sutton thought of himself as a gambler in the world of corporate decision making, and in the case of the TV cable project he was prepared to take big risks for the big payoff that seemed to loom. But as he pondered the many complexities of the matter, it seemed to him that he simply could not have his own Corporate Circulation director criticizing the project's fundamental marketing assumptions without taking action. Perhaps a meeting would be in order.

To the meeting in Sutton's office came the by now familiar cast: Zucchi, Dunn, Brauns, Crutcher, and now Meigher as well. After everyone had settled into chairs, Sutton turned to Meigher:

"Okay, Chris, what about it? Tell them what you told me."

Meigher replied, "What I want to say is, these response assumptions, the penetration figures, are *much* higher than anything we've ever had in this building. I mean, 60 percent penetration? Come on!"

Hearing this, Dunn became visibly agitated, and for good reason, since both he and Brauns were already on the record as saying the same thing—only instead of saying it privately to Sutton, the two young M.B.A.s had said it openly to Munro and the entire COO Group. Leaning forward in his seat, Dunn looked at Sutton:

"Wait a minute! We said that back in January! No one on this task force ever said these numbers were solid—because no one ever tested them!"

Now Sutton spoke up, saying to no one in particular, "Okay, so tell me again why we *shouldn't* test them."

A minute of silence ensued as task-force members pondered the abruptly shifting ground of the situation—for here before them was the company's group vice president for magazines, who, it must have seemed, was attempting to contend that the task force had already previously advised him *not* to test the magazine when, in fact, it was *he* who had told *them* not to test it.

The first person to speak was Zucchi, who actually began repeating back to Sutton the very reasons that Sutton himself had given in his office six months earlier for not testing—only now, Zucchi's recounting of them made it seem, whether unwittingly or not, as if these reasons were the task force's when, in fact, they were Sutton's.

Stunned by this reversal, Dunn grew even angrier, interrupting Zucchi in mid-sentence and demanding of Sutton, "Hold on! Hold on! We said you *should* test them! You tell *us* why we shouldn't test them!"

At this, Crutcher's mouth dropped open, for no one had ever seen Sutton spoken to that way before by anybody.

Back and forth the task-force members retraced all the reasons why the product needed to be market tested. Yet in the end the discussion wound up looping around to where the matter had come to rest the previous January: no test, rely instead on numbers alone, and the meeting broke up.

Yet no sooner had Meigher and Crutcher departed, leaving behind Zucchi and his task-force, than an even wilder scene ensued, as Sutton took a memo from his desk drawer.

"Listen to this," said the group vice president, and he began reading the memo aloud.

The players were transfixed, for the memo amounted to an indictment of the entire project; that the venture was a great risk, that there were too many uncertainties to justify a full-scale launch of the magazine, and that the writer doubted very much whether Time Inc. could pull this off successfully.

Having finished reading the memo, Sutton placed it on the desk in front of him and proceeded to ask the group for their thoughts on its contents. One by one the amazed task-force members affirmed that each risk and uncertainty was true, just as each had been true six months earlier when they had first recommended a test.

Then someone asked who had written the document. Sutton would not say. But, added the executive well known for his games playing with subordinates, "If you can guess, then I'll tell you." Whereupon he began encouraging the group to go ahead and start guessing. What now unfolded was the most bizarre spectacle of all, as the baffled task-force members reeled off the names of one Time Inc. big-wig after another, from corporate-level officials like President Munro and Chairman of the Board Ralph Davidson, to various Video Group executives.

"Give us a hint," asked one of the players. "Is it someone from Magazine Group?"

When Sutton nodded affirmatively, the members began calling out Magazine Group names, from the two executives who had just left the room (Meigher and Crutcher) to the project's former publishing side head, Durrell, even to officials in CM&D.

For many minutes the game continued, as the list of names grew to upwards of two dozen, to each of which the group vice president simply shook his head no and invited more guessing.

At last, Sutton stuck the memo back in his desk drawer and ended the meeting—without revealing who it was who had so scathingly criticized the project's prospects.

The players wandered out positively staggered. Just what in the world was going on? Here they were mere days from presenting what now looked like a full and final briefing on the project to Munro and the COO Group, and Sutton seemed not only to be ignoring reasoned warnings as to the dangers of pressing ahead on the basis of untested assumptions and hypotheses, but was actually taunting the group with sophomoric guessing games.

That afternoon Amax-7 buzzed as never before. Dunn was livid. "I may be a bit green in this company," he said to Zucchi. "But I wasn't born yesterday! I mean, come on! Dan, you weren't on the project back in January so you couldn't have known, but we said all that stuff to the COO Group six months ago! No way, José; *he* was the one who said not to test the magazine, not *us*!"

That night Dunn replayed the scene in his mind all over again—the intervention of Meigher, the maneuvers of Sutton, the surreal quality of the entire afternoon—and he thought, I've got to get off this project somehow, before it's too late. The whole thing could be out of control.

Later that week Zucchi called the players together. Sutton wanted him to stress the secrecy of their work. No one was supposed to talk about anything, and most especially "the numbers." As the financial forecasts of earlier in the spring had shown, Time Inc. was going to have to invest upwards of $100 million over the project's first five years—the largest such commitment in publishing history—and the group vice president did not want anyone outside of Time Inc., particularly investment analysts on Wall Street, getting wind of the huge scale of the expenditure.

After the meeting, Labich took Dukemejian aside. Though not involved in the business and marketing studies being done by Dunn and Brauns, Dukemejian had access to the project's financial details since he had been helping Labich work out production costs for the magazine. Dukemejian had gotten bids from over 100 different printing plants around the country, had visited large numbers of computer suppliers, had gotten price quotes from truckers and binderies. No more than half a dozen people on the task force knew the full financial details of the project, and Dukemejian was one of them.

"Remember," said Labich, "mum's the word." It was to be like Project Mustang, a deep secret.

That afternoon Dukemejian sat in his office and thought

about what he had been told. Organizing the production of the magazine was going to prove staggering. Everything would have to be coordinated down to the minute. The plain-vanilla listings would flow in from TV Data each Wednesday, be custom edited by Burgheim's staff on Thursday and Friday, then be transmitted to different printing plants in different parts of the country on Friday night and Saturday. The plants would then print the system-specific editions on Saturday night and Sunday. Meanwhile, other plants in other parts of the country would already be printing the national wrap. Then truckers would collect all the parts and transport them to binderies, where the right parts would be stapled together into the right system-specific editions. Other truckers would next take the completed editions to postal mail drops. If anyone missed a deadline, even by a few hours, the whole thing could fall apart.

To Dukemejian, it seemed an undertaking to challenge the organizing abilities of the German General Staff. Here he was, a young man who had just finished an M.B.A. night-school course at New York University, and suddenly he was involved in planning Time Inc.'s own Operation Barbarosa, the invasion of Russia. Now, Labich and Zucchi were making it sound even scarier—a veritable Manhattan Project, complete with its own aerospace company and hush-hush computer effort, Project Mustang. Yes, thought Dukemejian, in the last half-year he had come a long way from Pine Street. Now he was working on Time Inc.'s atom bomb.

Much of the following week Sutton spent rehearsing his subordinates for the presentation to Munro and the COO Group, scheduled to take place in only a few days' time. He wanted a presentation that was clear, easy to follow, and that made plain how thoroughly the market had been researched. If Munro and the others liked what they heard, there would be one step left—a presentation to Time Inc.'s board of directors

—then the cable listings task force would metamorphose from a project into an actual magazine, complete with an editor, a publisher, and a capital appropriation from the board to go into business.

But the rehearsals did not go well. For one thing there was the matter of the quadrant slides, which increasingly had become the centerpiece of everything the task force said and did. Now they were going to be the centerpiece of the presentation to the COO Group all over again—the same officials who had sat through the same slide show explanation of the marketplace once already. Would the performance hold their attention a second time? At a rehearsal several days earlier his subordinates had put on their slide show, then for a climax added a new slide at the end. It read:

RISKS AND UNCERTAINTIES
ALL OF THE ABOVE

Sutton had exploded; the presentation was terrible. He didn't want jokes and clowning around, he wanted a simple and easy to follow case for why the magazine would succeed.

The date was July 9th, and the setting was the same eleventh-floor conference room where the saga had begun the previous winter. For Time Inc.'s writers and editors—many of whom were not even aware that the meeting was occurring—the event was of no real significance. But to the company's business executives, the presentation had the drama and excitement of a Broadway opening.

Who attended, and who did not, took on its own drama. From the thirty-fourth floor came Sutton, Munro, Nicholas, Video Group's Levin, Grunwald, and his deputy Graves; from across the street came the task force, still reeling from speculation as to the identity of the mystery memo writer. One person conspicuous by his absence (at least to the task-force members who had only days earlier witnessed his anti-project skepticism first-hand in Sutton's office) was Meigher—apparently not invited.

Yet whatever doubts the task-force harbored about the project, they and Sutton kept them well hidden during the presentation. For what transpired, in a sense, was precisely what had occurred six months earlier, even down to the quadrants slide show and the talk about the project being akin to opening up China. Now, however, the presentation came bolstered by a new and elaborate set of mathematical projections, and resulting marketing strategies, from penetration levels to advertising, production costs, profit margins, and more.

In the face of such an array of appealing figures, the notion of not bothering to market test the magazine hardly seemed an issue. Instead, after the task-force members had finished their presentations, Munro turned to Video Group head Levin, who had been almost totally uninvolved in the project since January, and asked, "What about it? Is this going to fly?" From the one-time Wall Street lawyer came an enthusiastic thumbs-up—just as it had following the task-force's presentation six months earlier in the same room.

Chairman of the Board Ralph Davidson was equally hopeful. Though he had missed the presentation that morning, it was not for lack of interest. Davidson, a ruggedly good-looking man in his mid-50s, had little executive power in the organization, but as board chairman he possessed an influence that went beyond mere ceremonial duties. Ruminating in his office during a chat with Nick Nicholas on the project's prospects and the outcome of the presentation not long afterward, Davidson reflected on how important the project was to his company and, in particular, to Magazine Group. "There just aren't any other weekly ideas around," he mused. "This may be the last big weekly publishing opportunity this company gets."

That night Sutton took the task force to dinner at a nearby restaurant named Mercurio's. A favorite hangout of Time Inc.

executives, the restaurant catered more to a luncheon crowd than to dinner guests, and was largely empty as nearly a dozen of the players streamed in, led by Zucchi.

Drinks were ordered all around, and people began settling into chairs and banquettes. After the tension of recent days it was as if everyone just wanted to drink up and joke—forget about the computer wars, the intrigues, the quarrels, just tie one on and have a good time.

Of them all, Dunn and Brauns had plainly been through the most. Though Zucchi and Burgheim had been under pressure for months, the two young M.B.A.s had felt strains of a sort that only they could appreciate. Ultimately, the magazine had been their idea, not Burgheim's or Zucchi's, and they had been wary from the start. They had argued that it needed to be market tested before being implemented, and had done so in unambiguous and forceful language. They had given Time Inc.'s brass, as Dunn had put it, the publishing-world equivalent to the surgeon general's warning: Caution! These numbers may be hazardous to your financial health!

But what good had it done? At every turn, the brass had pushed the project forward, faster and faster. Before every presentation the two had gone over each other's remarks many times. "Are we covered here?" Brauns would ask. "Is there anything we've overlooked? Anything at all?"

Dunn was even more edgy. Nearly a year had passed since he had stood in that forty-seventh floor conference hall and heard Sutton mention his plan to market test a TV magazine. But there had never really *been* such a magazine—at least not until he and Brauns had invented it. Nor, as it now appeared, had there been any plan for a market test either. Instead, Sutton had apparently decided to put the project in the hands of Time Inc.'s own Italian stallion, Dan Zucchi, and let him pound it into shape come what may.

At about 10:30, Sutton called for the check, and people began to get up.

"Come on," said Zucchi. "The night's young! Kelso and I are going out on the town, who's for it?" and he looked around.

"I'll go," said Dukemejian.

Zucchi turned to Dunn. "What about it Jeff, want to come?"

Dunn shook his head. "Not tonight, Dan. I think I've had it."

"Me too," said Brauns. "I'm going home."

TWELVE

Fine, but Where's the Tar Baby?

AS PRESIDENT and chief executive officer of Time Inc., Dick Munro presided over a conglomerate organization that stretched from midtown Manhattan to the pine stands of the Texas/Louisiana border to satellite transmission facilities in the Far East. Yet wherever he was, whatever he was doing, one matter now loomed constantly among his concerns: how would the company's TV listings magazine be received on Wall Street?

On the evidence, Munro had no reason for worry. Time Inc. had a reputation among analysts for possessing a magic touch with new publications. Time Inc. had never launched a magazine that had not succeeded; moreover, in the case of this magazine, the company possessed undisputed leadership not only in the magazine field but also in the cable market where it was to be distributed.

Still, Munro felt troubled. He worried not so much that the magazine would fail, which he doubted, but that Wall Street analysts would fail to grasp the complexities of the business plan; would not realize that the magazine was *expected* to lose money, very large amounts of money, for several years before the profits began to flow in. He worried that analysts would see the losses and leap to a false conclusion: that the concept was not working. Somehow Time Inc. needed to get the message across that it was prepared to drop as much as $45 million of the required $100 million appropriation in the first year alone.

Munro had discussed the problem with his colleagues and they had decided on a public relations campaign to capitalize on the company's reputation for never having backed away from a startup. *Sports Illustrated* had been a classic example. Henry Luce, ignoring repeated advice to shut it down, had poured money into the magazine for eleven years before seeing a profit. Even *People*, the phenomenon of the 1970s, which took three years to move solidly into the black, proved that patience was essential on startups.

So the idea would be to stress Time Inc.'s "deep pockets" commitment to the project, which might require as long as five years to turn profitable. That was the theme, and Munro would soon be reading and approving press releases that would go out—once Time Inc.'s board gave the project its go-ahead—to newspapers, magazines, and media outlets around the country.

Munro had little doubt that the strategy would prove effective in convincing Wall Street. It should certainly drive home the point that the magazine's eventual success should not be judged by the early results, but that Time Inc. had staying power on the project.

Yet for all that, still something troubled Munro: what if the magazine failed? What if in spite of all the insisting and assuring, all the financial modeling and focus-group sampling, what if in spite of everything Time Inc. had done for the last year, it still failed and they had to shut it down? How would they then explain the press releases, or the five-year commitment that never materialized? The prospect seemed too Gothic to contemplate. Besides, there were more immediate problems to

attend to, such as rehearsing the task force for its presentation
to the board of directors.

Rehearsals had been taking place all week under Sutton's
direction in an eighth-floor chamber that adjoined a large, oak-
paneled auditorium and veranda. This was the complex in
which Time Inc. would from time to time hold annual shareholder meetings, but it had now been requisitioned for a final
dress rehearsal for the board presentation, and Munro had
come to watch.

Yet as the presentation unfolded, Munro seemed to grow
restive, as if troubled by something he could not quite identify.
After the presentations concluded, Munro turned to Sutton:
"It's not working for me. I don't know, maybe I've just heard
it too many times. We've got to do something. Liven it up
somehow."

The players knew very well what was wrong, but no one
wanted to say so since the problem stemmed from Sutton.
Munro could not understand the presentation because Sutton
had left the quadrant slides out of the presentation outline he
had given the task force.

If Sutton had left out the slides because he had simply
forgotten them, it would have been understandable. On the eve
of the board presentation the group vice president had much
on his mind—the size of the appropriation he would request,
the lack of a market test, the warnings of Meigher—and as the
fateful day had approached he had grown increasingly on edge.

But Sutton had left the slides out for a reason: by now he
hated the very mention of them. When the task force had first
shown the matrix to him the previous winter the two crossed
lines had seemed a stroke of organizing wizardry. But in the
months that followed, all he heard from the group was quadrant
this, quadrant that, as if without the concept the project would
lose its bearings completely. By now he wished he had never
heard the word quadrant. If they had to have the damned
slides, he was at least going to call them what *he* wanted—
sector slides—something to put his own stamp on the things.

Yet now was hardly the time to go into any of that.

An awkward silence settled over the group as people waited for a cue from Sutton. But the group vice president remained silent, and after several minutes Munro left. Yet no sooner did he depart than a much more urgent concern surfaced: what to call the publication. After all these months, and all the pleading, and all the arguing that he should not let it drag on any longer, Burgheim apparently *still* did not have a name for the magazine. "My God," groaned one of the group, "what are we going to do, ask the board to let us launch 'the thing'?"

A debate ensued, punctuated by suggestions to continue with the task force's working title, *TV-Cable Magazine,* a name that everyone agreed was hateful, then change it later when somebody came up with a better idea. But that notion was abandoned when it was pointed out that there would have to be a press conference following the board vote, and that it would look preposterous for Time Inc. to announce plans to publish a magazine for which the company could not devise an acceptable name.

Finally Sutton cut off the discussion. Earlier he and Grunwald had conferred on the matter, and now he revealed the results. "It's *TV-Cable Week,*" the group vice president announced with finality. "That's what we'll call it." Across the room, Jeff Dunn felt his stomach drop, and he thought, Oh no, not *that!*

Burgheim was also startled. He too had been discussing names with the editor in chief and had gotten the impression that Grunwald might have been leaning toward a name that Burgheim himself preferred: *Select.* Yet with time having run out and the need to decide the matter now immediate and unavoidable, Grunwald had apparently settled on a name that as far as Burgheim was concerned seemed to embody Grunwald's view of the magazine itself: boring, lifeless, and not worth a second thought.

Two days later, on August 12, 1982, the group reconvened in the conference room. Now it was the real thing: a formal presentation of the project to Time Inc's 23-member board of directors. More than a full year had elapsed since the project had first begun, and in that time, what had started as two men with vague instructions and no place to sit, had ballooned into a staff of more than 30 individuals, occupying half the seventh floor of a Rockfeller Center office building. Meanwhile, the trade press had begun to write stories about the project, the computer graphics industry had awakened to what looked like a potentially large new customer for editorial/production equipment, and from San Diego to Boston, cable system operators had begun to gossip and speculate about Time Inc.'s new project.

Keep the presentations short and clear, Sutton had told the task force, echoing his earlier advice from Grum on how to deal with the board: present a broad-brush picture, and under no circumstances digress into the project's complexities. Give the board the presentation, give them lunch, then get them to vote. That was the plan.

At about 11:15 A.M. the directors began to gather. Each had already received a briefing kit that contained among other things a two-page summary prospectus of the plan and a copy of the dummy, featuring the cover portrait of Dolly Parton.

Meanwhile, in keeping with the relaxed ambiance being orchestrated, Time Inc.'s executive catering service had set up a drinks bar next to the veranda and was now serving beverages, both soft drinks and alcoholic, to the arriving guests. As befitting purposeful gatherings of important people, the talk was cordial, muted, and the smiles sincere—though not every arriving guest seemed as at ease as some of the veterans.

New to the board was Clifton R. Wharton, Jr., chancellor of the State University of New York and a trustee of the Rockefeller Foundation. Wharton moved awkwardly among the others, finally seating himself next to another director, Donald Perkins, head of the Jewel Companies, Inc., a midwest supermarket chain. Momentarily, Perkins turned to a third director, James Beré, chairman of the board of Borg-Warner Corporation, a manufacturer of automobile parts, and announced where he stood on the idea, saying, "Well, *I'm* for it! If there's one thing this company knows it's magazines!"

First to speak was Grunwald, who tried to sound enthusiastic but wound up sounding more concerned with recording his doubts. He had heard plenty about the project's computer woes already, and had decided to make sure the record showed his worries, saying, "Ralph Graves and I are very conscious of the huge and risky unknowns involved. These unknowns are not only financial, but we also don't really know yet if technology will be able to cope adequately with an immensely complicated publishing proposition." So that no one should be unduly alarmed, however, Grunwald quickly added, ". . . although we feel this can be adequately tested before launch."

Then, in a remark that promptly became known among the players as "Henry's deal," Grunwald turned to his arrangement with Munro and said: "There is yet another problem, namely that the investment required for *TV-Cable Week* will hamper our ability to develop other magazines. Dick Munro and I have agreed, however, that work will go forward, and that if we indeed develop something worthwhile and promising, the resources will be found for it."

This was not as upbeat and positive sounding as one might have hoped, and as Sutton now rose to speak, the players wondered what he would say. How for example would he deal with the question of a market test, the absence of which seemed to hang over the project like a noxious odor.

Sutton chose to handle the situation this way: he simply left out the fact that his task force had long since prepared and urged upon the COO Group a detailed $9 million market-test plan—a test that, had it been undertaken, would by now be over and the results available. Instead, he told the board only that the cost of such a test would rival a "controlled launch," that the test itself would take "a very long time," and that undertaking a test would cause the company to miss its "window of opportunity."

"Given all that, you may wonder why I can stand here and comfortably recommend that we proceed," observed the group vice president. "I do so because of two bedrock convictions. The market is large, ready for this product, and as you will see, we have identified a section no one is serving. Few, we think, will have the industry or vision to see the potential of this section.

"Secondly, Time Inc.—with magazine, cable, and subscription television know-how—has a better appreciation and understanding of the consumer in this market than any company around." At this, Sutton rose slightly on the balls of his feet, and ended with a flourish: "And we intend to put the know-how to good use. So let's get at it!"

After Sutton came the players. Zucchi talked about advertising and the marketplace, Brauns discussed circulation questions, Dunn addressed the business plan financials, and bringing up the rear, Burgheim, who remained as seemingly mired as ever in plain-vanilla code words, saying, "The initial success of *TV-Cable Week* will ride on the comprehensiveness, accuracy, and utility of its listings." It was a statement that Burgheim believed as truth itself but that Dunn saw as more of his obsession with "perfect information," that Labich saw as a sideways dig at TV Data, and that Zucchi saw as more complaining about computers.

When the last speaker finished, silence filled the room. Was this magazine a good idea, a bad idea? Did any director even *understand* the idea? At least one man was having trouble. As the largest single shareholder in the company, with 15 percent of all Time Inc.'s outstanding common stock to his name or those of close relatives, Texas lumberman Arthur Temple had an important stake in the project's outcome, and had listened carefully to what had been said. But in spite of that, he felt unsure.

Temple prided himself on his down-home instincts, and in

his ability to ferret out the weakness in almost any business deal. If he did not like a deal, he would say so straight out. "A man can eat only so many beans," Temple would say. This cable magazine troubled him. Sure, he'd heard the talk about the cable operator "middlemen," and the computers that might not work, and why the magazine could not be test marketed. But what Temple wanted to know was how come, in spite of all that, these Time Inc. fellas were making it sound so easy.

Temple had to get to the bottom of this cable magazine somehow, and as the silence continued he realized that he would have no choice. Since no one else was going to ask anything, he would have to. He would have to hit them with one of his Arthur Temple boondocks specials. Heaving about in his seat, he removed the cigar from his mouth, blew out some smoke, and in a sleepy, Southern drawl asked:

"Fine, but where's the tar baby in this deal?"

As the succeeding weeks turned into months, and *TV-Cable Week* unfolded into a blunder of bigger and bigger proportions, the Texas tycoon's question would, if anything, seem too limited in scope, since it was not a matter of finding a tar baby "in" *TV-Cable Week;* rather, the magazine proved in its every dimension to be a complete tar baby deal all its own, sticking suppliers, customers, in fact anyone who came near it.

Yet not everyone in the room seemed as curious about the future as Temple did. One director, Beré of Borg-Warner, actually seemed to be having trouble staying awake. For as the speakers had droned on, the courtly gentleman's head had nodded backward and his mouth had slouched open, suggesting that at any minute there might begin to waft from it the soft, dozing sounds of snores.

At about 12:45 P.M. the task-force members were dismissed and, relieved that the ordeal was over at last, the group left for lunch at Romeo Salta's, a nearby Italian restaurant, so the board could discuss the matter in private and render its decision.

Munro was also glad that it was over, and as the directors headed to the elevator bank he detoured briefly into the men's room. There he found Clifford Grum already at a urinal. "Well, how do you think it went?" asked Munro.

"In my opinion it went well, Dick," answered Grum with a smile. "There weren't any questions we couldn't answer."

Several blocks away in Romeo Salta's, the task-force members settled themselves into chairs. "It's a done deal," thought Zucchi as he studied the menu. "The whole thing was cooked a long time ago, before I even got involved." Sitting nearby, Dunn was more doubtful. He simply could not believe the company was going to go ahead with the project without a market test, and he was sure the board members would feel the same. He turned to Zucchi and grinned: "Hey Dan, what about that crack by Temple! Where's the tar baby, can you beat it?" Zucchi laughed and began looking around for a waiter to take orders.

Later that afternoon Sutton came to Zucchi's office to deliver the news personally: the board had given its go-ahead, and *TV-Cable Week* was now in business. As the word spread through Amax-7, champagne was opened, and soon the hall was filled with joking, back-slapping employees. Among them was Burgheim. Like Dunn, he too had doubted the outcome of the board vote. Everything about the project had been tentative and vague—the computers, the marketing plan, even the vaunted cooperation of the cable operators. Was Time Inc.'s board going to authorize the launch of a $100 million magazine on the basis of that?

Even so, Burgheim had to admit that privately he had badly wanted the board to give its approval. In the final analysis, he really didn't care what name Grunwald and Sutton gave to the magazine, or how nightmarish and complex Labich's computer system proved to be, or about any of the other enervating squabbles that had consumed them all for months. What mattered was that Time Inc.'s board had at last voted its approval, and now the opportunity that he had hungered for was finally his: the editorship of a Time Inc. weekly magazine. And not just any weekly magazine, but one that was emerging as the most elaborate, complex new magazine in all of publishing.

That night Burgheim mulled over the many things that still
had to be done to prepare for a launch. September was obviously out of the question, just as he had felt back in June.
Though Zucchi's marketing and business-side staff had been
swelling by the week, Burgheim had been blocked until after
the board vote from recruiting the writers, editors, and computer personnel who would actually prepare the magazine.
Now he had to interview and hire them.

Burgheim had compiled a list of writers and editors from
within the company for key jobs on his staff and had already
quietly held exploratory conversations with many of them. Now
he would go back and make formal offers.

But where could he tell them they would be working?
Sutton had already made clear that he planned to move the
magazine out of the Amax Building, but he remained vague
about where it would ultimately be housed. Burgheim was em-
phatic that the magazine needed to remain somewhere within
the midtown Manhattan area and had said so repeatedly both
to Sutton and Grunwald. Over and over Burgheim had stressed
the importance not just of being able to recruit skilled and
experienced writers and editors from within the company, but
also of having quick and easy access to the Time & Life Building's research library and photographic archives. Now Burgheim wondered how much longer it would be before Sutton
revealed his intentions so that he could get on with the business
of assembling a staff.

Meanwhile, Burgheim wanted only to revel in the triumph
of the day, and sitting alone at his desk he took a piece of paper
from a drawer, spun it under the rollband of his typewriter, and
began to peck out a memo of congratulations to everyone in
Amax-7.

Thirty miles away, in the exclusive Greenwich, Connecticut, enclave of Field Point Circle, one of Time Inc.'s fourteen
outside directors, Thomas Watson, Jr., the recently retired

chairman emeritus of IBM, also reflected on the prospects for *TV-Cable Week*, but in a distinctly more troubled way. He wondered whether, after Time Inc. went to what was apparently going to be enormous trouble and cost, people would actually buy such a magazine.

Had they known his feelings, Watson's colleagues would have been astonished, for by all accounts he had far more important matters to concern himself with than the future of a television-listings magazine. A man of surpassing wealth and influence in the world of business, Watson was one of a handful of American businessmen—David Rockefeller, Walter Wriston, Irving Shapiro—who seemed to transcend the world of business altogether. Like global ambassadors of capitalism, they suggested the triumphant synthesis of morality and the profit motive, and of them all none seemed more patrician yet genteel than Watson. Under Watson, IBM had not only become the wealthiest corporation in the world, with a market value of more than $60 billion, but "Big Blue" had also become a paradigm of organizational efficiency—the corporate juggernaut that seemed to stand for all that was best in American technology, marketing, and management know-how.

Watson was more than the quintessential business leader; he was also a man of stature in the worlds of statecraft and diplomacy and had contacts that cut across the highest levels of international affairs. In 1979, upon reaching his company's mandatory retirement age of 65, Watson had stepped down from the chairmanship of IBM to become President Jimmy Carter's ambassador to the Soviet Union, a post he held until January 1981, when as protocol dictated, he submitted his resignation to the new president-elect, Ronald Reagan.

Now it was eighteen months later, Watson had returned to private life, and among other things had accepted an invitation to return to a seat he had held as an outside director on Time Inc.'s board from 1954 to 1966. Meanwhile, he and his wife, Olive, had decided to sell their home in Greenwich's Meadowcroft Lane, and in June of 1982 had paid $2.2 million for an eleven-room waterfront estate on Field Point Circle to be closer to Long Island Sound. At the same time, Watson had returned to his many civic commitments, from his membership in such organizations as the Council on Foreign Relations, to the River Club of New York.

Yet in spite of these many distractions, he still felt vaguely troubled by the prospects for Time Inc.'s TV magazine. Watson wondered whether the magazine was really the sort of well-conceived and well-designed product he had come to expect from Time Inc. Had they dry-run the magazine with potential buyers? Were they sure it would sell? Just how did they know? The dummy he had seen looked interesting, he agreed, but was there really a need for the product? After all, he could find out everything he personally needed to know about upcoming television programs from *TV Guide* or the *New York Times*.

Watson had been unsure how to deal with his concerns. On the one hand he did not want to be perceived as a meddler in Time Inc.'s internal affairs. On the other hand, he was a director of the corporation and had certain responsibilities, both to the company and to its shareholders. It seemed only right and proper that he get his misgivings on the record. But to whom, and in what fashion?

Perhaps the proper way would be to write Kelso Sutton a letter.

THIRTEEN

The Ultimate Focus Group

THE FOLLOWING MONDAY, August 16th, employees in Time Inc.'s corporate public relations department began telephoning trade reporters to announce a press conference. As far as the employees knew, the purpose of the conference was to announce the launch of the magazine. But behind the appearance lurked a more subtle thirty-fourth floor objective: to begin developing the theme of Time Inc.'s "deep pockets" commitment to the magazine and its staying power in the face of large early losses.

In recent weeks, President Munro had discussed the strategy regularly with his colleagues, and he was anxious that it prove a success. Much rode on Time Inc.'s ability to convince Wall Street that *TV-Cable Week*'s startup costs had been expected and planned for. Munro knew that getting that message across depended on getting it understood by the press, and it seemed obvious that Sutton was the man to begin the campaign.

The press conference took place in a room across the hall

from the eighth floor auditorium where the board had earlier met. Representing the company were three individuals: Sutton, flanked on his left by Burgheim and on his right by Zucchi. The new magazine's editor and publisher were on hand to answer specific questions about the magazine, and Burgheim's young helper, Ed Adler, was in an audio-visual projectionist's booth behind the far wall to run a slide carousel if the press wanted to see graphics.

The company's public relations people had hoped the press conference might attract coverage by publications like the *New York Times* and the *Wall Street Journal.* But the turnout proved a disappointment, as the only major news publication to send a reporter was *Time* Magazine. For the most part, the press was represented by upwards of a dozen young trade reporters from publications such as *Advertising Age, Adweek,* and *Multichannel News.*

One of these individuals was an eager young *TV Guide* reporter named Craig Copetas. His organization had been rife with speculation for months about the Time Inc. project, and Copetas saw the conference as a unique opportunity to find out exactly what lay behind the new effort. Copetas had come prepared to be polite yet forceful in his questioning. Rumor had it that Time Inc.'s new publication was going to be oriented toward TV listings for cable viewers, and Copetas wanted to know how the magazine could remain editorially independent and unbiased in its coverage if its owner, Time Inc., was also the largest single programming force in the industry.

But Copetas soon saw that asking that question was not going to be easy. Normally, press conferences consist of two groups of participants: the questioners and the questioned. But as Copetas now discovered, this press conference included a third element: observers, who began filing into the back of the conference room to watch as Copetas and his colleagues took seats at a horseshoe-shaped table at the head of which sat Sutton, Burgheim, and Zucchi.

Though Copetas did not know their names, the observers were plainly a contingent of Time Inc. brass. Were they there to judge the performance of the three men seated at the head of the table? This did not bother Copetas one way or the other, but it certainly seemed to be having an effect on at least one of the three, Burgheim, who had begun to perspire freely as he darted glances around the room.

The other two men seemed more self-composed. But when the questioning began, the man named Sutton pre-empted everything, and began leaping to answer question after question, no matter to whom it was addressed. Soon even Zucchi began to wilt, as his forceful demeanor gave way to helpless uncertainty as to whether to respond to the reporters at all. Copetas felt a certain pity, and he thought, Christ, what a spectacle! Those two guys have probably been working on this magazine for months, and here comes some big shot who's put three minutes into the thing and now wants to claim all the glory!

Oh, to hell with it, thought Copetas, and he asked his question: If Time Inc. were the biggest force in cable television, wouldn't the company face at least some temptation to use the magazine as a promotional vehicle? No way, said the group vice president, the notion was out of the question.

But Copetas would not let it go. Come on, he insisted, wasn't it asking a bit much to expect editorial independence under such circumstances? Sutton scowled at Copetas, as if to say, drop it, okay? But when the *TV Guide* reporter began to bore in all over again an elderly, silver-haired executive stepped from the group behind him and said, "I think we've covered that subject enough now."

Copetas fell silent, and the questions moved on to other matters, one of which was apparently a subject that Sutton seemed eager to stress: the nature of Time Inc.'s staying power and financial commitment to the project. *Sports Illustrated* had taken years to break even, Sutton declared, and Time Inc. was prepared to be no less patient with *TV-Cable Week*. This was, after all, the most carefully researched effort in the company's history, and Time Inc. believed it had the potential of eventually becoming the largest magazine in the corporation; all it would take is time and money, and Time Inc. was prepared to lavish both on the project.

To Copetas, the claims seemed to go down well enough with the assembled big-wigs behind him, who stood in respectful silence as Sutton's comments continued. Yet had the young *TV Guide* reporter been more familiar with the faces in Time's hierarchy, he would have been perplexed by the fact that the most important official in the company, President Munro, was not at the conference. Presumably, Time Inc.'s president had more important things to do than watch one of his group vice presidents perform for the press. Or did he?

Though no reporter in the room had even an inkling of Munro's whereabouts, a glimpse into the deeper drama of *TV-Cable Week*—with all its attendant concerns for Wall Street and the investment community—was available to anyone at the table curious (or paranoid) enough to get up and peek into the darkened audio-visual booth at the opposite end of the room. Anyone doing so would have discovered, crouched among slide projectors and extension cord wires, two grown and grinning men eavesdropping on the press conference as if it were an actual focus-group session—something that they wanted to observe but not really participate in. They were: Time Inc. President and Chief Executive Officer J. Richard Munro, and his Executive Vice President Clifford Grum of Texas. Sitting behind them, trying not to look: Burgheim's helper, Ed Adler, who had been hooking up his slide carousel when the two executives tiptoed through a side door and began whispering in anticipation.

What Sutton told the press conference was, in fact, what Munro and Grum had expected to hear: that Time Inc. had committed $100 million to its newest property, and was prepared to stay with it for years if necessary before earning a profit.

But that is not what the players had expected to hear. For weeks they had been told to keep quiet, stay mum, and say nothing about "the numbers." Then no sooner had the board presentation concluded than Sutton had begun announcing the secret details to the world. Moreover, Sutton had told the public exactly the opposite of what he had told the players to say to the board.

In its presentation to Time's board, the task force had been told by Sutton to stress that launching *TV-Cable Week* was not a long-term commitment. Rather, the magazine had been presented as a venture that could be quickly terminated by means of a secret "bail-out" scenario that was part of the business plan. The scenario detailed three different points at which the company could abandon the project (January, June, and December of 1983), as well as how much in pretax losses the company could expect to incur at each stage ($10 million, $38 million, and $59 million).

A detailed contingency plan was sound business practice, especially since the lack of a market test meant that no one knew the nature of the risks involved. But pretending such a plan did not exist seemed bizarre, even misleading, for instead of telling the public that the company was prepared to abandon the project at the first sign of trouble, Sutton was now saying that Time planned to stick with the effort through year after year of multi-million-dollar losses. The players were amazed.

Zucchi and Burgheim had planned an official "go-ahead" celebration at Amax-7 to follow the press conference. In preparation, Burgheim had mulled over and polished his memo to the staff. He wanted it to communicate his enthusiasm for the magazine, get people fired up and excited, put the fighting and feuding behind them—the battles with Labich and Zucchi, the quarrels over computers and office space, the draining, bloody struggle that had dragged on for a year.

Now the press conference was over, and as Burgheim sat in his Amax-7 office watching people gather in the hall outside, he wondered where they would all find the energy for what he knew lay ahead. The last year had been bad enough, but the hard part was still to come: actually publishing the magazine. Through his experience with the launch of *People*, Burgheim knew first-hand the ordeal of a new magazine—the late nights, the endless rewrites and revisions as the staff groped toward an identity and common voice. If this new effort were to succeed, people had to pull together and work as a team.

Earlier in the day Burgheim and Zucchi had jointly signed the memo, and now it was being distributed. He hoped the staff would appreciate its sentiments. The memo read:

"Four score and 78 plans ago, our fathers (or was it our grandfathers?) brought forth on this conglomerate a new magazine idea, conceived in haste, and dedicated to the proposition that all channels are created equal. It took us through barbed wire and through China, and other flights of metaphor, until Kelso told us to knock it off. And this is just the beginning. Our goal now: to be the largest magazine in Time Inc."

While the staff of Amax-7 was reading that, Kelso Sutton sat in his thirty-fourth floor office across the street, reading a letter marked "Personal." The letter was from Thomas Watson, Jr., of IBM, who had gotten around to recording his own misgivings about *TV-Cable Week*. Watson had, as he explained, taken a closer look at the dummy he had been given, and he was beginning to wonder: "The whole thing just doesn't unfold in an orderly fashion with clarity to this 68-year-old." Watson also wondered whether anyone really needed such a magazine, or whether a combination of *TV Guide* and local newspapers provided all the listings information anyone required. In conclusion, Watson added a reassuring afterthought:

"You have undoubtedly thought this through, and have dry-run it with various kinds of people, so that you know it will fly and that people will become familiar with how to find the data they are looking for in the publication."

Time Inc. had, of course, not "dry-run" the magazine with anyone, since as Sutton had explained to the board members, doing so would have taken "too long," and the costs would have been "too high." But as he pondered the letter, Sutton knew that it was a little late to be worrying about that now.

FOURTEEN

French Real Estate's a Steal

SEVERAL DAYS after the board vote, Zucchi walked into Dunn's office.

"Kelso's going to call you in a little while. He wants us to make the case for moving the magazine out of New York."

Dunn looked up. "Make the case?"

Zucchi nodded. "He says we can get secretaries out in the suburbs for twelve thousand a year; we'll save a lot of money."

Dunn stared at Zucchi. Make the case? Secretaries for twelve thousand a year? Move out of town? Every number the task force had just presented to the board had assumed that the magazine would at least remain in Manhattan, if not in the Time & Life Building like Burgheim wanted. If the project had to move out of town, the whole editorial infrastructure would have to be duplicated from what already existed in the building: clipping services, film developing facilities, research archives. It could cost millions.

But Zucchi was adamant; Sutton really meant it. "He's going to take next week off for vacation out in the Hamptons," declared Zucchi. "But he wants this stuff, and he's going to come back in on Tuesday to get it. He'll tell you all about it at lunch."

"This is impossible," said Dunn. "Burgheim doesn't even know how many people he needs. How can we figure out office specs if we don't know the size of his staff?"

"Then we'll have to figure it out for him," said Zucchi. "This stuff with Burgheim is driving me nuts!"

As soon as Zucchi left Dunn pulled out file folders full of earlier cost projections and analyses. He wanted to see if anything might be helpful. For all he knew, much of what they had done for the last six months might now suddenly be worthless. This is crazy, he thought, the dishes had scarcely been cleared from the board luncheon and already they were deviating from the plan. Everything was going so fast—the COO Group, the board vote, the frantic staccato of one surprise after another. It was as if nothing mattered anymore but the insanely rushing logic of the project. Make the case, get the numbers, up to speed, out the door. In his mind, *TV-Cable Week* had become a whirling blur of energy and motion.

After lunch Dunn went immediately to see Anne Davis. It was Tuesday, the 17th of August, and every minute counted. If Burgheim could not figure out how many computer people he would need, then Dunn was going to do what Zucchi said and figure it out for him.

"How are you going to set everything up, Anne? How many computers operators will you need? Where will they sit? What will they do? How's the whole thing going to work?"

Davis looked at him. "You tell me how many editions we're talking about, and I'll tell you how many bodies we'll need." Then she turned to her computer terminal and hunched forward in concentration.

Through that weekend Zucchi and his aides labored—not to "make the case," but simply to see if relocating out of New York would truly prove cheaper. Yet analyzing the relocation of even an existing business, with a known cost structure, is a complex effort most often handled by specialist firms and independent consultants who take many months to draw up plans and proposals. For Sutton to give the group four days to do the same thing seemed pointless.

By Tuesday, the Amax-7 executives had gotten no further than some speculative "guesstimates"—these built on the same assumptions and hypotheses that had been propping up the project for more than half a year. Zucchi had earlier scheduled a meeting that now conflicted with the briefing scheduled for Sutton, and he felt it wrong to cancel the appointment. The meeting was, after all, with Mr. Edward Ney, the chairman of the board of Young & Rubicam, the largest advertising agency in the world. Ney was anxious to land the *TV-Cable Week* account.

Zucchi thus left Dunn with the job of having to report alone to Sutton, who had just driven ninety miles from his summer home in Westhampton. But when Sutton saw the fragmentary nature of their work, he exploded and demanded to know not only why the two men had wasted his time, but why Zucchi wasn't there with Dunn.

"Dan's across the street with Ed Ney," said Dunn by way of explanation. At which point, Sutton exploded all over again: "Who the fuck is Ed Ney! He's just a goddamned supplier!" and scowled furiously.

When Dunn got back across the street he found Zucchi in the Zuke's Other Office, and broke the news, recounting in detail what had transpired.

Zucchi looked worried.

That afternoon the players were summoned to Grunwald's office to brief him on the relocation findings. When they arrived, there sat Sutton and Grunwald, along with his deputy, Graves, who wore a grim expression. Among those in attendance from Amax-7 were Zucchi, Dunn, and now Burgheim, who was so apoplectic at what was transpiring that he could barely speak. This left most of the presentation to Dunn, who reviewed the weekend's work. After Dunn had finished, the editor in chief spoke:

"Well it seems to me that there is no alternative. I don't think the economics justify remaining in New York."

Yet the "economics" that had just been presented to Grunwald were merely a weekend of guessing about the unknown —with the guesses based upon one assumption after another, from assumed rental costs, to assumed savings in labor costs by hiring employees in some assumed, imaginary suburb as opposed to New York.

Weighed against Grunwald's assertion that the evidence left no alternative but to leave New York was countervailing evidence that he did not even seem to be considering. Not only had all the numbers in the business plan that the board had approved been based on keeping the project in midtown Manhattan with quick and easy access to the Time & Life Building, but the economic rationale for now abruptly changing that plan had been put together in a single weekend. Moreover, even as Grunwald announced his decision, his own appointee to head the magazine, Burgheim, stood staring back at him in a silent fury, convinced that his opinion of the need to keep the project in New York was being ignored altogether.

Bad as this was for Burgheim, Grunwald's decision was great for Zucchi, who now did not have to worry about Sutton being angry anymore. After all, the editor in chief had ruled: the magazine would leave New York, which is what Sutton had wanted all along. Back in Amax-7 Zucchi turned to Dunn. "Thank God *that's* over with!" His subordinate was less confident and later said to his colleagues, "Just wait! Some day somebody is going to come looking for the numbers that justified this move, and they won't find them—*because there aren't any!*"

The scene in Grunwald's office had made Burgheim livid, and that night he nursed his rage. It seemed that he had been right all along, all the way back to January when Sutton had moved the task force out of the Big House and into Amax-7. The whole thing had been a corporate hustle from the start; they

were going to move his magazine out of New York whether he
liked it or not.

Even before the COO Group meeting Burgheim had
sensed that something was afoot, and he had sounded his warning. "I realize that it is tempting to consign a new cable publication to some low-rent district, or even outside New York. But
we are reporting on a Rockefeller Center-based industry, and
we need every advantage we can get. On behalf of the editors
of this magazine, I enter a bid today for space in this building."

But no one had listened. That was how it had gone with this
magazine from the start. No one listened. The bright guys at the
top had their own secret agendas, and that was all that mattered. But did they take him for a fool? He too had spent his
entire adult life as an employee of Time Inc. He too could hear
the struggle going on above him.

Sitting in the living room of his West-Side Manhattan apartment, a glass of scotch in hand, Burgheim wondered whether
the real source of these decisions was not Sutton at all, nor even
Sutton's superior, Grum, but further up the ladder still, to lum-
ber biggie Arthur Temple—a man who had a background neither in journalism nor even in the media, but in sawmills, who
hailed from Diboll, Texas, a town of seven hundred inhabitants
on the Louisiana border.

Burgheim thought back to an early press interview Temple
had given to a reporter from the *Village Voice* not long after
merging his Texas timber holdings into Time Inc. He recalled
how Temple had sounded the skepticism and distrust of New
York that one often hears from business executives of smaller,
less cosmopolitan cities—complaints about the $100 expense
account lunches, the clubby world of midtown media men. He
recalled how Temple had remarked that he could see no logical
reason why *People* Magazine should not be relocated to less
expensive quarters in, say, Los Angeles; why *Fortune* should not
be moved to Atlanta; why *Money* should not relocate to Austin;
Sports Illustrated to Chicago.

Ruminating in this way, it seemed possible that behind

Sutton's action and Grunwald's indifference did indeed lay the desires of Temple, desires that perhaps had smouldered from the start, from the moment he had acquired the Time stock a decade earlier. At the time, the merger had been described in Time Inc. press releases as a nice "fit," because Time had owned a much smaller logging operation in the area since shortly after the war. Yet the huge size of Temple Industries, the largest family-owned logging enterprise in the world, made it possible to wonder: which was fitting into which?

Now a decade had passed, and the tom-toms of the Big House had for more than a year beat the message that the next magazine Time Inc. developed would be brought to market outside New York. Was Temple behind it, or did he even feel strongly either way anymore? Maybe Grum simply *thought* he did; maybe Sutton in turn thought *Grum* did. Who cared! What counted was the manipulation of the task force.

For more than a year now, he had worked to design a quality product to please readers instead of simply cable operators and the people at HBO. Anything less and he would have bargained away the editorial integrity of the publication. Time Inc. had already been charged by labor attorney Theodore Kheel with writing a glowing cover story about New York mayor Ed Koch in order to win the cable franchise of the borough of Queens, potentially the most lucrative franchise in the country. Now, if the company unfurled an entire magazine that seemed a cable house organ, Time Inc. would look craven.

Burgheim had spelled out his fears to the COO Group on that point, too. "Will cable operators be reading page proofs? Hell, no! They can never be allowed to smudge the editorial integrity of Time Inc. We will have to re-prove every week something that this building takes for granted: the bristly independence of Time Inc. editors. We will have to demonstrate that we are not a house organ for Home Box Office."

Now Burgheim began to wonder whether Grunwald or Sutton had listened to a word he had said on anything.

The next day, Burgheim gathered his colleagues together and headed back to Grunwald's office for a rehearing. Dunn and Zucchi felt uncomfortable attending the meeting, but Burgheim had insisted. The editor in chief sat behind his desk expressionless as Burgheim stated his case again. To Burgheim's assistant, Demargitay, Grunwald seemed to be listening attentively. But to Burgheim it was just more of the same: the editor in chief had already made up his mind.

As the meeting drew to a close, Burgheim's fury boiled over, and his lips began to quiver as he read an actual, prepared protest statement from the clipboard in his hand. "With respect, Mr. Editor in Chief, your decision stands, and we will do our best. But I hereby declare that I play this game under protest."

There was an awkward silence, and back across the street Dunn summed up his thoughts on the matter to Demargitay: "Gida, you've got to hand it to the little guy; he's really got guts."

A few days later came another blow to Burgheim when Sutton announced that *TV-Cable Week* would become Time Inc.'s first non-unionized publication. The decision was of no real significance to Zucchi and the business staff, but for Burgheim it was devastating. For months, Burgheim had been planning to begin recruiting from within Time Inc.'s own ranks once Grunwald gave him permission to start building a staff. But under the rules of the National Labor Relations Board, Burgheim could now recruit no more than a handful of Time Inc. employees onto his staff under any circumstances. The rest would have to come from outside the company.

The decision to make *TV-Cable Week* non-unionized was based on rumors that had reached the thirty-fourth floor that the New York Guild, which maintained a Time Inc. chapter, was preparing to merge with the International Typographer Union. The ITU had a reputation of militant confrontation with management over automation issues and had put a number of newspapers out of business as a result of strikes. Sutton feared that the ITU might do the same to his magazine, especially since it depended so critically on computers.

But a decision not to grant union recognition to the project meant that the magazine had to be a completely separate entity from the rest of Time Inc., physically removed from the premises. The decision also meant that the staff would have to come from outside the company, or Time Inc. would be open to an unfair labor practice suit.

As soon as Burgheim heard the news he demanded to see Grunwald all over again. But the editor in chief had departed for vacation at his weekend home on Martha's Vineyard. Later that week Burgheim learned that a Time Inc. labor relations expert named Deane Raley was scheduled to brief Grunwald on the labor question at his home on the Vineyard. Raley was going to take a company jet, accompanied by Sutton, Zucchi, and Graves, who also had a summer home on the island. Burgheim got himself invited and went along.

The trip began as a black Cadillac stretch limousine headed through mid-morning traffic from one Manhattan neighborhood to the next collecting the Time Inc. executives. When the last was aboard, the limousine swung south on Park Avenue. Twenty minutes later the group pulled into the Pan Am East Side heliport just north of the United Nations Building, where a Time Inc.-leased helicopter sat waiting, its rotor spinning slowly in the summer air. When the executives were settled aboard, the chopper's engines rose to a scream, and in an instant the group was winging northward above Hell's Gate and the Triboro Bridge.

Another twenty-five minutes and the helicopter settled onto the tarmac at Westchester County Airport, home of one of the largest fleets of corporate aircraft in the country. From the helicopter, the group transferred to one of Time Inc.'s five business jets, and in another hour were touching down at the community airport of Martha's Vineyard, the summer home of not just Grunwald and Graves, but a long list of celebrities, literary notables, and media executives.

Grunwald was a fixture on the island, and enjoyed participating in intellectual "panel discussions" arranged by Henry Beetle Hough, the crusty and colorful editor of the *Vineyard Gazette*. At one such symposium on "Power and Politics," Grunwald endorsed Ronald Reagan's way of making use of power, saying, "He has a kind of wonderful detachment from the issues. He has a certain air of being above the battle, of being an inspirational figure." That was how Grunwald liked to see himself as well—only now the battle he had been trying to hover above was about to come into his living room.

A widower for nearly three years, Grunwald had done his best to make the visiting executives feel comfortable, and had placed a plate of cold cuts, cheeses, and bread on the coffee table. He was curious to hear what Raley had to say on the union question, and wondered what Graves and Sutton would offer as well. He only hoped that Burgheim would not bring up plain vanilla.

But Burgheim was determined to talk about nothing else. In the editor's mind, every issue confronting the magazine— from moving out of New York, to union non-recognition, to editorial quality and integrity, even to freedom from meddling by HBO—eventually came down to Burgheim's right to custom edit and improve TV Data's listings. He was the managing editor of the magazine, and he was determined to edit and approve every word in it. That was how Time Inc. editors worked. It was how Grunwald had edited *Time* Magazine. It was how Burgheim was going to edit *TV-Cable Week*.

So, no sooner had the meeting begun than Burgheim began laying out his case anew: moving to the suburbs would make it impossible to recruit skilled journalists; non-recognition of the Guild jeopardized the quality of the magazine; the computer system still had not been tested and proved workable . . . and on and on.

Grunwald looked at him.

Here it was all over again. The man was a broken record.

At last Grunwald spoke:

"Dick, why don't you just publish the plain vanilla and forget it."

Burgheim started to answer, then stopped. Why bother? The man was just not listening.

At the end of the discussion the group rose to leave. Burgheim felt crushed. And his spirits hardly improved when Grunwald offered him some parting advice:

"Ten to six, Dick, run a happy ship."

Then the front door closed and it was back to the airport.

By mid-September, Time Inc.'s real estate staff had found the magazine a home, but it was a curious choice: a White Plains, New York, high-rise that was still under construction, with plumbing still being roughed in, wiring being pulled through walls, even many of the walls not yet erected. Sutton wanted the editors to move and start work anyway. Burgheim was agog. The place did not yet have bathrooms!

At about this time, Burgheim's assistant managing editor Bill Marsano arrived from Canada, ready to go to work. Burgheim broke the news:

"There's been a slight change, Bill. We're not going to be working in Manhattan after all. Ever hear of White Plains?"

Marsano panicked. He hated commuting, and so did his wife. He had taken the job to work in Manhattan, not some suburb in no where.

"I've got to do something," said Marsano, and he called up New York City Mayor Ed Koch's Task Force on Business. The task force had been formed to discourage businesses from leaving New York for places like White Plains, and Marsano wanted to start gossip that would embarrass Time Inc. into changing its mind. He got an aide on the phone.

"This is going to be the biggest weekly magazine in America," Marsano explained. "It's all about cable TV, right here in

New York. But Time Inc. wants to move it to White Plains. We've got to stop them."

"Look," said the man. "We're very busy here. Can you put it in writing?"

On September 12, 1982, the ever-growing staff of the magazine gathered in the Hunt Room of 21, one of the establishment's private upstairs salons, to celebrate two events of note: the board go-ahead for *TV-Cable Week*, and the 41st birthday of Zucchi, who had now been officially named the magazine's publisher by Sutton.

On such occasions, the appropriate tone is one of happy conviviality, punctuated by polite laughter at reminiscences over funny stories like Arthur Temple's tar baby remark. That was how events began to unfold in the Hunt Room of 21, as the assembled Time Inc.'ers sipped Beefeater and tonic, and vodka martinis with a twist ("white goods" being the preferred inebriate in Magazine Group) and regaled each other with stories from the lengthening lore of the project.

Yet Sutton was having trouble getting into the swing of the thing. As the cocktails gave way to dinner he seated himself awkwardly next to the magazine's art director, a man named Eric Seidman. Besides their involvement in *TV-Cable Week* and their corporate identities as Time Inc.'ers, the two men had little in common, which was not surprising given the wide disparities in their income levels and lifestyles (Sutton's income of $465,506 in salary, stocks, and bonuses was nearly ten times that of the Brooklyn-born Seidman's). The fact was, neither man had any clear idea how to make small talk with the other.

Befitting his senior position in the corporate hierarchy, Sutton took the initiative and, seeking a way to break the ice with the young man seated next to him, turned to Seidman and commenced an enthusiastic discourse on the opportunities that the collapsing French franc now afforded the shrewd investor in Loire Valley castles and chateaus. "Really," he said to Seidman, "at 6-plus francs to the dollar they're practically giving the

stuff away. You can get fabulous chateaus for under a million.
I'm telling you, French real estate's a steal!"

Seidman was dumbfounded.

Doing his best to respond, the art director offered that he
too had dabbled in real estate lately (leaving out that it consisted
of putting his life savings into a downpayment on a converted
Greenwich Village loft).

Nearby sat Burgheim, holding an altogether different view
of Sutton's real estate acumen. After dinner came speeches—
jokes by Dunn, go-get-'em cheering by Zucchi—and through it
all sat Burgheim, nursing his resentment at the man who was
moving his magazine out of New York. When he could stand it
no longer Burgheim rose and stared slit-eyed across the room
at the group vice president: "Kelso," he said at last, "you and
I went to the same school I'm afraid to say, and this idea of yours
about moving out of town is the dumbest damned thing I've
ever heard of."

His voice trailed off in mumbling, causing the assembled
revelers to shift even more uncomfortably. But Burgheim
would not sit down, and though Dukemejian began clapping
politely to invite him to end, still he remained standing. Then,
abruptly, he seemed to regain his thoughts and lit out at Sutton
again, attacking his business wisdom, lambasting the relocation
idea from one perspective after another. Through it all Sutton
sat grim-faced and silent.

The next morning Zucchi's first telephone call was from
the group vice president. "What the Christ was *that* all about?"
Sutton wanted to know. Zucchi answered with aplomb: "Now
you know what *I* gotta put up with, get it?"

A week or so later, Sutton took Grunwald to inspect the
magazine's new premises for himself. As publisher of the new
magazine, Zucchi went along. The *TV-Cable Week* offices were
to occupy the top three floors of the seventeen-story high-rise,
the Centroplex, the tallest building in downtown White Plains.
But there was little to see, for the floors were filled largely with

workmen and construction debris. After a quick tour, the group gravitated across the street to the city's premier local attraction, a two-year-old indoor shopping mall called the Galleria.

As students of the subject know, malls are much the same nationwide, at least when it comes to the people who visit them and the products they go there to buy: food, clothing, posters of rock stars, and different species of household pets. At the Galleria—an almost exact mirror image of the Sherman Oaks, California, Galleria mall that was the site of the movie, *Fast Times at Ridgemont High*— the amphitheater-like environment of glass and chrome featured potted palms and climbing philodendra. It was the autumn of 1982, when the "Valley Girl" craze was at its zenith, and as Grunwald could see upon entering, the place swarmed with them.

Wherever Grunwald looked, there they were: gum-chewing 15-year-olds in white pullover shirts by Esprit; collars up, eyelids encrusted with mauve All-day Performing Eye-color by Aziza; lashes daubed with hypoallergenic Colorplus Thickening Lashcolor by Almay; lips smeared with Cherry-Smash Kissing Slicks flavored automatic lip gloss by Maybelline; cheeks alive with Frosty Fresh Sponge-on blusher by Max Factor; fingernails erupting measle-like in Diamond Dust and Purple Passion Hot Dots by Cutex; legs wriggled into pin-striped hot-pink jeans by Sergio Valente; bodies drenched head to toe in Baby-Soft cologne spray by Love's; and scampering from one shop to the next in Grendha turquoise plastic pumps from Brazil.

There were, as Grunwald could also see, plenty of shops to choose from. No sooner had he and the others entered than they found themselves in a culinary theater-in-the-round, ringed wherever they looked by one junk-food eatery after another: Danish Supercone, Pasta Mania, The Golden Egg Roll, Taco Don's, Weinerfest, Wings 'n Things, Not Just Bagels, Greater 'Tater—and at the far end of this trencherman's gaunt-let, a hamburger eatery called Mr. Greenjeans, which served such throat-choking sized portions of everything that it seemed in some mysterious way to be a culinary representation of *TV-Cable Week* itself.

As residents of nearby Briarcliff Manor, Zucchi and his family had shopped often at the Galleria. But the baffled expression on the face of Grunwald suggested, to Zucchi at least, a man entering a world he had until now only known from magazines and movies.

The man who had first held the position of Time Inc.'s editor in chief, Henry Luce, possessed a mind of limitless curiosity, and found it equally as fascinating to hob-nob with Winston Churchill as to experiment with psychedelic drugs like LSD. But here was his latest successor, Henry Anatole Grunwald, the perfect embodiment of intellectual self-possession; whose own father had written the lyrics for the operettas of Franz Lehař; a man who had never learned to drive a car, since he was accustomed to taking corporate limousines everywhere; who numbered among his "friends" the heads of government of half of Europe. Here was Grunwald wandering around inside the Galleria shopping mall, past Quick Snax and Salad Scene, past The Magic Pan and Pastrami Delights, even as pubescent teenagers swarmed about him clutching posters of Michael Jackson and licking triple scoop ice cream cones from Slurps.

As the tour continued, Zucchi snuck a sideways glance at the look of bewilderment and confusion that had cemented itself to Grunwald's face, and he thought, Christ, I don't think the guy's ever *been* in a mall before!

Gorillas, Granola, and Maggots

I T WAS around this time that Brauns became pregnant with her first child. Consumed by her work, she did not let her pregnancy slow her in any way, and continued to dash from meeting to meeting as she worked to fashion a circulation strategy that would both satisfy cable operators and prove economically viable.

Sometimes in a reflective moment Brauns would wonder whether what she was doing was worth it, or whether some radical change in career might bring her more satisfaction. Would she be wiser to cease working all together for a while? Her husband was a rising young New York investment banker in the mergers and acquisitions department of Lazard Freres, and they certainly could get along without her second income for a while. Perhaps satisfaction might come from the challenges of a smaller, less complex world. Such thoughts would linger for a time on the rim of her consciousness, then the airport public-address system would call her flight and she'd be off for another meeting with a cable operator.

For his part, Dunn had long since made up his mind to try to be removed from the project. But when a job offer was forthcoming through a colleague elsewhere in Magazine Group Zucchi told him that Sutton wanted him to stay where he was. Now he was beginning to feel trapped, and when he learned of Brauns's pregnancy he started counting the months to term, until he came to the spring of 1983. How do you like that, Dunn said to himself. Right when the whole thing is going to go to hell, Sarah's going to get to go on maternity leave—and I'll still be here!

But the project was in deep trouble already. Not only had no cable operator signed a deal, but the decision to relocate the magazine to White Plains had caused staff quotas to swell overnight, even as it added $5 million to the business plan that had been approved by the board. Now Sutton was telling Zucchi to prepare for launch in March of 1983 anyway—with no computer system as yet debugged and running, with no technicians as yet hired to operate it, with no writers or editors as yet on the payroll to produce the words that would go on the magazine's pages.

In the autumn of 1982, *TV-Cable Week* was not the only cable venture in deepening trouble. Even as Kelso Sutton's project struggled to launch, every week seemed to bring more bad news for the CBS Cable project across the street at Sixth Avenue and Fifty-second Street. Born of the same internal pressures as *TV-Cable Week,* CBS Cable had long since become a political football within the company's broadcast group, and was now suffering the combined effects of inadequate planning and poor market research.

CBS's chairman and founder, William Paley, had seen in cable an opportunity to provide "quality entertainment" for TV viewers, and in that spirit the network had lavished enormous sums on the project's programming. But "quality entertainment" had more appeal to the media executives gathered around the bar at 21 than to the cable viewers who would have to pay for it, and subscriptions never reached more than a fraction of initial projections.

"It was a wild time, a crazy time," recalled the service's director of research, Thomas Delaney, "with everyone wanting to get aboard the cable bandwagon, especially now that Wall Street was calling the broadcast networks 'dinosaurs.' All the way through the planning it was a case of people making suppositions and then acting upon them as if they were facts backed up by research."

Other ventures were also foundering, many having made precisely the same mistakes as CBS. One of these services was The Entertainment Channel, launched in June of 1982 with great expectations but now struggling to stay afloat.

A creature of RCA and the Rockefeller Corporation, and headed by Arthur Taylor, a one-time president of CBS, The Entertainment Channel from its inception had been built on sloppy market research and a disdain among the brass for having to deal with pole climbers in the hinterland. Michael Rihimi, the venture's director of national accounts, described the problem in the simplest terms possible: "Between the programmer and the customer stands the cable operator. Programmers say the operators just don't understand marketing, but the operators look upon programmers as being arrogant." Though the men at the top spoke bravely of TEC's "potential," the troops in the trenches gave the programming service six months more at most.

By now it was becoming increasingly easy to see that cable's future had been oversold, and that the industry as a whole was in for a retrenchment. Yet the clearest signs came late in November, when the *TV-Cable Week* executives flew to Los Angeles to attend the second of the industry's annual gathering rites: the Western Cable Convention, held in Anaheim, California.

Once on the scene, the players found not the self-delusion of Las Vegas six months earlier but an industry reminiscent of, say, Berlin in 1944. There was the dancing and cheering and the parties that ran all night. But though no one wanted to mention it, the Russians were already at the Vistula, and down in the Fuehrerbunker the talk was turning to secret weapons to swing the tide of battle. Unable to pay the costs of equipping their systems to provide interactive cable, addressible converter systems, and other promised high-tech features for subscribers, many cable operators were now threatening simply to walk away from their franchising contracts unless city councils let them install cheaper systems and charge more for the service.

Meanwhile, up at street level things were getting increasingly kinky. Unable to attract audiences for fare like *Daytime* or the soon-to-be-launched *Games Network*, programmers were turning to more reliable ways to draw a crowd. At its mildest, there was the Playboy Channel, counting heavily on R-rated soft-core programming, while further along could be found offerings of, say, The Pleasure Channel. Movies available to those with more specialized tastes included *Wanda Whips Wall Street, Garage Girls in Bondage, Wrestling Women versus the Aztec Mummy,* and perhaps most memorable, *Teenage Virgins versus Nuns with Whips.*

At one booth, a man looking as if he had just stepped from behind the wheel of an Eighth Avenue pimp-mobile beckoned passers-by to step inside and watch a film segment featuring a woman being raped by a gorilla. Over and over the same scene would replay itself on a loop, as the raped woman would crawl off in the dirt, only to be dragged back by her ankles and raped anew by the crazed beast.

Nearby was the booth of a struggling programming service called the Cable Health Network. There, ruddy-faced attendants passed out snack-food packets of natural, healthy-sounding granola mix. So natural was this mix that, as horrified CHN officials discovered upon inspection, some of it had arrived from the manufacturer infested with maggots. This led to a furious argument between a CHN advertising executive, who wanted to give the packets out to conventioneers anyway, and corporate higher-ups, who finally overruled the idea.

In keeping with the surreal quality of all they surveyed, the players were also afforded an opportunity to behold a woman of such traffic-stopping proportions as to be the instant center of attention wherever she went. Bearing the name Aphrodite Jones, she worked as a reporter for United Features Syndicate Inc., covering the cable industry, and had been dispatched to Anaheim to report on the event.

Ms. Jones, with raven-black hair, an hour-glass figure, and a fondness for clinging black dresses slit to the thigh, was one journalist who had no trouble getting the attention of busy executives. For into a press conference she would slink, draped in a fur coat, her legs flashing like polished marble, and instantly all conversation would cease, all heads would swivel, and silence would envelop the room as all in attendance simply stood and gawked. Such, when it came to Aphrodite Jones, was the power of the press.

One individual anxious to make her acquaintance as quickly as possible was an eager young journalist named Richard Zacks, then a trade reporter for a Washington, D.C., based publication known as *TV Digest.* Besides his interest in Aphrodite, Zacks had been growing increasingly interested in joining Time Inc.'s *TV-Cable Week* project, especially after covering the company's postboard vote press conference and hearing Sutton stress how much money and patience Time Inc. was prepared to commit to the venture. Two weeks before the convention, Burgheim had offered Zacks a job on the magazine, which Zacks was continuing to weigh.

Now by a stroke of luck, Zacks found himself afforded an opportunity for a close-up inspection of both Aphrodite and Burgheim simultaneously. The occasion, it turned out, was a double date to a Mel Tormé supper-club concert, Zacks and Aphrodite, and accompanying them, Burgheim and *his* companion for the evening, an exotic-looking Chinese-American woman named Flora Ling, a senior editor on *Money* Magazine, who had been recently assigned by Grunwald's aide, Graves, to serve as Burgheim's administrative helper.

In her early thirties, Ling was a study in contrasts, mixing a background in journalism with detours into everything from hippie communes to mingling for six months with CIA agents and the son of a high Laotian general in Vientienne, Laos, during the height of the Laotian Civil War. An expert shot with an M-16 automatic rifle, and familiar with the use of a NATO-standard grenade launcher, Ling was also attractive and fluent in the Laotian language.

Now she was sitting next to Burgheim, Zacks, and Aphrodite Jones, a mellow smile on her face, listening to Mel Tormé croon "Foggy Day in London Town" next to the piano in front of them. Sitting so, Flora Ling felt confident in herself, in the future, and in her ability under pressure. She too had heard the rumors of what lay behind the project in Amax-7; she too knew that Time Inc. was a company under pressure. But to Ling, these things simply whetted her curiosity, for in business as in life, Flora Ling welcomed the opportunity to drop a coconut at five hundred yards, then disco till dawn with spies and not bat an eye. But Flora Ling had not yet entered the real-life world of Time Inc.'s new venture, and once she did, life at the office would begin to give her symptoms of a bleeding ulcer.

SIXTEEN

Let's Make a Deal

IN THE WEEKS that followed Anaheim, one cable
personality was beginning to wonder if he and his
sales staff had contracted some social disease that
no one would mention.

Here he was, Dan Zucchi, publisher of the biggest, most
heavily promoted magazine startup in Time Inc.'s history. It
was a project that the company had proclaimed itself ready to
spend $100 million to make viable, and on which it had already
made a sizable downpayment: millions of dollars worth of computers on order, a staff that had by now grown to well over one
hundred, a five-year lease signed on enough White Plains office
space to contain one and one-half football fields, printing contracts with five different plants around the country, deals with
truckers, with binderies, with a high-tech aerospace firm to pull
off Labich's secret Mustang Project.

Yet with all that happening and more on the way—not to
mention the eyes of Dick Munro, Kelso Sutton, and the corporation upon him, along with orders to get the project up to speed

and out the door by March, little more than three months away
—what did Zucchi have to show anyone?

Nothing!

The biggest startup in his own career, in the company's
history, and he had not one distribution deal with a single cable
operator. The thought made Zucchi writhe.

The cable operators kept giving him one excuse after another: their plans were "on hold," they felt "no particular
hurry" to sign with Time Inc. "at this point." The foot-dragging
made him wild. Especially so with ATC. This was Time Inc.'s
own cable system, the second largest in the country, and he
could not get them to sign anything. We're not sure, they would
tell him, we're "reevaluating our guide plans." Reevaluating?
Zucchi *was* their guide plans! What was going on?

He would constantly try to put the best face possible on
events—giving Sutton his salesman's pitch that the project had
life: that cable operator reaction to the concept remained "very
positive," that all sorts of deals were "firm" ("pending contract
signing"). Sure, Zucchi would say, no one's said yes yet, but no
one's said no either. He hoped to God something broke soon.
The marketing people had already gotten letters of intent from
two cable systems at the Anaheim trade show—Buffalo, New
York, and Providence, Rhode Island—but when it came time to
sign, they had had second thoughts and backed off. The deal,
the deal, Zucchi needed a deal.

One possible solution might have been to buy Peter Funt's
On Cable, acquiring his cable operator contracts in the process.
But now Zucchi got what he thought was a better idea. Stories
had begun to circulate within the industry that Funt had run
into cash flow problems and might be approaching bankruptcy.
Great, thought Zucchi, we'll just wait until the guy keels over,
then we'll snap up the Sterling Manhattan contract and be
riding high again. Zucchi lit a cigar and went to discuss the
matter with Dunn.

Although Zucchi did not know it, Funt's cash flow problems

were actually the result of a corporate reorganization that occurred when one of his two partners bought out the other and ran into a liquidity squeeze in the process. Now the surviving partner wanted to sell *On Cable* and had hit upon approaching the two magazine consultants Time Inc. had used to see if *On Cable* had been for sale the previous spring. Might Time Inc. still be interested? It won't work, Funt thought, they know we've got problems, so why should they make an offer at all? They'll just wait until we go out of business.

Yet to Funt's amazement, talks actually developed, not with Zucchi, who had taken one look at the operation and said to Dunn, "Offer him twenty-five grand, the operation's a dog," but of all people, Larry Crutcher, the very executive who had earlier threatened to sue Funt. Though Funt remained perplexed by Crutcher's interest, it was not until Crutcher invited Funt to a private dinner for two at a Greenwich, Connecticut, restaurant, Cinquante Cinq, that the mystery began to clear. In part, the dinner amounted to a "feel you out" encounter: a get-together designed to see, in effect, if Funt could be regarded as a "team player."

Yet there was more to it than that, for as the evening progressed, Crutcher kept moving the discussion around to something he called "the thing." Among the executives of Amax-7, this so-called "thing" was known as "the filler guide," and though Crutcher did not go into details, Funt quickly recognized it as a sign that *TV-Cable Week* was in trouble.

The problem, basically, was this: in system after system, cable operators apparently wanted assurance that if they discontinued supplying their customers with free guides provided by themselves or others in order to help market *TV-Cable Week,* and it developed that not every cable customer actually bought the Time Inc. product, then the system operator would still have some sort of listings guide to offer nonsubscribers free of charge—a quick and cheap summary of what was on.

When Burgheim first heard of the filler guide idea he had dubbed it cable-viewer "methadone," suggesting an ersatz narcotic for cable vidiots unable to afford the genuine article. But when Funt heard Crutcher explain it, the thought came to him that cable operators were proving wary of the Time Inc. publication. Funt's doubts about the competition's prospects only deepened when Crutcher next began describing what the *On Cable* publisher would later, out of deference to Burgheim, characterize only as "editorial management" problems. Hearing all this, and from a vice president of the company, not only amazed Funt but gave him enormous encouragement. Here was the dreaded Time Inc., caught between what its delegated representative in the Cinquante Cinq restaurant was revealing as the company's twin miseries of "editorial management" and "the thing," and hoping to find a way out by acquiring a nearly bankrupt magazine. Boy, thought Funt, maybe I'm not in such bad shape as I thought I was.

Energized by Crutcher's revelations, Funt launched himself on a month-long whirlwind of deal-making, and in a frenzy of financial razzle-dazzle, the *On Cable* publisher paid $100,-000 to his business partner and backer, Omni Cablevision, to acquire a thirty-day option to all rights to *On Cable*. Then Funt went to Cox Cable of Atlanta, Georgia, and to the Wall Street investment banking firm of Warburg Pincus, and struck a deal that made *On Cable* part of the Cox group, providing the capital not just to stay in business but to expand.

Said Funt of this period later, "What I had to do was convince Cox Cable that Time Inc. was going to fail, and I did. Why else would they have wanted to get in front of a $100 million freight train?"

But no train is too big—or company too rich—to derail, as Dan Zucchi was discovering. Recalled to life by Crutcher's dinner-table disclosures, *On Cable* now began blocking Zucchi's marketing efforts in one system after another, as word spread that Funt was suggesting a way for cable operators to exploit Time Inc.'s troubles. Explained Dunn in a memo to Zucchi on the matter, "Monthly guides are suggesting that cable operators

charge the same $3.00 price for a monthly as they would for
TV-Cable Week, thereby improving the cable operator's mar-
gin because of the difference in physical costs between a weekly
and a monthly." In other words, the monthlies were using Time
Inc. as a pricing umbrella under which to raise their own prices
without fear of being undercut.

One day Dunn went in to Zucchi's office, pulled up a chair,
and sat staring at his boss. Finally Dunn spoke:

"That fox, Funt, he's killing us with this gimmick."

"Yeah," said Zucchi, kneading a clenched fist. "What I can't
figure out is how come he didn't go bust back last fall. The guy
was on the ropes. Now all of a sudden he's got the Cox people
behind him and he's knocking us around. Jesus, I don't get it."

SEVENTEEN

The Kludge that Ate
White Plains

THREE DAYS before Christmas, Group Vice President Sutton came to White Plains for a party. It was held on the sixteenth floor of *TV-Cable Week*'s unfinished offices in the Centroplex Building and had been organized by Labich to encourage the building's union contractors to work faster. The staff was due to start arriving in less than two weeks, and the premises were a shambles. The employees needed offices to sit in, desks to sit behind, chairs to sit on. They needed toilets that worked, doors that locked. Get the job going, Labich had told them, and Time Inc. was going to throw them a bash they would not soon forget. Now it was time to make good on the promise, and Sutton had come to observe.

The festivities were due to begin at 12:30 P.M., and were to take place in a huge and largely empty room that was labeled on the architect's plans as the "Operations" area, where several dozen computer operators and electronic page-setters were to work. For now, however, there was nothing in the room but bags of cement, piles of rolled carpeting, coils of electrical wire

—and several folding tables butted end to end against each other.

Atop the tables Labich had arranged the most elaborate selection of Italian antipasto and delicatessen food imaginable: proscuitto and melon, pimientos and olives, scungilli, fettucini, calamari in oil; eggplant parmesan, ravioli, peppers and sausage, macaroni salad, and potato salad—complete with paper plates, plastic knives and forks—and at each end of the banquet, two fifty-gallon, corrugated steel garbage cans filled with crushed ice and cans of Budweiser beer.

The food was for the workmen. Feed them, stroke them, get them to work harder and faster, that was the plan.

At about 12:20 pm the men started drifting in, second- and third-generation Italian-Americans, with names like Vinny and Sal and Rocky and Nick, the kind of guys seen downing tools in beer commercials after a hard day of Building America. Grimy and dust-covered, with hammers and T-rules hanging from their work belts, these were the workmen upon whose shoulders the fate of the project now rested.

What one would have expected was for a lot of muscular arms to start digging into the crushed ice and pulling out cans of frosty cool ones, then for the men to belly up to the banquet and slap their plates full of pepperoni slices and potato salad.

But that was not what happened.

For at the opposite end of the room, in an effort at hospitality, Labich had arranged for an executive catering service to set up an actual cocktail bar for the construction crew—not unlike the one that had been set up for the directors at the August board meeting.

As a result, as the hungry workmen drifted in, first a few at a time, then by the dozens, all eyes fell not on the antipasto spread before them but on the incongruous cocktail bar across the room—and on the uptight-looking business executive, cocktail at the ready, standing next to it: Sutton. Next to him stood a littler version of same—Kelso Jr.—while nearby in shuffling silence stood Labich, Dunn, and the others.

It was Labich who finally broke the ice, gesturing first to the antipasto spread, then to a Christmas tree that had been set up at the far end of the room. Under the tree were Christmas presents for the men. Since there were 86 men on the job, there were 86 Christmas presents, each one a *TV-Cable Week* tote bag, inside of which was not more antipasto, but a bottle of Dewers' blended scotch whiskey. Said one of the workmen later: "Jesus, we'd hardly started the job and they were already giving away free booze. This deal looked like the pig trough of all time."

After the party the men went back to work. Though they *looked* busy enough—hauling galvanized steel L-beams, drilling holes in the wall—progress proved elusive. Two weeks later, when the editorial employees arrived, conditions had not changed appreciably from what they were on the day of the party.

To the scream of power saws and drills had now been added the day-long pounding of pneumatic air hammers, as workmen began blasting ten-foot wide circular holes in the floor. According to the architects' plans, these would become internal circular stairways so that, as Company Services Manager Karen Domanick explained it, "staff could move about easier."

In reality, the stairways were the end result of weeks of scheming by Zucchi, Dunn, and Labich to find a way of "controlling" Burgheim, a man over whom they had no direct authority but were convinced Grunwald was unwilling to remove. Zucchi wanted to have his office not on a separate floor from Burgheim's—the usual form of separation for Magazine Group's editors and publishers—but on the same floor and as physically close to Burgheim's as possible. This way, Zucchi could maintain a continual hovering presence over the managing editor, being able to spot instantly whenever Burgheim did something that he did not like. When that happened, Zucchi planned simply to light up a cigar, stroll into Burgheim's office, and give *TV-Cable Week*'s managing editor a dose of the publisher's patented "hey paisano" medicine.

But putting both officials on the same floor meant that portions of their staffs had to be scattered to other floors. To accommodate easy interfloor movement, Labich hit upon the "stairways solution," thus enabling Zucchi to pursue his tactics unimpeded. To Burgheim, what little he knew of Zucchi's staircase schemes amounted to yet more psychological warfare against the editors in general and himself in particular.

Occasionally, Grunwald, Grum, and other officials would come from Manhattan to see for themselves what was happening. Though the 30-mile trip took approximately 45 minutes by chauffeured limousine at a cost of $50, Grunwald preferred arriving by helicopter, a means of transportation that not only took longer but cost ten times as much—and always made him late.

When the executives arrived, Labich would issue them plastic construction-site hardhats emblazoned with the *TV-Cable Week* logo. Suitably protected, the officials would then begin climbing around through the junk, inspecting the "progress."

During one such visit, *TV-Cable Week*'s newly hired technology adviser, Milton Carter, attempted to hold a conference to alert everyone to the chaos ahead. A black man of disarming wit, Carter had been hired a week earlier, after months of battling between Zucchi and Burgheim, to head up a crash effort to develop a replacement for Labich's computer system. Now Carter was in a state of shock at the conditions in which he would have to work. He had hoped his meeting with Grunwald would drive the point home, and in a way, it did. No sooner had the executives seated themselves around the conference table and Grunwald had begun to speak, than there erupted not three feet behind him on the far side of a thin sheetrock partition, the skull-shattering roar of a pneumatic jackhammer that made him literally jump from his seat.

"Can't somebody do something?" cried Time Inc.'s editor in chief, but his words were scarcely heard above the din.

Some of the most captivating scenes of all were to be found down the hall, where work crews had set up their heavy construction equipment and noisiest power tools. In one room, cement mixers churned away day after day as if making ice cream, and every few minutes workmen would come out pushing wheelbarrows full of the wet mix, slopping it onto floors and walls.

Often, the workmen would take a "shortcut" through a cavernous space that was identified on the architects' plans as "the computer room."

This area was supposed to be kept dust-free and at controlled temperatures at all times in order to protect the sensitive equipment within. In this room, a group of electronics engineers headed by Zucchi's "can do" guy Siringo were already wiring up hardware: banks of hard disk drives the size of washing machines; neatly aligned rows of central processing units the size of refrigerators; floor-to-ceiling shelves of 9.6 kilobaud modems that looked like ultra-sophisticated stereo preamps; a circular chamber that belonged to a videocomp machine but called to mind an isolation booth from a 1950s game show; a row of pagination processors to fit logs and grids to pages; exotic-looking gear to crop, scan, and store thousands upon thousands of black-and-white publicity photographs from movies and TV shows.

On and on it went, the whirling tape drives, the panels of blinking lights—it was technology on parade, the electronic brain center of *TV-Cable Week*— and what seemed astounding beyond words was that right in the middle of it were workmen slopping around wheelbarrows of wet cement, nailing up sheetrocking, sweeping up clouds of dust. One day Siringo came out shaking his head, saying, "This is insane! Insane! We're hooking up this fucking kludge in the middle of a construction site!"*

Even as Siringo and his colleagues worked to connect up the kludge's various organs, other technicians were at work on

*A "kludge" is computer jargon for an assembly of processors and associated equipment that is neither graceful nor imaginative in design or function.

its tentacles as they snaked out through the building. Day after day the work went on, then week after week, as lengths of computer terminal wire were pulled up through walls and false ceilings by union electrical workers who barged into meetings, disrupting whatever was going on.

Count Demargitay moved about in a seeming state of shock, while Anne Davis's demeanor veered toward silent fury. For the last nine months she had warned time and again what would happen if Labich's system was used to publish magazines. Now she had to use it. In her office she kept what amounted to a living embodiment of her mood: a vicious little Pekinese dog called Fang, which would rush from under a couch snarling and snapping at anyone who came near it. Fang, one supposed, was there to eat Labich, Zucchi, Sutton, or Dunn, whoever came in the room first.

Around the corner sat some twenty writers and editors, a number that both Zucchi and Dunn constantly berated Burgheim for being excessive. But neither man seemed to realize that all these people were not nearly enough for what Burgheim actually had in mind.

Burgheim's writers and editors were not going to write just feature stories but upwards of 100 program "highlights" each week, 200 to 300 movie reviews each month, rush back and forth to New York to screen TV shows at the networks, edit plain-vanilla channel files from TV Data—in short, bring up to Time Inc. standards every word of every edition of what was shaping up as the most complicated undertaking in magazine publishing history.

To Burgheim's new administrative assistant, Flora Ling, fell the job of "organizing" all this. At the trade show in Anaheim six weeks earlier, Ling had been the soul of composure; now she seemed permanently on the edge of hysteria, rushing from one meeting to the next, notes in hand, eyes squinting, black hair flapping behind her. At the meetings her questions would come out like fifty-caliber machine-gun bullets: who's in charge of this, what's the state of that? Through it all, Burgheim would stand aside, suspended in confused amazement at what the forces of bureaucracy had unleashed. He simply could not believe it had gotten this far.

Even under the best of circumstances, bringing a new magazine to market is no easy matter, and often it can take many months before a new publication begins to acquire an appealing and marketable personality. But here was Time Inc. on the verge of unfurling what seemed literally the impossible magazine: a publication that had to be an immediate smash hit wherever it was sold, instantly achieving unheard-of penetration levels in every market, or else the entire business plan would collapse.

According to the plan, Zucchi would be signing up deals with new cable systems all the time, with the result that week after week, month after month, *TV-Cable Week* would, in effect, be premiering somewhere. Thus there would never be a minute's rest for the staff, never a week in which writers or editors could "coast." For them, every week had to be their best week, or else in some new market somewhere, *TV-Cable Week* might not make its required penetration level.

This level of editorial pressure existed nowhere else in Time Inc., and considering the stakes involved, probably nowhere else in American magazine publishing. Yet it was now placed on a staff of largely young and inexperienced people, nearly all of whom had quit jobs with other magazines and trade journals in order to join this heralded Time Inc. venture. Once aboard, they found themselves in a world they would never forget, as dust, debris, and wandering workmen filled the halls, even as Burgheim fought with Zucchi, Labich fought with Carter, Dunn fought with Ling, and Dukemejian fought with Davis—while the magazine's dumbfounded writers and researchers tried to get the knack of producing "Time Inc. quality" articles and program reviews amidst the bedlam.

Appalling though the situation was, it abruptly got worse. Mere days before the premiere of the magazine's first issue, which was to carry a cover date of April 10, 1983, two whole years' worth of warnings came true: the kludge reached its technological limit. Since November, Zucchi had managed to sign deals with five cable systems, exactly one-fifth the number anticipated for the launch date in the business plan. Yet Burgheim's insistence on custom-editing every word of every edition had by now so overtaxed the kludge that it proved itself incapable of processing even dry-run test editions for Zucchi's five systems before coming to a halt.

"The thing's got basic database corruption," announced Carter solemnly. "There's nothing worse that can happen to a computer."

Siringo analyzed the problem this way: "The system is overloaded. We're asking it to do too much. Something's got to give!"

Yet with the computer room already packed with nearly two-thirds as much editorial computing power as was contained in the Time & Life Building for all the company's other publications combined, Burgheim was not prepared to budge on anything. The magazine that he had spent nearly two years designing was not going to be ripped apart and redone two weeks from its debut!

This led to some of the most desperate fights of all, as Burgheim and Zucchi raged back and forth over what to do now, on the very eve of the magazine's premiere. Should Burgheim start trimming back his editorial design, or should Zucchi just shut up and get the editors more computers?

At midweek, Zucchi called a meeting in his conference room, attended by upwards of a dozen angry executives from Business and Edit.

"What the fuck's going on?" boomed Zucchi. "Why do we need all these goddamned computers anyway?" He turned to Carter. "Lookit, Milt, we're going to have a smaller meeting in two days, right here in this room all over again. And up there on that wall I want you to put a diagram of what these goddamned computers are supposed to do. I want to see the whole thing on one wall, got it?"

Two days later the group reconvened. On Zucchi's wall Carter had taped a ten-foot-long schematic diagram of the magazine's editorial "process flow" through the kludge. But the diagram was so confusing, with so many subloops and processing routines, that not even Carter understood it; and after five minutes of explanation he had thoroughly confused everyone, including himself.

"Goddamnit," barked Zucchi, as he slapped his hand on the table. "This thing is an ocean of shit!" At that, *TV-Cable Week*'s publisher looked to Burgheim for a response. But *TV-Cable Week*'s managing editor just picked up his clipboard and left the room.

The resulting standoff terrified everyone. What would happen now? If Burgheim did not publish at least *some* plain vanilla, the magazine would not premiere at all. But Burgheim was adamant. It was *his* magazine, not Zucchi's. Zucchi had his own problems—like finding cable operators to buy it! Burgheim wanted more computers, and Zucchi was going to get them, period.

The two men stayed eyeball to eyeball as their aides tried to put together a compromise. Perhaps Burgheim could be persuaded to publish "just a little plain vanilla," while Zucchi bought "just a few more processors." On Friday the publisher blinked: "Cut a check," he said to Dunn. "Get the guy what he wants."

Yet the bigger the kludge got, the more complex and confusing grew the problems it created. With part of the kludge wired to processors on the fifteenth floor, and another part wired to largely noninteractive computers two hundred miles away at TV Data, and still other parts wired to duplicate versions of the fifteenth-floor computer room in each printing plant, the kludge in reality was not one computer system but many—each of which had its own inherent technological limitations. Said Carter to Grunwald of what that meant, "Publishing this magazine is going to take human wave tactics," but the editor in chief seemed either not to understand or not to care. Siringo knew what it meant very well. The more the kludge expanded, the more people he had to hire to serve it. Some days the breakdowns and glitches came so frequently that Siringo had to grab the first body he could find. One day Dunn came to work and wondered why the elevator security guard was not at his post. The mystery cleared later that morning when Dunn went to see Siringo about hooking up some more computer processors for the editors and found the security guard, now dressed in a suit and tie, working in the computer room as a "trainee systems engineer."

Siringo looked at Dunn. "Hell, I'm up to my ass in alligators, Jeff, what do you want me to do?"

By mid-March, Davis already had 28 people on her own staff serving the kludge. Then came the two assistants who worked for Count Demargitay, the six assistant editors who worked for Burgheim, four of the programmers who worked for Siringo, three senior editors, both assistant managing editors, and even Ed Adler, Burgheim's all-around helper (by now promoted to news editor). In short: nearly four dozen people to wrestle the kludge for only five test editions—and this for a magazine that was supposed to be gearing up to produce live editions by the dozen. Said Eric Seidman, the art director: "If this keeps up we'll have to hire the state of Connecticut!"

Some foolish staffers thought they could handle the kludge. There was, for example, Billy O'Connor, who had been an infantry point man in Vietnam, won a bronze star, and figured he could take on the kludge with no problem. The kludge straightened him out immediately. First task: the kludge wanted a list, figured out by Billy, of every possible combination of every professional team sporting event ever seen on American TV— and the kludge wanted it in *two weeks*. The kludge was going to use this list to check TV Data's weekly sports listings, so that Burgheim's magazine never referred by chance to the Cleveland Yankees playing the Birmingham Astros.

Chicago Cubs versus Philadelphia Phillies; Los Angeles Express versus Tampa Bay Bandits; Arizona Wranglers versus Oakland Invaders; New Jersey Generals versus Michigan Panthers. On and on it went—baseball, basketball, indoor soccer, football—if it involved professional team sports, the kludge wanted it on the list.

The list ran to the hundreds, to the thousands—for Billy it was like the North Vietnamese Army; the more you counted, the more there were.

Day after day, night after night, Billy would sit there, putting away the beer, typing up the lists. Team after team, combination after combination, beer after beer.

One day Billy got up from his desk and went over to his supervisor, a lady named Hope. He said:

"Hope, I think I'm losing it. I think I'm going out of my mind!"

Hope knew exactly what Billy meant. Her job was to be responsible for a staff of people as shell-shocked as he was. These were the "DEC-hands,* whose misfortune it had been to demonstrate the powers of concentration and memory needed to master the kludge's evilest dirty work of all—actually editing the plain-vanilla files from TV Data. This was the job that Grunwald did not want to hear about, the job that Sutton did not understand or care to learn about, the job that Labich and Zucchi figured no one would be willing to do; but the job that Burgheim had insisted from the project's inception was the very heart of the magazine.

So complicated was the work of the DEC-hands, and so intimately linked to the far-flung operations of the kludge, that one erroneous DEC-hand keystroke in 10,000 would cause the kludge to freeze up, printing plants to stop, and from all over the building people to come running and shouting at Hope, "What happened! What happened!"

One night, Billy and a few of the DEC-hands went across

*So named because of the Digital Equipment Corporation (DEC) "VT-72" terminals on which they worked.

to the Galleria for some beers to cogitate on the situation. They talked about this and that, and before they knew it, everything had become a metaphor for Vietnam. The whole larger-than-life scale of the thing, the jerks who thought it up—for Billy O'Connor it was the Au Shau Valley in 1972 all over again, and he was clawing through jungle so thick he could not see three feet in front of him. Billy pronounced this feeling "very strange."

But to see something *really* strange, all Billy needed to do was come around the following Sunday morning at about 9:00 A.M. and stand in front of the Centroplex Building. If he had, he would have seen a scene to top any in *Apocalypse, Now:* Time Inc.'s version of an actual airborne assault mission, as a giant cargo helicopter flown in all the way from Wisconsin would drop out of the sky and lower onto the roof of the Centroplex Building not Editor in Chief Grunwald but more parts for the kludge.

The device in question, a 75,000-volt generator so huge that it would not fit in the building's elevators, had been bought by Time Inc.'s executives in case the ultimate catastrophe imaginable occurred: a power blackout. If all else failed, at least the kludge would have its own supply of electricity.

Because the kludge swallowed up the energy and attention of everyone, no one had any time to follow up on annoying details. Take the so-called "movie-syndie project," otherwise known as the "Case of Andy's Little Piles."

It all took root many months earlier, when Burgheim started insisting that TV Data's movie and syndicated series program descriptions were not up to Time Inc. standards. One favorite example of his concerned a TV Data movie review that had identified nineteenth-century Austrian-born novelist Franz Kafka as "Frank."

"So what," shrugged Zucchi, and the fights began.

By the time Edit had moved to White Plains in January

1983, Assistant Managing Editor William Marsano had somehow gotten the movie-syndie project rolling. Having done so,
Marsano tossed responsibility to keep it rolling to an editor
named Peter Young. "It's sort of a little cottage industry," explained Marsano. "You'll like it."

But as Young soon found out, calling the movie-syndie project a little cottage industry was like calling the Cologne cathe-
dral, the largest Gothic structure in Europe, a little cottage. For
lurking behind the 16,000 movies was a detail Marsano had
overlooked: Burgheim also wanted Time Inc. quality reviews of
more than 40,000 syndicated-series episodes as well—every episode of every series ever seen on American TV, from "The Life
of Riley" to "The Many Loves of Doby Gillis," from "Make
Room for Daddy" to "M*A*S*H."

On and on it went—"Get Smart!," "My Three Sons," "Petti-
coat Junction," "The Jeffersons." Every episode, every plotline:
Ralph and Norton invent no-cal pizza; Beaver Cleaver wants a
suit like his big brother Wally's; Lucy wants to be in Ricky's
show; Hazel gives Mister B. his comeuppance.

All of it had to be researched, written, edited, fact-checked,
top-edited, proofread, then fed into the kludge—the trivia challenge of the age.

On and on the project went, as freelance movie and TV
trivia buffs from everywhere began getting in on the action:
$3.50 per item to *write;* $175 per day to *edit.* In came the
reviews, out went the checks.

At last, the whole colossal thing seemed to be nearly done,
and Peter Young looked up from his desk with a haggard smile.
It was now March of 1983, virtually the eve of the magazine's
debut, and what had taken *TV Guide* years to accomplish, Time
Inc. had thrown $400,000 at, more or less, and knocked off in
a mere six months!

But wait. Hadn't something been overlooked?
Yes.
It seemed that although the writers had been writing the

reviews, and the editors and researchers had been editing and
researching them, no one had been keyboarding them into the
computer.

Instead of becoming part of the kludge, the movie-syndie
project now consisted of 56,000 scraps of paper piled up on the
floor. No one had told the young man being handed the pieces
of paper each day, one Andy Grossman, what to do with them.
So Andy just squirreled them away in neat alphabetical piles: a
pile for the As, a pile for the Bs, and so on and so on. Every day
the piles got bigger. When they got so big they looked ready to
topple over, Andy used his noggin. He started another pile.

Eventually, the whole back area of the Ops room was filled
with Andy's little piles of paper.

When Ling heard of this, she went to look for herself.

"What *is* all this?" she asked.

Andy looked at her like she was an idiot.

"It's the movie-syndie project," he announced.

At which point Ling began rushing around shrieking, "Oh
my God, oh my God, don't you understand? There's half a
million dollars lying on the floor back there! We've got to do
something—hire more people!"

EIGHTEEN

The Genius of Dick Burgheim

BY EARLY SPRING, the staff of *TV-Cable Week* totaled nearly 250 employees. In one way or another, most worked on the kludge, many of them reporting either to Anne Davis or to Labich. Feuding between these two had grown so severe that Davis had taken to hanging Do Not Disturb signs on her door whenever it seemed she might have to attend a meeting called by either Labich or one of his associates.

Barricaded in her office, Davis spent her days hunched over a computer terminal, trying to devise workable techniques for moving plain-vanilla listings from TV Data through the custom editing process, then placing the results in the right system-specific editions of the magazine. Sometimes listings would appear with the wrong channel markers, or the wrong titles, or the wrong airing times. Sometimes the right program would appear in the wrong edition, sometimes the data would disappear altogether.

At last Davis reached a fateful decision: the kludge was

essentially worthless; everything in the magazine was going to
have to be checked by hand. In the end, human beings were
going to have to do the work of Labich's system.

Davis was not shy about making her feelings known to
anyone who asked, and from time to time she would post com-
puter-typeset signs on her office door. These included such sentiments as "Magazines Are Run by Editors" and "Writers Are
the Highest Form of Human Life"—all designed to show passers-by precisely where she stood on the issues dividing Burgheim and Zucchi. Now her plan to hand-check the listings
seemed to call for the most unambiguous proclamation of all;
soon there it was, another sign appearing Luther-like on her
office door:

> THERE ARE SOME THINGS WORTH DYING FOR
> BUT KELSO SUTTON
> IS NOT ONE OF THEM

In the days prior to the launch of *TV-Cable Week*, President Munro knew little of the circumstances in White Plains,
but the magazine remained on his mind nonetheless. Six
months earlier he had authorized a public relations campaign
in which Time Inc. had gone out of its way to impress the Wall
Street investment community of the company's five-year, $100
million commitment to the magazine. Now, on the eve of the
magazine's launch, he and his aides Levin and Nicholas returned to that theme.

The occasion was a private party given for Munro and the
others by the Wall Street brokerage firm of L. F. Rothchild,
Unterberg, Towbin. The purpose of the gathering—typical of
many such Wall Street-sponsored get-togethers—was to enable
the brokerage house to bring together investment clients and
the top executives of companies whose stock the firm was currently recommending for purchase.

On this occasion, the prime topic of conversation was *TV-
Cable Week*. Munro still regarded the publication as a triumph

of synergism, wedding together the talents and know-how of the company's two largest and most profitable divisions. To impress the gathering, he had brought along several copies of the latest update of the dummy.

The dummy looked interesting, everyone agreed, and there was a *pro forma* question or two about the marketing strategy and the computers. But so far as Munro was aware, neither presented serious obstacles, and he thus remained both positive and convincing throughout the evening.

Yet Munro and his associates were preaching to an audience that was eager to believe. One of the analysts at the gathering, Alan Gottesman, summed up his reaction to the presentation this way: "Hell, if you hear the company's top men say they've got some new breakthrough computer system to publish the magazine, you're going to believe them, right?"

It was this very "wanting to believe" that discouraged Wall Street from probing deeply into the claims for the magazine. Here before the analysts were the top executives of a highly respected corporation, enthusing about a high-tech publishing product that no company in the country seemed better positioned to bring to market than Time Inc. Yet in reality, the product they described had no state-of-the-art technology, no effective management oversight, and no solidly grounded market research to indicate that the effort had a chance of succeeding.

In White Plains, of course, all this was well known, adding an ironic undertone to the countdown to launch. In addition to the five cable systems from which Zucchi had by now gotten firm commitments, the publisher was also at last making headway with perhaps half a dozen more, to be phased into the publishing cycle later in the spring and summer. Yet few of the systems were large enough to be an attractive market for the product, and no one knew how many editions of the magazine the kludge would be able to turn out. Labich's early claim to the

COO Group of being able to produce 250 editions "untouched by human hands," now looked to be a sick joke; Anne Davis had begun advising Burgheim that the kludge's limit would probably be no more than 20 editions, regardless of how many people she hired.

In spite of all that, Time's public relations apparatus was already in high gear, and coverage of the project was growing rapidly. Lengthy articles had appeared in *Business Week, Newsweek*, the *New York Times*, the *Village Voice*, the *Christian Science Monitor, New York* Magazine, *Los Angeles* Magazine, the *Miami Herald*, the *Detroit Free Press*, and hundreds of different trade journals and lesser known newspapers around the country.

The company's "deep pockets commitment" strategy had worked well. Nearly all coverage had picked up on the theme that Sutton had sounded at his press conference the summer before. Reported *Newsweek*, in a full-page article on the publication: "Time is spending at least $100 million to launch *TV-Cable Week*. . . . This is by far the largest investment ever made to launch a new magazine." The article included a photograph of Zucchi and Burgheim posing in shirtsleeves with this caption: "Zucchi and Burgheim: Betting $100 million."

Broadcast and cable television and even radio provided coverage. There were segments on ABC's "Entertainment Tonight," the ESPN cable network's "Business Times," Public Broadcasting's "The Nightly Business Report," and a joke on "The Johnny Carson Show." Meanwhile, a mini-cam crew from "CNN," (Ted Turner's Cable News Network), had come to White Plains and shot interview segments with Zucchi, Burgheim, and Demargitay.

Though coverage in the press was almost universally fawning, two media interviews suggested darker possibilities. Viewers of the "Today" show could have tuned in one morning early in April to see the following exchange between Zucchi and "Today" show co-host, Jane Pauley:

Pauley: "A hundred million dollars is unprecedented to

start up a new magazine. Time Inc. then is betting on a cable explosion, and yet 1982 was not a banner year. There were some major cable network collapses."

Zucchi: [awkwardly] "Uh-huh."

Burgheim as well was brought before the public's eye, though his withdrawn and bashful personality made radio seem a safer medium. But an on-the-air telephone interview with New York radio talk-show host Barry Gray did not go quite as planned:

Gray: "I have here Mr. Richard Burgheim, who is the editor of a brand new publication, called *TV-Cable Week.* Mr. Burgheim?

Burgheim: "Hi, Barry."

Gray: "You're in White Plains, aren't you?"

A long pause.

Burgheim: "Yes indeed."

Gray: "Boy, that's a long distance call."

Silence.

Gray: [sounding confused] "I don't hear anything."

Burgheim: [Inaudible mumble]

Gray: You don't like White Plains?

Burgheim: "It's Sixth Avenue where all the broadcasting action is. . . ."

Gray: "What's your background, Mr. Burgheim?"

Burgheim: "I was show business editor at *Time* back in the sixties and came to *People* with the launch of that back in 1974. And there until July 1981, when we began about an eighteen month study of whether this magazine was viable, and if so, how to do it."

Gray: "So for eighteen months you've been walking around trying to explain to people what you do for a living because they didn't see anything that you've done."

Burgheim: [sounding evasive] "Packing my bags and moving to White Plains."

Gray: "Obviously you're a Manhattanite. Well, White

Plains looks a lot different than it did twenty years ago."
Burgheim: "I'll take your word for that."

Such was the prevailing spirit on the evening of Monday,
April 4, 1983, as more than 350 staff members and friends
gathered in the grand dining salon of the La Reserve Hotel, two
blocks from the Centroplex Building, to celebrate the magazine's premiere. Though President Munro had more pressing
commitments elsewhere, he could rest assured of receiving a
full briefing on the proceedings since he had sent in his place
Executive Vice President Clifford Grum, the same individual
who had listened in with Munro on Sutton's press conference
the previous summer.

Also present were the two executives whose widely differ-
ing views of the project had contributed so much to its present
circumstance: Grunwald and Sutton. Sutton had even brought
his aide, Crutcher, whose dinner-table disclosures to Funt, still
unknown to Zucchi and his aides, had unwittingly given *On
Cable* a new lease on life.

The proceedings began when Zucchi stepped to the microphone to welcome the officials from New York. Turning the
microphone over to Sutton, Zucchi tried to conclude his remarks on a light-hearted note, and said casually to the audience:
"Well, thank God we got the signs taken down."

There was a murmur of amusement through the crowd, for
the anti-Sutton sign on Anne Davis's door had by now become
the subject of staff-wide joking that worried Zucchi no end. The
murmur only grew louder when Sutton stepped to the microphone and began muttering, "Signs, signs, that's all I've heard
since I got here."

Sutton as well had come prepared with some humor, and
at one point in his remarks observed, "Clifford Grum and I
racked our brains for a gift for you. We were thinking of what
we would need if we were working for Dick Burgheim and Dan
Zucchi. A punching bag was our first idea." Sutton went on to
announce that Time Inc. was giving *TV-Cable Week* a room full

of Nautilus exercise equipment ("so the next time you are tempted to give Dan or Dick a swift kick you can pump a little iron and *then* give them a swift kick"). Yet the crack did not get the laughter the group vice president might have hoped for, since a poll of the assembled listeners would surely have revealed that it was not Burgheim or Zucchi but Sutton himself whom the assembled Time Inc.'ers wanted most to "give a swift kick."

Probably the most off-key note of all was struck by Grunwald. Rising to the microphone, a plastic goblet of champagne in hand, he pronounced *TV-Cable Week* to be, as he put it, "really sensational"—a tribute to "the genius of Dick Burgheim."

What Time Inc.'s editor in chief left out was the most sensational part of all: that the magazine had even emerged. Yet in spite of everything—from computers that did not work to executives who could not communicate with each other or agree on anything—there they were, exactly as Burgheim had promised: five, separate, system-specific "Time Inc. quality" editions of the magazine, each printed in full color on heavy, coated paper; each with breezy *People*-like feature articles and personality profiles; each with different system-specific channel lineups, distinct pay services, and local-access programs unique to that system alone—over 50,000 interrelated and cross-referenced items of listings information, all written, edited, proofread, and checked for accuracy and internal consistency not by the kludge but by Burgheim's editors and writers.

Yet now, at the celebration festivities for this achievement stood Grunwald, champagne glass held aloft, toasting the very magazine he had earlier scoffed at as only "partly journalistic in nature," as well as the man he had snubbed from the start. To all who knew what had gone before, it was a moment of surpassing gall, and the person who seemed to sense it the most was Burgheim. When it came time for him to speak, the bashful and withdrawn little man delivered a line of such devastating and sharp-edged humor as to sum up in a sentence what the entire previous two years had really been all about.

With the crowd arrayed before him, and Grunwald, Grum, and Sutton at his side, Burgheim hesitated in brief reflection, then said, "To paraphrase what Winston Churchill once said under somewhat different circumstances, when it comes to *TV-Cable Week* and Time Inc.'s stockholders, never will so many have owed so much to so few."

There followed several seconds of silence as the full import of Burgheim's words sunk in, then the room erupted in gales of laughter and applause.

NINETEEN

Playing in Peoria

THOUGH they had not shared their fears with Burgheim, Zucchi and his aides by now were desperate, and spent hour after hour debating whether to hang tough or admit failure and advise Sutton to shut the project down. As all realized, the failure to sign up more than a handful of cable systems for the magazine's premiere made the launch little more than the very wet test that Dunn and Brauns had urged on Sutton over a year earlier. Only now, the test was not a "test" at all, but the actual publication and marketing of a new magazine—one with an elaborate physical infrastructure and staff already in place, and with the aroused interest of Wall Street waiting for the pay-off.

Meanwhile, costs had escalated alarmingly. In their original COO Group presentation, Dunn and Brauns had estimated the cost of a wet test to be $9 million. But the cost of the project had already climbed past $20 million, and six months of actual publication now seemed likely to push the figure to nearly $50 million.

The most immediate problem was getting subscribers to

buy the magazine in the five systems where it was being offered. That was Brauns's job, but she was having no more success at it than Zucchi was having in getting cable systems to sign
up. The very complexity of the marketing effort seemed to
overwhelm her. There were too many details to look after, too
many interwoven responsibilities involving too many different
departments and groups—of which hers was only one; the project had gotten too big and confusing to coordinate and market
at all.

Originally, the idea behind the marketing of *TV-Cable
Week* had been to "soften up" each cable system market with
a blitz of advertising about *TV-Cable Week* approximately a
month or so prior to the launch of the magazine in that system.
Media devices were to include billboard posters, radio and TV
commercials, and newspaper ads.

Once the market was softened up, Time Inc. would attempt to skim off charter subscribers to the magazine by offering cut-rate prices if they signed up prior to publication. Then,
when publication in a given cable system actually commenced,
each cable viewer in that system would get four free issues of
the magazine to read and examine before being asked to subscribe. In some systems, the marketing drive would also use the
services of cable system door-to-door salesmen, who would
move through neighborhoods selling subscriptions to *TV-Cable
Week* even as they sold subscriptions to cable service itself.

Unfortunately, the softening up blitz, prepared by the New
York advertising agency of Ted Bates, emphasized slogans such
as "The whole TV scene in one magazine," and "Suddenly
there's so much more to see," which confused more people than
it enticed. As a result, few people placed orders for charter
subscriptions. Said one project executive of the result: "It was
amazing—the lowest response rate the company had ever
seen."

This led, in turn, to what another project executive characterized as "virtual panic" in the marketing department, as the
marketing plan moved on to the four free issue giveaway stage.

Brauns herself began to think in terms of the Iranian hostage rescue mission. At a planning meeting with Zucchi she explained her strategy this way: "We don't want to make Jimmy Carter's mistake and go in there with only one or two helicopters; let's take the whole Air Force!"

TV-Cable Week's version of napalm turned out to be a magazine marketing device known as "the negative option." In it, the recipient of a free sample offer in effect implicitly agrees to become an actual subscriber once the "free sample period" lapses—unless he takes an overt step indicating that he does not want to continue receiving the magazine.

But *TV-Cable Week*'s marketing strategy artfully fudged over the fact that after the fourth free issue the magazine would start to cost money. The results can only be described as extraordinary, as in market after market, people leaped to the conclusion that they were being tricked. Soon hate mail began to arrive, as furious cable viewers charged the company with everything from bully tactics to invasion of privacy.

"I don't know, Dan," said Dunn at one meeting on the matter, "Before this thing is over we'll be wanted by every Better Business Bureau in America."

In Illinois, Texas, and Florida, complaints went beyond mere Better Business Bureaus and wound up involving actual law enforcement agencies. One cable system executive, Jeffrey Chandler, marketing director for General Electric's Peoria, Illinois, system, recalled the time well: "We were getting 50 to 75 complaints a day from our customers. On some days we just couldn't get anything else done in the office. The complaints were all the same—the Time Inc. marketing people just would not take no for an answer. *TV-Cable Week* had been represented to us as a 'retention tool,' but before any of our customers ever saw the first copy of it, Time Inc.'s marketing people were driving them away."

Because the heavy-handed marketing was being concentrated in tightly defined cable markets in which literally everyone in a neighborhood could wind up feeling bullied, the pressure on cable system operators was severe. Said Chandler of the reaction in Peoria: "Our customers would come in and say, 'If you don't stop *TV-Cable Week* from coming, I'll downgrade my service.' Other customers would say, 'I'll sign up for this or that pay service just so long as I don't have to get *TV-Cable Week!*' Other customers would come in and throw their bills at the switchboard operator. Some would say that they never wanted to see another Time Inc. publication in their lives."

By far the most bizarre incident occurred in Springfield, Missouri, where the cable system manager found himself under seige from the moment his customers discovered that the magazine they thought was free turned out to cost money. Most just yelled. But not a Korean War veteran who many years earlier had gotten himself caught in a negative option trap set by a different publisher. Like a familiar tattoo of doom, the bills kept coming—for a magazine that he did not want.

When he could stand it no longer, the Korean War vet took action.

Storming into the cable company office, he demanded to see the manager, and once the man appeared, the vet announced his intentions:

"If you don't stop this magazine from coming, I'm going to come back here and waste you! The only people worse than you are *My Weekly Reader!*"

As soon as the man left, the shaken manager called White Plains with the news. Yet there was apparently nothing that *TV-Cable Week* could do. It seemed the Korean War vet's name was already imbedded in the kludge, and it would take weeks to get it out.

Weeks?

The cable manager could be dead by then!

After urgent talks, *TV-Cable Week*'s executives came up with a solution: for the first time in the sixty-one-year history of the corporation, Time Inc. would provide round-the-clock bodyguard protection to keep one of its business partners safe from one of Time Inc.'s own readers.

As the turmoil in the marketplace worsened, Brauns grew anxious. Already eight months pregnant and nearing maternity leave, she began to fear that with her departure she would be gossiped about—just like in the old days in Corporate Circulation, when she had first arrived in the company from the B-School. Then the gossip had preceded her arrival; was it now destined to follow her departure? Didn't anyone remember that she had not wanted the magazine to get this far in the first place? that she, like Dunn, had urged a market test before actually starting to publish? One of the few senior female executives on the project, Brauns began to wonder what was being said about her when Dunn would go into Zucchi's office and close the door.

Her fears were far from groundless, for behind the closed doors the men did indeed talk about Brauns. We've been braunzed, they would say. This whole thing isn't our fault, it's Sarah's. She was the one who thought up the marketing plan, not us.

That of course was not only not true—since the marketing plan had been the creation of Dunn, Brauns, Durrell, and ultimately, Sutton—but the accusation simply illustrated the heightened anxieties of the men themselves. They were as frightened as Brauns was, for their own areas of responsibility were in as much turmoil as was hers.

At the bottom of the hierarchy stood Dukemejian, still in charge of Project Mustang but instructed by Labich to pay the bills and never mind about the details. Then came Labich, in charge of a computer system that he had designed and proclaimed to the COO Group to be capable of 250 editions—but which was struggling to produce half a dozen. Then came Dunn, the smartest of all the business players, and perhaps in a way the most desperate. For the project had gotten so complex and huge, and was growing so rapidly, that it was no longer really possible to manage *TV-Cable Week* at all. Yet Dunn carried the title of General Manager. And all around him, everywhere he looked, was evidence of his plight—from telephones that did not work, to construction workers who never finished their jobs, to message vans that never arrived from New York.

Twelve months earlier the two Harvard M.B.A.s had stood before Time Inc.'s highest officials and warned them not to move forward with the project without ascertaining whether the computers would work; whether cable operators would cooperate; whether customers would subscribe. But Time Inc.'s brass had dismissed the warnings and pushed ahead anyway, and now each and every warning was coming true, just as Dunn and Brauns had feared, only *they* now presided over the mayhem—or at least appeared to.

Meanwhile, complaints from the field began to mushroom. They ranged from the pushy sales representatives to, at the opposite extreme, pleas from people who actually wanted to receive the magazine but kept getting rebuffed. Said one elderly man from Overland Park, Kansas, "I've had triple by-pass surgery, and I can't get out of bed anymore. All I want is to start getting your magazine. I've paid for it *twice* already, but all you do is send me more bills! I'm an old, sick man. I just want to know what is on TV. Can't you help me?"

When Burgheim learned of this call, the managing editor's shoulders sagged and he looked for an instant actually ready to cry. As he wandered off, he turned to a colleague and said, "Jesus Christ, this is a tragedy. This whole thing is a tragedy."

Day by day the staff seemed to grow edgier and more anxious. The magazine had officially been in business for no more than a few weeks and suddenly people were asking questions for which no one had answers. Where were the big new deals that Zucchi kept talking about but that always seemed to evaporate at the last minute? What happened to the Tulsa deal that was "nailed down solid" but then got away? What about the

deal in San Francisco, the one in Atlanta, the one in Memphis?
One day one of the writers came up and asked, "What happened to the Nautilus machine that Mr. Sutton said we were getting? When is it going to arrive?"
It was another question without an answer.
Burgheim was probably the edgiest of all, as the strain of two years began to take its toll. Undisciplined in the management of his time, yet determined to be open and accessible to every staff member who might want to see him, Burgheim now found his office besieged day and night by various departmental officials. His secretary, a kindly though increasingly haggard-looking woman named Mary Anne, kept a jar of jellybeans on her desk outside Burgheim's office for the waiting petitioners to snack on as they queued up for their audiences each morning. By noon, the jar usually needed refilling, and by mid-afternoon she had often switched from jellybeans to Hersheys chocolate kisses. Meanwhile, the parade of hopefuls continued.
At 6:30 each evening most of the staff would leave for home —but not Burgheim. Now freed at last to do actual editing, he would swing his chair around to the computer terminal behind his desk and begin editing the mountain of stories and program reviews that had piled up during the day.
Yet even his evenings were not his own. As the hours passed, art designers would enter bringing page layouts to approve, photographic researchers would present him with pictures of celebrities to illustrate the stories, and operations personnel would interrupt to brief him on the kludge.
It had been this way from the day Burgheim had moved to White Plains—the constant roar of people clamoring for decisions. Now, with the magazine at last being published and in the marketplace, he sensed a new undercurrent of muttering and sideways glances that he could not quite explain.
One day he went to see Ling, and found the door closed. He could hear voices inside, but when he turned the handle and looked in the conversation abruptly halted and he found several of his colleagues staring back at him in embarrassed silence.

"Excuse me," he said, "I didn't mean to interrupt," and backed quietly out of the room. Yet no sooner did the door close than he could hear the whispering resume.

Burgheim went back in his office and thought, What was *that* all about? After a while he poured himself a glass of wine, swung around in his seat, and resumed his editing.

In contrast to Burgheim, Zucchi became an energized blur as the bad news grew—walking faster, talking faster, rushing to more and more meetings with more and more cable operators. "We gotta push this thing harder," he would say to Dunn, "get a bigger hit quicker." It was as if the publisher of *TV-Cable Week* thought his problems could be made to go away if he simply moved about at lightning speed.

But it was not many weeks after the magazine's debut that Zucchi as well began to see that the project was foundering. Not only had only a mere fraction of the required number of cable operators signed deals, but instead of 40, 50, or even 60 percent penetration in each market, *TV-Cable Week* was getting less than 10 percent penetration, with subscriptions not in the tens of thousands per system but in some cases merely in the hundreds.

"These returns are dog shit," moaned Zucchi, as he worried over how to explain the shortfall to Madison Avenue. Advertisers had taken the company at its word regarding the magazine's potential, and Zucchi had already gotten commitments for more than six hundred pages of national advertising for the first year. But Zucchi knew it would not be long before the truth would start to leak out, and the most heavily promoted magazine in Time Inc.'s history would become the laughing stock of every advertising agency in New York. The thought of it made his skin crawl. Something had to be done, and fast, but the question was, what?

Zucchi was sitting at his desk worrying over the question one Friday afternoon toward the middle of May when the telephone rang and on the other end was Brauns.

"Dan," she said rather matter-of-factly. "I won't be in Monday. I don't think I'll be able to come to work."

"Why not?" asked Zucchi. "You gotta. What's up?" There was a pitch to his voice, urgent and concerned, as if everything depended upon her turning up for work.

"It's the baby," said Brauns. "The doctor said I'll never make it beyond the weekend. It's going to happen any minute."

"Oh," said Zucchi, as the reality of her circumstance sunk in. He began offering reassurances, urged her to keep in touch, then rung off and returned to the reality of *his* circumstance.

Before him on his desk sat a confidential memo he had just received from Dunn. It was a devastating critique of the crisis in the marketplace, from the lack of cable operator support throughout the industry, to the galling failure of Time Inc.'s own cable subsidiary, ATC, to sign a deal.

In Zucchi's mind, *TV-Cable Week*'s ace in the hole all along had been ATC, the second largest cable TV network in the country, by now with more than 2.5 million subscribers in over 100 different systems. As Zucchi saw things, if all else failed, there was at least ATC; they would have to buy the magazine —Munro could *make* them! But every time it came time to sign, the deal just slipped away. Why?

"Time Inc. is the largest cable company around," read Dunn's memo. "We *have* to have ATC allow us to establish the product. If it takes Time Inc. involvement to make this happen, this should be requested. I'd suggest that you give ATC's brass one more shot first, in person over dinner, where you explain the stakes involved."

In the week that followed Zucchi fretted over the matter. Something was wrong with ATC, seriously wrong, and he had to find out what. At last he called Dunn to his office. "Get out to Denver," he said. "Find out what's going on out there. Find out why we can't get a deal."

By now, Dunn too was frantic. Nearly two years of his life had been swallowed up by *TV-Cable Week*, his future at Time Inc. seemed in doubt, and, like Brauns, he feared he would be somehow tarred forever by this business misadventure.

So on the evening of Sunday, May 22, Dunn and a marketing associate boarded a flight from New York to Denver to meet with ATC's president, Joseph Collins, and find out exactly what it would take to nail down a deal.

Though neither Dunn or Zucchi knew it, the answer to that question was not in Denver at all, but much closer to home, in the internal files of Video Group head Gerald Levin.

In those files sat the confidential memo that Collins's assistant, Gary Bryson, had drafted enumerating ATC's doubts about the prospects for *TV-Cable Week*—drafted immediately after the task-force's COO Group presentation in January of 1982. But since Levin had not seen fit to share Bryson's memo with the task force, an entire year and a half had passed without anyone on the project knowing its contents.

Now Zucchi was to learn the truth.

The scenario began to play itself out on the morning of May 23, in the Englewood, Colorado, headquarters of ATC, in the shadow of the Rocky Mountains. Though ATC's glass facade headquarters, completed in 1980, seemed typical of many such corporate "ice palaces" that dot the American landscape, the two visitors quickly noticed a fundamental difference: this one featured an "open office" environment—an arrangement in which offices have neither walls nor doors but are simply open-air "spaces," separated by potted plants, shelving, and portable partitions. Anyone who passed by was thus able to observe what now followed, as the two visitors from White Plains settled themselves into chairs in Collins's "space" along with Collins and two marketing associates.

For the next two-plus hours, the group listened to one reason after another from Collins why *TV-Cable Week* was something that no right-minded cable operator wanted to get involved with in any way, and least of all ATC. Instead of a *weekly* magazine, Collins now revealed that ATC could fill all its needs, and at a much lower price, by providing subscribers simply with *monthlies.*

Dunn was astounded.

Long before the task force had gone before the COO Group to describe the Durrell/Burgheim plan for a weekly publication, both he and Brauns had already concluded that Time Inc. simply could not make money publishing on a monthly cycle no matter how many editions it offered; the advertising revenues would be too small, the circulation returns too limited. Publishing on a monthly basis was not even worth the effort.

Now, here was the president of ATC, the company's own cable system, suggesting the task force should have developed a monthly from the beginning. In other words, there had been no point to *TV-Cable Week* at all—or even, for that matter, a *TV-Cable Month*. One formula yielded no market, the other yielded no profits. The last eighteen months had been a total and complete waste of time.

Shattered by their discoveries, the two executives returned to New York, wondering how Zucchi, a man who seemed not to know the meaning of the word failure, would take the news.

"Jesus," said Zucchi as his two assistants spelled out the facts for him back in New York. "Kelso had better hear this."

TWENTY

Why Not Give It Away!

WHILE BURGHEIM'S STAFF put the finishing touches on the ninth issue of *TV-Cable Week* in White Plains, Zucchi and Dunn sat in the thirty-fourth floor office of Group Vice President for Magazines Kelso Sutton, in an atmosphere charged with tension.

Neither man had ever been in a situation like this before. Here before them sat one of the most powerful and feared men in Time Inc., a man whose consuming goal for the last eighteen months had been to get a TV cable magazine to market. Now, with the marketplace in turmoil and the project collapsing before his eyes, he was being told that the project's synergism—the factor that was to give the magazine a criticial edge—had been an illusion from the start; that ATC was not about to buy *TV-Cable Week* and perhaps had never intended to.

Not fifty feet from where the three men sat was the office of Gerald Levin, the man who ran Video Group, and who one might reasonably have assumed would have known the facts of the situation. Further down the hall was the office of President Munro, a one-time Video Group head. And the man who now presided, in theory at least, over both Magazine Group *and* Video Group seemed oblivious to the fact that his two prime lieutenants were apparently not communicating on this issue. Also nearby was the office of Executive Vice President Clifford Grum—the man who on the corporate flow chart had been responsible for carrying the messages back and forth between Video and Magazines from the beginning, but had apparently missed out on the key one. In short, it had taken two entire years for a piece of information crucial to the success of the biggest publishing effort in the company's history to travel exactly fifty feet—from Gerald Levin's office to Kelso Sutton's— and only then by means of a four-thousand-mile detour through a Denver, Colorado, subsidiary.

Though the meeting in Sutton's office concluded without any clear indication of what the group vice president had in mind, it was plain that he now knew that the publication upon which he had bet so much and counted so heavily was in "very very serious trouble."

A few days later the magazine's executives got the first glimmerings of how Sutton proposed to deal with the situation. He summoned several of them back to New York for a luncheon meeting with an outside management consultant named Bruce Hiland, whom he had brought in to help analyze the situation.

What Sutton now had in mind was to view *TV-Cable Week* not so much as a Magazine Group quagmire as a kind of corporate-wide annoyance that could be tolerated when one looked at the bigger picture. For instance, he said, suppose Time Inc. were to print editions for all of ATC's systems and virtually give them away. At a stroke, one could create a magazine with two million-plus circulation, wiping out ATC's "guide" expenses overnight. Meanwhile, ad revenues would begin to flow, and the project would be on sound footing again.

In fact, Sutton continued as he warmed to the subject, why

not do similar deals with systems operators everywhere? Overnight one would have a magazine with five million circulation, ten million. . . . Indeed, Sutton exclaimed, when you got right down to it, why not just give the thing away to everyone!

But when Sutton looked to Zucchi and his aides for a response, he met only blank stares. Why not give the thing away? The physical costs of simply printing the issues would devour the whole project. That was the reason they were *selling* it in the first place. If *TV-Cable Week* were to be given away, the bigger the circulation got, the deeper into the red the project would sink.

"Let's do some numbers," Sutton instructed. "See what they show."

Back to White Plains went the stunned executives to inform their staffs of the new idea—to analyze the numbers that would prove the obvious: that given enough time, Sutton's solution could bankrupt all of Time Inc.

Down the hall from Burgheim and his editors, Zucchi and his staff of M.B.A.s now began desperately reexamining every publishing option Dunn and Brauns had looked at more than eighteen months earlier—and all to see if the cost of a Time Inc. listings magazine could somehow be reduced to a level that would allow the publication to meet the competition of the low-cost monthlies.

Yet no matter how they looked at it, there was no solution. Whether they published on a weekly or a monthly cycle, the project's overhead and production costs, even as originally set forth in the business plan, now blocked the company's ability to compete. Not only did the project entail high-cost printing contracts with plants around the country, but there were deals with binderies, with truckers. Meanwhile, marketing and sales offices had been opened in Detroit, Chicago, and Los Angeles, even as Zucchi continued to maintain a marketing and sales operation in Amax-7.

Beyond all that loomed the millstone of White Plains—a kind of Time Inc. version of CBS Cable's Arabian tent village at the Las Vegas trade show—from its payroll staff of 251 employees, to its five-year multi-million-dollar lease on the Centroplex Building, to the project's ever-growing investment in the kludge.

As Zucchi and his aides now saw things, the problem was how to explain all this to Munro, who was to appear in White Plains along with other thirty-fourth floor officials for a previously scheduled "management update" meeting on June 10th, only days away.

The time had long passed for putting an optimistic gloss on the facts; the players now realized there was no genuine solution left. The only way out was for ATC to buy the magazine whether the cable division lost money by doing so or not.

Somehow Munro had to be made to understand this, and by the morning of the meeting, the players had worked out a strategy for breaking the news: first, they would proceed through the scheduled routine update. Then, when that was finished, they would recap the news from Denver and drive home the point that the whole future of the magazine was in jeopardy, that the only hope for survival lay in making ATC "eat a money-losing deal."

Now it was Friday, and though not yet 11 A.M., a steamy summer haze hung over White Plains. Yet in the newly finished audio-visual conference room across from Zucchi's office, the atmosphere felt almost chilly by comparison. The room had been designed for Zucchi and his sales staff to make presentations to cable operators, and had been equipped with every convenience imaginable, from a quadraphonic sound system and multimedia screening facility to a kitchen and catering pantry. Rounding out the ambiance, newly installed recessed ceiling lights cast overlapping and mottled pools of illumination across the room, as if the executives for whom this space had been designed might move from one spotlight to the next in the course of negotiating their deals.

Yet gathered now under the spotlights of this room, so recently decorated that it still smelled of paint and freshly laid carpeting, were not sales executives and cable operators, but the heaviest collection of thirty-fourth floor brass the Centroplex Building had ever seen. They sat seated around a large horseshoe-shaped chrome and oak conference table in the center of the room, waiting for the update to begin. Among the attending big-wigs were not only Munro, Sutton, and Levin, but Sutton's consultant-aide Hiland (soon to be appointed a Time Inc. vice president), and Grunwald's aide, Graves, who had flown in from his vacation home on Martha's Vineyard wearing khaki slacks, a denim workshirt, and a funereal scowl. Also in attendance, and making his first *TV-Cable Week* on-site appearance, was Chairman of the Board Ralph Davidson, who had interrupted a honeymoon with his new wife of eight days to be at the meeting.

When the last of more than a hour's worth of middle-management reports concluded, Zucchi and his aides presented their last-chance strategy of making ATC "eat the deal." The White Plains executives had naturally assumed that Munro would have been told at least something about the grim news from Denver; yet his reaction suggested a man who had been left almost completely in the dark about a crisis that was now exploding in his face. Seemingly flabbergasted at the disclosures, Time Inc.'s soft-spoken president burst forth in swearing.

"Goddamnit, why am I hearing all this *now!*"

It was a question that no one in the room cared to answer, especially since the two group vice presidents who could most obviously enlighten their leader—Sutton and Levin—sat mutely at his elbows.

A brief silence ensued as Munro regained his composure. Then, in steadier tones, he proceeded to dress down Zucchi and the others for wasting his time with the trivial matters that had occupied the first hour of the meeting. After that, Munro surveyed the group and declared:

"Obviously, if it is right for the corporation, ATC will fall into line. But if ATC itself won't voluntarily buy this magazine, then why would anyone else?"

At this Levin nodded his agreement.

Munro turned to Sutton: "Okay Kelso, what do *you* think about all this?"

Sutton answered with a sideways scowl at Zucchi and Dunn: "I don't think it's really all that bad." He then began to spell out his reasons why Time Inc. should force ATC to sign a deal. *TV-Cable Week*, the argument seemed to run, could prove beneficial to Time Inc. from a corporate-level perspective, even if the magazine made no sense to ATC as a business.

Bleaker and bleaker grew the mood of the meeting until even Munro seemed to notice it. During a break in the discussions, he seized the chance to lighten the gloom and remarked to Zucchi that MTV, the rock video station owned by Warner-Amex, had so mesmerized his children that they no longer seemed interested in athletics but would return home from school to watch hour after hour of their favorite rock stars. Said Munro of how he had dealt with the situation, "I got MTV removed from my cable service; now my kids *can't* watch it!"

At this, Zucchi offered his own view of the quality of cable TV programming, and what to do about it, saying with a determined look, "You think *that's* something? Hell, with my kids it's not MTV but goddamned HBO! Well, I just ripped the damned wire right out of the wall altogether!" at which point he reached forward two meaty hands and made a yanking gesture in the air.

Yet for all the small talk, by meeting's end no one seemed clear what to do about the crisis itself—or even what had caused it in the first place. For as the gathering drew to a close, Munro announced to the group with steely resolve, "Well, I'll tell you right now, we're not going to fold it yet!"

Picking up on the theme, the assembled executives began to congratulate each other on how "gutsy" Time Inc. was to be involved in the project at all. Even Sutton's newly enlisted consultant on the crisis, Hiland, chimed in, saying in a voice of dead seriousness, "If you want to know how gutsy Time Inc. is, think of this: we launched this magazine without ever even testing it!"

TWENTY-ONE

The Big Jump

THE JUNE 10th meeting had unnerved all the corporate officials in attendance, but no one was more acutely embarrassed by the revelations than Sutton and Levin. Having ridden high on the company's now-dashed hopes for *TV-Cable Week*, both men were due to be elevated, along with Nick Nicholas, to Time Inc.'s board of directors later that month. Now they would have to attend their first meeting in that capacity to report on a foul-up in which they were both implicated.

Within a matter of days Time Inc. had convened its second cable listings task force in as many years—this one installed not in White Plains, where logic might have dictated, but behind closed doors in a large suite of thirty-fifth floor offices in Time Inc.'s Manhattan headquarters. Unlike the earlier effort, which had begun with only two individuals sent off to "write on a blank slate," this one—given the uplifting name Operation Sunburst by Sutton—consisted of dozens of people, many from HBO and ATC, and all charged with finding a solution to the crisis.

The participation now of Video Group in the salvage effort signaled the drama's final act. Behind the closed doors of Operation Sunburst the two-year-long political struggle over *TV-Cable Week* was coming to a climax, as the executives of Video Group and Magazine Group grappled not just for control of the project but in a sense for control of the corporation itself. Would Sunburst decide to continue with the publication of a high-cost weekly magazine such as Sutton had backed from the start, or would the new team abandon that effort and shift to a less ambitious monthly of the sort that Video Group apparently had preferred all along?

It was a question freighted with significance, for if *TV-Cable Week* were to be successfully relaunched by Sunburst as a monthly guide, Gerald Levin would rise to Time's board wreathed as a corporate savior as Video Group outflanked Sutton, Grunwald, and the entire bureaucracy of the Magazine Group old guard.

This is what *TV-Cable Week* had been about all along. For in the new Time Inc. of conglomerate growth, with its intergroup rivalries and intrigues, it was no longer enough to be the "brightest guy" on the "fastest track" in Magazine Group. What had historically been a single ladder to the pinnacle of power had been joined by a second, parallel set of rungs. For the bright and the ambitious, the trick was to climb them both, to "pull a Munro"—coined for a man who had begun as a nameless face in *Time* Magazine's circulation department and had risen through the Magazine Group ranks before making the big jump to Video. As his reward for making that jump, Munro had become the president of Time Inc.

In its way, *TV-Cable Week* had been Sutton's opportunity to make the jump, acquire Video credentials, and make the final reach for the top spot. No two people were thus more astounded than Dan Zucchi and Jeff Dunn to find whose turn it would become next: none other than S. Christopher Meigher's —the man who had sat in the group vice president's office with them a year earlier and warned against going forward with the project; Meigher now became Sutton's choice to lead the Magazine Group contingent on Sunburst itself.

On the evidence, Meigher was certainly qualified for the job. He was the company's leading circulation expert, and the lack of subscribers was, after all, the cause of the magazine's woes. But what staggered Dunn was that Meigher should be involved at all.

In his way, Jeff Dunn had always thought of *TV-Cable Week* as *his* magazine, not Sarah Brauns's, or Dick Burgheim's, or Dan Zucchi's. True, those people were paying in blood, as he was, for the failings of their superiors. But with the magazine in tatters, who was once again entering Dunn's life than the individual who had been his first mentor in the company—now reappearing as a critic of all he had done for the last year and a half. It blew Jeff Dunn away.

The week following the June 10th meeting, Meigher and Hiland emerged from the Sunburst offices and convened a luncheon meeting with Dunn and some others from White Plains. The mood was arctic. Though the luncheon had been called at Sutton's orders to help the Sunburst group develop a *TV-Cable Week* "cost analysis," the discussion quickly opened up into broad-ranging arguments that strayed into every topic imaginable, from marketing to manufacturing, from penetration levels to distribution methods.

To Dunn and his colleagues from White Plains, the men from midtown seemed "like babes . . . mere infants in this thing." To Meigher and *his* colleagues, Dunn and the others seemed negative and noncooperating. For Zucchi, time was running out.

In White Plains itself, the mood was captured by a late June cover image Burgheim chose for the magazine: a scowling portrait of Mister T., complete with a clenched fist. In the rumor-filled atmosphere of recrimination and finger pointing, accusations and counter-charges flew like artillery shells between the entrenched troops of Zucchi and Burgheim.

Meanwhile, Sutton had taken over the office of one of the

magazine's advertising executives, and begun round after round of closed-door meetings with Zucchi. Among the subjects: plans to oust Brauns, who was still at home recovering from the birth of her child. The project was in desperate straits, and Sutton and Zucchi agreed: removing Brauns was the thing to do. They would take her off the project, find a job for her in New York, and bring in somebody fresh.

Brauns got the news when Zucchi called her into his office from home, told her she was being removed, then instructed her to say nothing to anyone about it. At the right time they would have a farewell party for her, and her accomplishments would be remembered. It was just that now was not the right time, the situation was too delicate.

At lunch, Sutton weighed in, shifting from Zucchi's grim demeanor to a kind of beaming camaradarie, emphasizing that she should look upon her new assignment—working in strategic planning in New York, directly under Sutton himself—as a real opportunity.

"I'm being set up," Brauns thought. "I'm being made the scapegoat."

Her anxieties only intensified when, not long afterward, she went to her office to look through her files, the full two-year-long record of what she had done, and found that her file cabinets had been emptied out—by whom she did not know.

Left in the dark through all of this was Burgheim, one of the few senior executives on the project doing what he was paid to do: edit the magazine. Organizationally inept, and naive in the ways of office politics, he was under attack from the business side for all manner of alleged offenses, some of them bizarre in the extreme.

One day Labich came into his office and sat down with a huff.

"Dick, we've got a problem. It's the fresh air—the bills are getting too high. Last weekend we paid $20,000 for fresh air.

We've got to do something about it, these fresh air bills are killing us!"

Then Labich got up and headed back down the hall.

Labich's air bill woes had not been caused by Burgheim but by Labich's kludge, which needed cooled fresh air to operate. But the Centroplex Building had central air conditioning that could not be regulated floor by floor, and would shut off automatically for the entire building at 6 P.M. Yet no weekly magazine in America keeps normal business hours—and this was arguably the nation's most abnormal magazine anyway. So whenever staffers worked late or on weekends, the air conditioning system had to be started up for the entire building—and *TV-Cable Week* had to pay the bill.

That afternoon, Flora Ling came to Burgheim and looked about anxiously:

"Listen to this. Jeff says we've got to cut back on Federal Express and messengers. He says they're out of sight."

Burgheim looked at her.

"That's nothing. Labich came in here this morning and said to cut back on breathing."

The more absurd the attacks grew, the more despondent Burgheim became. He felt he had been manipulated and misled, that high above him a struggle was going at the corporate level in which he and his employees had become pawns. Meanwhile, where was Grunwald? With Sutton and Zucchi now closeted down the hall while the staff gossiped wildly, Burgheim needed support from Grunwald lest his subordinates conclude that the magazine was being abandoned altogether.

Finally, in early July Grunwald succumbed to Burgheim's pleadings and appeared for what came to be remembered as The Big Lunch. Accompanying Grunwald to White Plains was an individual named Gil Rogin, the managing editor of *Sports Illustrated*, who had lately been serving as a note-taker and all-around aide for the editor in chief. Though Rogin's name appeared along with Grunwald's on the masthead of *TV-Cable*

Week as a member of the magazine's editorial board, he was so infrequently seen in White Plains that few at the luncheon even knew who he was. Burgheim himself seemed to judge Rogin's detachment as total, remarking of him at one point, "Forget about Gil, he's even worse at this political crap than I am. He's *totally* out of it."

But the most detached was Grunwald, and for good reason. Unlike Burgheim, the editor in chief knew what was taking place behind the closed doors of Sunburst. When it came time for the editor in chief to speak, he turned to Burgheim and offered a single, needling comment:

"Dick, I must ask what you think about perhaps running some more 'serious-minded' articles from time to time."

Burgheim's face became a study in controlled fury as he simply stared back and said:

"Frankly, Henry, I don't plan *any* new direction to our editorial coverage."

At one point, Flora Ling seemed to grow so frustrated with the course of the discussion that she put down her eating utensils and started actually squeezing the air with her fingers, saying, "This is not a healthy atmosphere we have up here. We've got to clear the air with the business people."

At this, Rogin looked at Grunwald in alarm and declared, "Sounds like it's time for a meeting to me, Henry, don't you think?"

Responded Grunwald without looking up from his dessert plate of kiwi fruit and sherbert:

"No meeting yet. It's not time."

Hearing this, Rogin produced a pen and paper and scribbled some words while slowly muttering aloud:

"No meeting . . . too early. . . ."

Watching the performance, Bill Marsano recognized a familiar situation, and knowing exactly how to relieve the tension with Time Inc.'s editor in chief, picked up where he had left off during his job interview the year before, and began regaling the man with funny sounding titles of pornographic movies as well as some anecdotes from his days as the editor of an ice cream magazine. Grunwald's face lightened up, the eyebrows lifted, and all could see that here at last were subjects with which Time Inc.'s editor in chief felt more comfortable.

Late that afternoon Burgheim called Ling, Marsano, and one or two others into his office and closed the door. He wanted to talk about what to do. With his back to the wall, with the editorial independence of the magazine at stake, it seemed to Burgheim as if, once again, Grunwald just could not be bothered.

Sitting on the couch, Marsano began to stroke his beard, while Ling climbed over some unpacked book cartons and took a seat next to Burgheim's desk.

"Maybe Kelso could help," she said. "If we could get an agenda for a kind of clear-the-air summit, maybe. . . ." but her thoughts trailed off. Burgheim did not respond. Gloomy as things were, he knew that involving Sutton would only make them worse.

As the group drifted out, Burgheim walked to the window and stared out, past the roof of the Galleria below, beyond the smog and factory fumes of New Rochelle, and on and on until over the rim of the horizon he could imagine midtown Manhattan with its glass and aluminum towers, its bumper-to-bumper executive limousines, and its $250 expense account lunches at the Four Seasons. And he said softly, "They have done nothing to help me on this. Nothing at all."

In the days that followed, life at the office became almost surreal. In Austin, Texas, two local residents set out to break the *Guinness Book* world record for being "buried alive." Spotting an opportunity for some free publicity, executives of Austin Cable Television, a *TV-Cable Week* system, offered to wire up the men's coffins with cable. Who should spot a public relations opportunity for Sutton in all this but Labich, who promptly informed the group vice president that he had made arrange-

ments for complimentary free copies of the magazine to be
delivered right to the gravesite each week, to help the dare-
devils "maintain their sanity." For Sutton, of course, preserving
one's sanity was not a matter of arranging to be buried alive
"with" *TV-Cable Week* but figuring out how to avoid being
buried alive *by* it.

Then came the "reassignment" of Brauns. Just as she had
been promised, she now got a farewell party. But as she might
have predicted, no one laughed when Dunn presented her with
a copy of Frank Sinatra singing "I Did It My Way" as well as a
desktop model of a burned bridge to commemorate a fear she
had often expressed regarding Chris Meigher. The icy ambiance heated up when two *TV-Cable Week* security guards
slipped in, got drunk, and for no apparent reason started beat-
ing each other up.

And if it is indeed important to "dress for success," no one
had his timing off more than Bill Marsano, who came to work
in a wool suit on a scorching midsummer day that pushed the
Centroplex Building's air conditioning system beyond its limit.
Late in the morning, maintenance men shut the system down
for repairs, and by noontime Marsano was soaked through with
sweat. Determined to make a point of his discomfort, he stalked
out of the office and headed across the street to a Galleria
clothing shop to, as he put it, "slip into something more comfortable."

After lunch Marsano returned and began parading around
the office in his new duds: an undershirt, gym shorts, and
shower clogs. As it happened, that very afternoon proved to be
the occasion for one of Larry Crutcher's rare appearances in
White Plains, and it presented the Sutton aide with a perspective on the listings business that he would never forget. For as
Crutcher sat sweating in a suit and tie in a conference room
adjoining Zucchi's office, he beheld floating past in the hall
outside the bearded and grinning spectre of Marsano—in gym
shorts and flip-flops.

"What was *that?*" blurted out Crutcher.

Answered an editor sitting opposite him:

"That guy's our A.M.E. You ought to come around more often, Larry."

The weirdest adventure of all involved the discovery by Milton Carter, the magazine's technology adviser, of just how far the tentacles of the kludge had actually spread.

For the last six months, Carter had been working to develop a replacement system for the kludge, and had spent many hours in deep technical discussions with experts from a wide range of computer firms. What Carter did not know, but what Labich now at last decided to let him in on, was that for more than a year the project had been pushing ahead with a super-secret computer development project all its own.

"We're putting you in the picture on Project Mustang," said Labich in hushed tones. "But whatever you do, don't tell TV Data!"

Shortly after breakfast the following morning, the two men, accompanied by two other magazine executives, climbed into Labich's car in front of the Centroplex Building, swung onto the Saw Mill River Parkway, and headed toward New Jersey.

When they reached the town of Wood Ridge, headquarters for the Curtiss-Wright Corporation aerospace firm, Labich turned off the highway and pulled up in front of what appeared to be a sprawling machine shop and hangar complex. At the gate was a guard shack. Labich stepped forward and signed a register. Everyone waited until a man came out with lapel pin-on "Visitors' Passes" for the executives. Then the group followed the escort inside.

Deeper and deeper into the Curtiss-Wright complex they went, turning left and right through silent hallways. Finally they reached an unmarked door. The escort stopped, turned the handle, and beckoned the group to enter.

Inside the windowless room was a large, round table and six chairs, in front of each of which was positioned a yellow-lined notepad and a sharp-pointed pencil. At the opposite end of the room was a smaller table, upon which sat a computer console and keyboard of undetermined manufacture.

There now followed a "briefing." But instead of being filled in on what he had been led to believe was an high-tech project of immense significance, Carter found himself being questioned by a smallish man who wanted to know the answer to a question that had bedeviled him for months:

"When you copy a TV program schedule into the computer, should you start with the title, with the channel, or with the time?"

Carter gaped at the man. Was this for real?

As Labich had explained it, Project Mustang, secretly under development for over a year, was intended as a kind of fallback system in case TV Data should stop providing listings for the magazine. But as Carter could now see for himself, in all that time Project Mustang had not gotten beyond the input stage.

On the way back to White Plains Labich had an idea:

"Maybe we could put a Project Mustang terminal right in your office, Milt. What do you think of that?"

Carter looked at him blankly for several moments before responding.

"And do *what* with it?"

"You know," said Labich. "Figure out input formats and things."

Carter said nothing, realizing by now what Dukemejian had known for months: Project Mustang had been a complete waste of time and money from the start.

TWENTY-TWO

Rats in the Big House

IN THE SMOTHERING HAZE that blanketed White Plains, shoppers moved through the streets slowly, or gave up and nursed glasses of iced tea under the canopies along Main Street. Yet inside the isolated and nervous world of *TV-Cable Week*, the atmosphere seemed to Burgheim, at least, to be even more oppressive and close. It seemed that whenever the managing editor entered a room an awkward silence would ensue, as people began self-consciously shuffling papers or engaging in forced and unconvincing small talk.

By nature a reticent person, Burgheim had felt a dread growing for weeks—that in some unimaginable way it would not be Sutton or Grunwald or Zucchi or Dunn or Brauns who would wind up being blamed for *TV-Cable Week*, but himself. What was really going on behind all these suddenly closed doors? Were people working on upcoming issues of the magazine or concocting evidence for some star-chamber inquisition?

Sitting at his desk, Burgheim glanced at his calendar. The date was July 5, 1983, his 50th birthday, ordinarily a moment of importance in anyone's life. Yet to Burgheim, the birthday seemed almost incidental to the larger anniversaries the date suggested. Almost exactly two years had passed since Grunwald had assigned him to the taskforce—an assignment that had begun with such high hopes but had so quickly soured into rancor and disappointment.

It was also almost six months to the day since the magazine had been relocated to White Plains—six months during which not a day had passed without interruptions by workmen, breakdowns by computers, and all the other nerve-jangling dislocations of being removed from New York.

Burgheim thought back to the blustery January day when he had arrived, and not long after that to when Zucchi as well had settled in. It had taken the publisher all of one day to get his own office into shape—as if in the midst of bedlam Zucchi had somehow just *willed* it into being by the force of his personality. One day his office was filled with packing crates and piled furniture, and the next day it looked like a showcase display of an office furniture manufacturer, with potted palms, neatly filled book credenzas, and precisely positioned lithographs in brass and lacquered frames.

By contrast, Burgheim's office had remained a jumble of boxes and books from the day he had arrived. Running his eyes across the confusion, he wondered what sort of an impression the contrast must have made. Could people be expected to follow a leader who couldn't clean up his room? Was he failing on some level for which he had never been prepared? How in the world had everything gotten this far? A crushing despondency pressed down upon him as he saw more clearly than ever that his dream of a lifetime had crumbled into just another disappointment for a middle-aged man.

Burgheim looked up and saw Flora Ling standing in his doorway. She looked at him oddly for a moment, then said:

"Dick, can you come down to the conference room for a minute? There's something you should see about the plain vanilla. Milton's almost finished with his computer design and he's got some slides he wants you to see about how it will work."

Burgheim rose from his desk and headed down the hall behind Ling. He felt wave after wave of ennui break over him. Was he doomed to this forever—this torture rack of slide shows and computer fights and battles over cable operators and plain-vanilla program listings?

The corridors and offices were strangely empty for 3 P.M., as if all except he had decided to hell with everything and not even bothered to come back from lunch.

The conference room was dark, and Ling said, "Wait a minute, let me get on a light."

She disappeared into the dark, feeling her way toward a light switch on the far wall.

"Here it is," she called out at last, as her finger found the light switch. "Okay!"

And as she flipped on the lights, the entire editorial staff of the magazine, 125-strong, burst into a chorus of "Happy Birthday" to their managing editor. Stunned, Burgheim surveyed the crowd. It included not only his own *TV-Cable Week* colleagues, but those from other magazines as well, who had been secretly brought to White Plains for the surprise.

Along the conference room's walls Burgheim could also now see the reason for the weeks of conspiratorial huddling by his staffers. In addition to preparing *TV-Cable Week* each week, the staff had also been preparing a 64-page, four-color "collector's edition" of the magazine devoted entirely to Burgheim— a kind of journalistic "roast" in the spirit of the Friars Club.

Layout artists in the magazine's art department had secretly arranged to have the pages of the magazine enlarged to three-foot-by-four-foot dimensions, and that morning the results had been positioned one after another along the conference room walls. The pages contained articles about Burgheim's career ("Would You Give This Man $100 Million? Hah!"), a profile of life in the Centroplex Building ("TV's Shameless Tower of Sin"), and page after page of project lore stretching back over the years.

One after another, Burgheim's staffers now read excerpts to their boss, and when they were finished, one of the editors presented him with a large watercolor painting of Burgheim adrift in a sea of sharks. The painting was signed by every staff member, all wishing him happy birthday, and most going on to express admiration and support for his leadership in the crisis.

Though it provided a kind of momentary respite from the enveloping tensions, Burgheim's birthday bash did little to ease the strains on the project's executives, and in the days that followed relations between the magazine's business and editorial executives continued to deteriorate. The person in the middle was Burgheim's administrative assistant, Ling, who rushed from one meeting to another trying to mediate disputes.

In desperation she at last turned to Zucchi and Burgheim. The situation was appalling, and one way or another the air had to be cleared. Would they *please* make a joint address to the staff, give them some reassurance? If not, soon no one would be doing any work at all, just moving from office to office gossiping about the latest rumors.

At noon on the 15th of July the magazine's entire staff of 251 employees assembled in the conference room. To judge from the somber faces it was an audience that was going to need convincing. And before many minutes had passed it was clear that not even Zucchi's best sales effort was up to the task.

The meeting reached something of a low point when an employee asked what the magazine's long-term prospects were and Zucchi declared with a determined look: "Listen, all that has happened is that we've gotten in the ring with a guy who can fight, and he's landed a couple of solid punches. But it's okay. Right now as we stand here, Time Inc. has got three dozen of the best brains in the company working away on the thirty-fifth floor on this problem. We need to find a way to hit the market harder, move this thing faster, and we're gonna!"

There was a smattering of applause as people filed out, but the level of conviction seemed best expressed by a single razor-edged one-liner from Burgheim on his way out the door: "I forget, did he say it was thirty-four people working on the *thirty-fifth* floor, or thirty-five people on the *thirty-fourth* floor?" Then the managing editor of *TV-Cable Week* cackled strangely and headed off down the hall toward his room.

Visibly worn from the ordeal of recent weeks, Zucchi had planned to take the following week off for some badly needed rest and relaxation with his family. But had he more closely examined the cover subject of the magazine that was rolling off the presses as he spoke, Zucchi would have had second thoughts about removing himself from the action for a single minute. Even as the sixteenth and latest, issue of *TV-Cable Week* presented readers with a cover portrait of *Dallas*'s handsome young star, Chris Atkins, with an actual live rat nibbling at his ear, so too were the rats in the Big House ready to devour Zucchi.

Ling knew nothing of what was being planned for Zucchi, but she did know the present situation was intolerable. From the moment she had gone to work for Burgheim her life had been one unending psychodrama of disputes between the editor and the publisher, and nothing she did seemed to help. Had conditions been like this from the very beginning of the project? Why hadn't someone intervened from above before now?

At last she turned to the person who had assigned her to the project in the first place, Grunwald's aide, Ralph Graves. Someone had to bridge the gulf between church and state, and if Graves could not, then no one could.

Ling did not share her plan with Burgheim, but on the morning of Saturday, July 23rd, she and an associate boarded a flight from the Marine Air Terminal at New York's La Guardia Airport, to fly to Martha's Vineyard for a meeting that she knew would cause pandemonium if it were discovered. She had arranged to meet Graves at his home, unburden herself of her fears for the future of the magazine, and plead for intervention. Someone had to take control of the situation, and as she had

seen for herself at the Big Lunch, Grunwald was unwilling to
to so. What about Graves? Like Grunwald, he was a member of
the board of directors and shared in the ultimate authority in
the corporation; perhaps he could be persuaded to act.

Graves had been uncomfortable about meeting with Ling,
and for good reason: she was coming to discuss a supremely
embarrassing subject, the inability of Time's top management,
Graves included, to seize control of *TV-Cable Week*. Here was
a project that Graves had tried to warn his colleagues against
from the beginning; a project that spelled trouble from the first
time he had heard of it. Now, eighteen months later, this publishing extravaganza had turned into a fiasco. How would he
explain having encouraged Ling to become part of it?

Much of the sensitivity of the situation traced to Graves's
complex relations with his boss, Grunwald. Outwardly, the two
got along well. But privately Graves did not particularly care for
Time Inc.'s editor in chief, and would sometimes let his feelings
show in casual asides that suggested a view of the man as gruff
and self-possessed.

The problems began in 1977 when Grunwald, then in his
ninth year as managing editor of *Time* Magazine, was elevated
by the company's editor in chief, Hedley Donovan, to the
thirty-fourth floor position of corporate editor. In that capacity
Grunwald became the third-ranked editorial executive in the
company, reporting not to Donovan but to his second-in-command, who happened to be Graves.

Two years later, in June of 1979, Donovan stepped down
as editor in chief, designating as his successor not Graves, who
held the second-ranked title of editorial director, but Graves's
subordinate, Grunwald. Now instead of Grunwald reporting to
Graves, Graves reported to Grunwald.

"I would have made a hell of an editor in chief," Graves
said sadly later of his situation, but it soon became much more
awkward and unpleasant than that. The problem involved his
wife. Like many Time Inc. employees, Graves was married to
a woman who was herself a Time Inc.'er. A person of patrician

bearing, striking good looks, and a deserved reputation as a world-class epicure and cook, Eleanor Graves had risen through a variety of editorial positions within the company before being appointed assistant managing editor of *Life* Magazine by Donovan in 1978.

As *Life*'s assistant managing editor, Eleanor Graves ostensibly reported to the magazine's top editor, Philip Kunhardt. But Kunhardt was in failing health, and placed much of the day-to-day management of the publication in the hands of his assistant, Eleanor.

Eleanor Graves naturally assumed that in due course she would succeed Kunhardt as managing editor. She felt this for two reasons: not only was she qualified for the job, but she was also a woman, and Time Inc. was under pressure to begin promoting females to top editorial positions, all of which were then filled by men.

Ralph Graves would think back often to what happened next, for now, in the summer of 1983, the events of the spring of 1982, nearly eighteen months earlier, had taken on a significance that only hindsight could provide. At issue was a routine-seeming series of executive reassignments by Grunwald, but like the shot at Serajevo, they had set in motion large and ultimately unstoppable forces.

Looking back on it now, the problem seemed a simple one: Grunwald needed a female managing editor, and in all the company in the spring of 1982 there were only two credible possibilities: Eleanor Graves at *Life,* and over at *People,* Patricia Ryan, the magazine's third-ranked editor. Ryan held the title of assistant managing editor, reporting first to Burgheim, and above him to Burgheim's boss, Richard Stolley, the magazine's managing editor.

At the time, Burgheim had already been assigned by Grunwald to the cable listings task force, Stolley was back as *People* managing editor after a temporary tour as a Grunwald assistant on the thirty-fourth floor, and Patricia Ryan was now serving as Stolley's second-in-command.

People Magazine had been an embarrassment to Grunwald from the beginning. But with Burgheim consigned to the cable project, it seemed to Grunwald that now might be the time to begin upgrading the magazine's editorial tone. Patricia Ryan would do perfectly. A former researcher on the staff of *Sports Illustrated,* she had little interest in pop culture subjects but seemed ready and eager to do as Grunwald wanted and begin elevating coverage beyond the magazine's steady diet of rock star profiles and stories about Hollywood.

But there was a problem: Stolley, who continued to serve as *People*'s managing editor. Like a chess player studying the board, Grunwald had pondered his moves carefully, and the more he did so the more he realized: the key to the whole thing was Eleanor Graves.

When Kunhardt stepped down from *Life* Magazine Grunwald would not promote Eleanor to the job, but bring in Stolley from *People* instead. That would open up the *People* top spot, and with Burgheim out of the way on the cable listings task force, the job could go to Patricia Ryan. The moves would simultaneously get the company a female managing editor, upgrade *People,* and find a new use for Stolley.

Unfortunately, the victim was the wife of Grunwald's own deputy, Ralph Graves, both of whom were mortified by the move. First Ralph had been humiliated by having his subordinate, Grunwald, made his superior; now Grunwald had engaged in a convoluted executive shuffle that publicly humiliated Eleanor as well.

Eleanor was enraged and announced her intention to quit forthwith. The company offered her a lucrative severance package that included editing a series of culinary books for Time & Life Books, but at her farewell party her anger boiled over. When Grunwald offered her a toast that included praise of her culinary talents, she rose to the podium, her face framed elegantly in a silver-gray coiffure, and responded cooly to her host:

"Yes, and four forks to you, Henry!"

Graves's bitterness only deepened when Grunwald in the

wake of Eleanor's departure began pushing more and more oversight responsibility for the cable listings project off on Graves himself. For Graves the awkwardness of the situation was enormous; he had not wanted the project to go forward to begin with, yet Grunwald was now, in effect, putting him in charge of it anyway.

The greatest difficulty of all involved what to do about Burgheim. For nearly a year now Sutton had been pressuring Grunwald, apparently at Zucchi's urging, to do something about Burgheim—either replace him or at least appoint an administrative aide to handle the man's day-to-day managerial chores. Grunwald in turn had pushed the chore off on Graves. But Graves lacked the power to do much more than lecture Burgheim, and at last had settled on Ling as a way to provide the man with some administrative support in what was obviously a difficult situation.

Now Ling was coming to see him personally, presumably to reveal the obvious: that the situation was hopeless, and that higher authority had no choice but to intervene. How could he tell her that his hands were tied—and had been so all along?

Looking back on it later, Flora Ling could not imagine what had possessed her to make the trip. She had had no clear objective in mind, no agenda for action, but had wound up sipping drinks with Graves and his wife at poolside and talking vaguely of life in White Plains.

The house was lovely, with a weathered terrace and pool deck that looked down across meadowlands at the center of the island. Soft breezes washed the hillside, and finches and orioles chirped in the branches of a poolside shade tree.

"Well," said Graves, "I'm sure what's on your mind is important or you would not be here. Does anyone else know you've come?"

"No," said Ling, "just the two of us." She nodded at her colleague seated beside her.

"Good," said Graves. "We have a secure meeting." His wife

walked onto the veranda and pulled up a chair and Graves looked at her. "Don't worry about Eleanor," he said. "You can speak freely. So what is on your mind?"

Ling began to speak, but as she did Graves leaned forward in his chair.

"Excuse me, but there is something that I think you should know first." He eyed her face, this trusting young woman who had gone so far out on a limb to share her concerns. Now he was going to saw the limb off. It was a hideous situation, but what choice did he have? He had something to reveal, and not to reveal it now would be to compound the damage already done. For all practical purposes Graves had been a lame duck from the moment Grunwald had been named his boss in 1979; "All I do in this job is talk to people," he had said of his role. Beginning next week he would be a lame duck for real.

Graves took a sip of his drink, let his eyes wander across the meadows below, and as if speaking to no one, declared:

"As of next Wednesday a memo will go out in New York announcing my early retirement from the company. I shall be leaving Time Inc. Whatever you have in mind to discuss with me ought to be weighed in that light."

Ling felt a slight gasp escape from her throat. Graves quitting? The man who had encouraged her to take the job in the beginning? This was not possible. Her colleague muttered an awkward acknowledgment, and as if to change the subject began reeling off the problems in White Plains. But Ling hardly heard a word, for abruptly and without warning her mind had leaped halfway around the world and a decade into the past. She had been through this all before.

It was the summer of 1972, and she was high on a hillside on the outskirts of Vientenne, Laos. Below her coiled the Mekong River, brown and heavy, and against the banks opposite the landscape stacked itself in undulating green hillocks to the horizon. Next to her sat a friend. They were sipping coconut drinks in the shade of a palm tree, watching a Laotian woman delicately bathe herself, fully clothed, in the river below. It was mid afternoon, airless and still, and the woman moved dream-like as if in a trance.

"See," Ling said, "they can wash their whole bodies and never take off anything. They are very clever people."

The young man seated next to her nodded in agreement. He was a Laotian—the son, as it happened, of a general in the Royal Laotian Army.

Deep in the hillside opposite them a column of smoke suddenly appeared . . . then another, and another. Then a long streak of smoke sideways through the jungle, and a *pfumpf, pfumpf* sound distantly in the air.

"Look," said the young man, "we are striking the Pathet Lao."

"I think we'd better go," said Ling as she stood up and watched the strafing attack grow in intensity. She had come to spend a quiet afternoon, and the next thing she knew she was in the middle of a war. Now in Martha's Vineyard it was if anything even worse; she had come hoping to talk her commanding officer into ending a conflict, only to learn that he was retreating from the battlefield.

The following Monday was a day Dan Zucchi would never forget: it was the day he was fired. In the same way that he had called Brauns in from maternity leave four weeks earlier and ousted her without warning, Zucchi now found himself being given the same treatment by Sutton. The shortest-lived publisher in Time Inc.'s history got the news on the day he returned from vacation, and in a way that left his subordinates in the dark and anxious as to what was happening. Instead of coming to work in White Plains, Zucchi had been told by Sutton to report directly to the group vice president's office in New York. There, he was informed that Chris Meigher was replacing him, effective immediately, and that he was being demoted to the position of *People* Magazine's associate publisher.

Zucchi was staggered. The humiliation was bad enough, but what about the effect his ouster would have on the magazine? Here it was already in turmoil over Sunburst, and now all of a sudden he was being ejected to make way for one of the project's most outspoken critics. What possible good could come of that?

Zucchi left in a daze. All that day and well into the evening he dwelled on the ouster. Here he was, the quintessential team player, a man whose sole concern had been to get the project up to speed and out the door like Sutton wanted: get through that window of opportunity.

Well, Zucchi had done that. He had followed the business plan; he had done everything asked of him. And now he was taking the dive. Was he being set up as Sutton's personal scapegoat? Why hadn't he simply been told to go play golf for a month? The way this was being handled would wake up the whole world. What cable operator would want to sign a deal now? What advertiser? In all probability, what Sutton had just done was destroy the project's last remaining shreds of hope for survival.

There is an expression among ad men about a certain kind of person—an "empty suit"—a person devoid of substance or self-esteem, who has been so ground down by a career of glad-handing and vacuity that there is nothing left to him except smiles and insincerity and martinis for lunch.

But Zucchi was not an empty suit, he was a person with feelings and depth, and he had just been publicly humiliated in front of everyone in the world he valued: his family, his friends, his contacts on Madison Avenue. Yet what could he do about it? In New York, Zucchi belonged to a health club a few blocks from the Time & Life Building, and when he felt tension growing from the office he would sometimes duck out during the noon hour and slug away at a canvas punching bag that hung in the club.

This was Dan Zucchi, Time Inc.'s regular Joe. No chrome and leatherette exercise machines for him but canvas punching bags and sweat, and the strain that comes from pouring his last ounce into everything. That is what he had done with the project; he had tried to bench-press *TV-Cable Week.* And with the whole wobbly edifice looming above him, Sutton had come by and kicked him in the kidney.

Sitting at his dining-room table, in Briarcliff Manor, not twenty minutes from downtown White Plains and the scene of the wreckage, it occurred to Zucchi that there was something he just had to do.

He pushed back his chair, went to the kitchen, and swept up in his arms every "TV-Cable Week" coffee mug, cup, and glass he could find—promotional giveaway items from various trade shows and conventions. Next, he headed for the garage. There, in the darkened room beside the Zukemobile, he let rise within him an anger of such proportions that there was but one course of action possible: and in a rage at Sutton, or Meigher, or perhaps just life itself, he began hurling the mugs and cups and glasses one after another against the far wall.

TWENTY-THREE

The Three Cheapos

SUTTON HAD ANTICIPATED the shock that Zucchi's firing would give to the magazine's executives, and the next morning he went to White Plains to explain the decision personally. He had had considerable difficulty in figuring out how to present his reasons, for however he examined them he could find no face-saving way to fire his subordinate.

Maybe the way out would be to assert that the last four months had in effect been a kind of market test all along—that launching the publication had really been intended to see if consumer demand existed. Removing Zucchi could then be represented as the end of the test phase and the beginning of something new. It was a flimsy reed, but what else could he lean on?

So unsure of himself was he that he had at last written his remarks out on paper to be read Burgheim-like to the group. Once in White Plains, he went directly to Zucchi's office, where Labich, Dunn, and some others were waiting. Then all proceeded to the sixteenth-floor conference room.

Determined to strike an optimistic note, the group vice president read his remarks, stressed that the magazine had been satisfactorily launched, then argued that now it was time to concentrate on circulation; hence, the appointment of Meigher. At the conclusion of his remarks, he looked around the room.

"Any questions?"

Across the table from Sutton Dunn cleared his throat.

"Kelso," he began, wondering if he should press on with a question that was certain to prove both embarrassing to and unanswerable by the group vice president. "Kelso, I think we've got a real public relations problem with the staff because of this. Last week Dan stood in this room and told a meeting of the entire magazine that everything was going to be fine. Now he's been replaced. It's like, how do we explain it?"

Sutton gave Dunn a look that seemed to say "You again!" Then, letting whatever private thoughts he may have had pass unsaid, Sutton answered only that a memo had been prepared that would be delivered to everyone shortly.

The next day, Meigher arrived, trailing accountants, computer experts, and a group of McKinsey & Company consultants that quickly became known as "the Goon Squad." The staff observed the new arrivals warily, not knowing much about the tumultuous recent events beyond the pep talk by Zucchi and Burgheim, then the ouster of Zucchi. Now Zucchi's office was occupied by a preppily dressed business executive who looked ten years younger than he was, and who had arrived for work not in a Zukemobile but a late model leased Volvo. As a command center, the group took over the conference room off Zucchi's old office, into which they moved personal computers, desktop calculators, and stacks of printouts and note paper. Passing by, Milton Carter looked in, then went to report to Brugheim: "Dick, you won't believe it. They've got *thousands* of pencils in there, each one with a perfectly sharp point!"

Apprehensive about everything, the employees grew more so as the McKinsey & Company consultants fanned out through the building, looking through departmental records, interviewing large numbers of people. One after another the project's executives were called into the consultants' command post and questioned. Why were their staffs so large, why were there so many computers on the premises, how exactly did "everything work?"

That afternoon came Dunn's turn. Dunn probably knew more about how "everything worked" than anyone else on the staff, but Meigher had not said as much as hello to him all day, remaining sequestered instead in Zucchi's old office with various lieutenants. The cold shoulder was bad enough for the young M.B.A., but what happened next stunned him beyond words. For once in the Goon Squad command post, Dunn found himself in conversation with a young McKinsey consultant who seemed thoroughly astounded by the prevailing chaos and wanted to know how everything had been permitted to get so completely out of hand.

"After all," she said, "didn't anyone pay attention to Ralph Graves's memo?"

Dunn was baffled; this was the first he had heard of such a document.

"Ralph wrote a memo? What did it say?"

Whereupon the consultant began to recite its contents: that the project was a great risk, that it was full of uncertainties and doubts, and that he feared very much whether Time Inc. would succeed with the project.

"Where did you get *that?*" gaped Dunn as sweat formed in his palms.

"It's in the files back in New York," answered the consultant, now wary of Dunn's interest. "Why do you ask?"

But Dunn hardly heard her, for his mind was reeling back crazily through the months—back and back until he was suddenly in Kelso Sutton's office the summer before, with Sarah and Dan, and the board vote looming before them. And once again he saw Sutton reach into a drawer and pull out a memo and begin to read it to them—that the project was a great risk, that it was full of uncertainties and doubts, and that the writer feared very much whether Time Inc. would succeed with the project. Who had written the memo? Sutton had refused to say, and now Jeff Dunn knew why. Ralph Graves had written that memo—Graves, a member of Time's own board of directors. Graves had said the project was imperiled, and Sutton had turned the warning into a guessing game.

Dunn stared at the consultant. "You may not believe this, but I *know* that memo! Kelso read it to us in his office last summer."

"Uh oh," said the woman as Dunn's amazement seemed to register. "Maybe I shouldn't have said anything," and she began shuffling papers to tell him it was time to leave.

Though the stated purpose of the interviews was for the consultants to "get a grip" on the situation, the net effect was to spread rumors and stories like oil on a mud puddle. By the end of the week, *TV-Cable Week*'s staff buzzed with the project's innermost details, spread by the Goon Squad. "We've got to get to the bottom of this mess," announced a Goon Squad member grimly. "The money is going out at a million a week!" Soon even drivers for White Plains's Central Cab Company knew the figure.

It was just before lunch of his first day on the job when Meigher got to meet Burgheim face to face. This summit of sorts had been arranged by Flora Ling in a large conference chamber appropriately known as the War Room. Along one wall of the War Room hung a Teflon-coated board for planning future issues of the magazine, while in the center stood a large circular table around which Burgheim and his staff would meet three times a week for editorial planning sessions. Now the table was ringed by Meigher, the Goon Squad, and several of Burgheim's top assistants. But no Burgheim.

As everyone waited and fidgeted, the wary managing editor could not bring himself physically to enter the room; he kept approaching the door, clipboard in hand, only to turn about abruptly and scoot back into his office as if he had forgotten something important. To those who knew him well by now, it was Burgheim's way of saying "I don't give a damn about your Sunburst crap, Chris, *I'm* the managing editor of this magazine, not you, so sit there and think about *that* for a while."

When Burgheim finally did make his entrance, the manner in which he and Meigher shook hands called to mind H. L. Mencken's description of two women kissing: like prize fighters touching gloves at the start of Round One.

As soon as they sat down, one of the Goon Squad executives rose from her chair, went to the Teflon board, and unfurled what all had been waiting for: the details behind Sunburst. This was what "three dozen of Time Inc.'s best minds" had come up with for a listings guide, and everyone was anxious to see the result. Who had won the struggle behind Sunburst's closed doors? Would the new publication be a weekly or a monthly, a magazine or a guide, high quality or low?

The consultant took a felt-tip pen, turned to the board, and marked off three columns. Atop one she wrote, "30 Cent Cheapo." Atop the next she wrote, "60 Cent Medium Cheapo." Atop the third she wrote, "$1 El Cheapo Grande." She turned and declared, "It'll be like Burger King—three monthlies, any way you want 'em."

Burgheim's eyes bugged out. This was it? This was what two whole years of his life had come to, why he had fought with Zucchi and Sutton and Grunwald on every issue imaginable? He was now to be the editor of three monthly "cheapos"? He began darting glances around the table as if appealing for help. But the parade of cheapos continued, as Meigher and the Goon Squad began explaining the concept behind them: each would be, in effect, a modular building block assembled out of mass produced parts. The cheapest version would have only pay TV listings; the medium priced version would contain pay TV plus basic cable listings; the top-of-the-line version would have all that plus broadcast listings.

For several moments no one said anything, as all eyes locked onto Burgheim. But Burgheim sat motionless, as if in a trance.

At last Meigher spoke:

"Well there it is. So what we need now are dummy mock-ups to show the cable operators."

"When?" asked Flora Ling, worried that the staff would buckle if any more work were placed upon it.

"Right now," answered Meigher. "Next week at the latest." They would try, replied the editors, but what if Meigher actually signed a deal? The kludge could barely handle its present workload; if the publisher found takers, he would be committing the project to something it could not produce.

As the quarreling continued, Meigher grew impatient. Look, he said at last, the computer question could wait. The problem now was to sign some deals, hit the road with the three cheapos and get some cable operators signed up. The technology could be handled later.

If he had been able to have his way, Meigher would have preferred to push aside the technology problem altogether. But there was a problem: Milton Carter. For the last six months, Carter had been working to design a replacement system for the kludge, and now he had apparently succeeded. Initially, Carter had believed the task of building such a device lay beyond the capacity of the American computer typographics industry. But by bringing together experts from a number of different firms, he had developed a design configuration for a 4.5 gigabyte system—enough capacity, he said proudly, to process the next decennial census of the People's Republic of China. Equally at home in the design labs of IBM or the street corners of Wilmington, Delaware, where he grew up, Carter proclaimed his creation a "motengator" (an ethnic word, he allowed, for "ten thousand motherfuckers").

Carter was extremely proud of his motengator, partly because of the many technical obstacles he had had to overcome in the course of developing the design, but also because of what his work represented in terms of improved efficiency in the editing of program listings. With the motengator, *TV-Cable Week* would no longer need the services of TV Data; Burgheim's staff could collect their own program listings and edit them directly.

Now Carter wanted to present his work to Time's brass, and he had invited Sutton, Grunwald, and Graves to come to White Plains for a formal presentation. Designing the motengator was, after all, why he had been hired in the first place.

Yet Meigher knew that Carter's presentation would be a waste of time. Though the new publisher had reassured Burgheim and the editors that they would continue to publish the weekly version of the magazine along with the cheapo monthlies, Meigher also knew that behind the closed doors of Sunburst the decision had already been made to terminate the weekly as soon as Meigher could sign a deal for a monthly. In this way, Time could hide the fiasco from public view, claiming, in effect, that the weekly was simply being reborn as a monthly rather than put it out of its misery.

Moreover, from the moment that he had replaced Zucchi, Meigher had been planning to junk the kludge and publish the cheapos by hand, and he had no intention of purchasing some new state-of-the-art system as a replacement. Yet he could hardly say so after having already said the opposite to Burgheim. The only way to salvage the situation would be to split the meeting into two parts: first Carter could present his computer system, then the brass could turn to the more urgent matter of the cheapos. With luck, Meigher would even have dummy mock-ups to show them.

Carter of course knew nothing of his looming role as a warm-up act for the cheapos, and he had been working feverishly to get his presentation into shape. He had brought in a commercial photographer to take pictures of the kludge to be made into acetate slides; he had hired a graphics design house to prepare schematic drawings of the motengator's various interlinked parts; and he had printed up individual spiral-bound presentation booklets, complete with pricing lists and order schedules, for each of the guests. He was determined to make his case clearly and cogently, in simple dollar-and-cents terms that even the most distracted executive could understand. The motengator was going to cost $2.3 million, but without the expenditure *TV-Cable Week* might as well call it quits.

Now it was the following Wednesday morning. Meigher had been on the job precisely one week, and as a team of free-lance art designers touched up cheapo mock-ups on the floor below, Sutton, Grunwald, Graves, and Grunwald's assistant, Rogin, settled into chairs in the sixteenth-floor audio-visual screening room. Opposite them sat Burgheim, Ling, the Goon Squad, and Meigher. At the podium stood Carter, arranging his notes.

Carter realized that $2.3 million was a great deal of money to request, especially when one considered the magazine's present prospects, so to make his case for an appropriation more powerfully he had decided to lead the executives step by step through the actual program editing work being done by the DEC-hands.

After a brief introduction, Carter began his presentation, first spelling out the key elements in his design, then explaining as best he could in plain English how the system would work. At last he came to the climax: the slide show of DEC-work. One after another the slides flashed by. As they did, the Time officials finally saw for themselves, two full years after the computer wars had first begun, what the technology disputes were all about: learning to edit the plain-vanilla listings on the kludge, turn them into "Time Inc. quality" custom listings, then dispatch them to printing plants, required mastery of a computer language so dense and baffling as to look like Urdu.

As the last of the slides was finished and the room's lights came up, Carter said:

"What has happened here, gentlemen, is that we have created a situation in which a handful of the lowest paid employees on the staff have evolved into a high and mysterious priesthood. What they do, no one but they understand." Carter paused, then added, "Everything that you see around you—all of it—is potentially hostage to people whose work remains a mystery to everyone but them."

The room was dead silent.

Sensing the awkwardness of the moment, one of the editors spoke up:

"With this new system, we'll be able to customize individual editions in a way that is now impossible. We'll be able to produce lists of individual movies carrying various ratings for kids, segregate out sports programs, all sorts of things. The magazine can become far more useful then ever for readers."

Sitting next to Grunwald, Rogin responded:

"Who wants to do that? What do we want to do that for anyway?" and looked hopefully at his boss. Grunwald said nothing, and the room lapsed again into silence.

When Carter's presentation concluded at 12:30 P.M., the discussion quickly switched from computers to a matter of more urgent concern to Sutton and Meigher: the cheapos. In keeping with the no-time-to-waste spirit of the proceedings, someone proposed that instead of adjourning for luncheon, the assembled executives "order in." A secretary appeared to take orders, and about twenty minutes later a box arrived from one of the fast-food shops in the Galleria. There was the usual: pastrami on rye, chicken salad on whole wheat, cartons of chocolate milk, cans of Pepsi Light, plastic containers of coleslaw.

Yet no sooner did people start reaching into the box and passing around its contents than something unexpected happened: Editor in Chief Grunwald rose from his chair, stared briefly into the middle distance, and went quickly out of the room. Though several at the table exchanged glances, no one said anything; and when Grunwald returned moments later, the luncheon proceeded as if nothing had happened.

But something *had* happened, and although no one in the

room but Grunwald knew what it was, there was one *TV-Cable Week* employee destined to remember the event forever after.

That person was an attractive young secretary named Katherine Speer, whose desk was in the hallway outside the audio-visual screening room. With her colleagues having now departed for the noon hour, and the officials from New York apparently settling in for their working luncheon, Speer was preparing to leave when she looked up to find staring down at her the bushy-browed visage of Grunwald. Said he to the startled secretary: "It's getting late! Please order me a helicopter!" Then Time Inc.'s editor in chief turned and headed back into the conference room.

Speer was speechless. Order me a *helicopter?* Was he talking about some new Galleria delicacy, some triple scoop dessert with a propeller in it? For several moments she sat motionless before the message sank in: the man was apparently serious— he wanted her to order him an actual helicopter!

Speer opened the Yellow Pages and started looking for "Helicopters," then gave up and called the editor in chief's secretary in New York. "He wants a *helicopter?*" exclaimed the woman. "In *this* weather? We're going to have thunderstorms any minute down here! Order him a limousine instead!"

Meanwhile, across the hall in the Ops area the DEC-hands faced the most immediate crisis of all. It was already two hours past deadline, and the thunderstorms that Grunwald's secretary had warned of were darkening the sky in all directions. The danger: a power outage, not in White Plains, where the kludge had its own rooftop generator, but across the Hudson River in TV Data's Glens Falls headquarters, where the system did not have standby power. Moving to the windows, the DEC-hands watched as minute by minute the sky grew darker, sending jabs of forked lightning into the countryside.

Suddenly the phone rang, and it was a technician from TV Data on the other end. An Adirondacks electrical storm had just knocked out all power to Glens Falls, destroying nearly an en-

tire day's worth of plain-vanilla editing by the DEC-hands. In
that instant, after all the planning, effort, and expenditure of
treasure, it was impossible to escape the feeling that not just the
DEC-hands, but indeed all of *TV-Cable Week*, were caught up
in forces beyond anyone's control.

Meigher soon came to much the same conclusion. After all
the months and years of first bragging about, and then actually
producing, its weekly magazine, Time Inc. had not frightened
the competition but had strengthened it. To begin with, there
was *TV Guide*. Dismissed by Time's brass as a lethargic organization incapable of responding to a challenge, *TV Guide*
proved an exceptionally agile opponent. Tactics ranged from
deep discounts off the cover price to in some markets offering
what amounted to actual system-specific deals to cable operators to block Zucchi's own efforts.

But Meigher's biggest problem concerned the competition
generated by the low-cost giveaway monthlies that had been
breeding like bacteria for the past two years in what the Dur-
rell/Burgheim task force had labeled "Quadrant 3." By the
time Meigher hit the road with dummies of his three cheapos,
every cable system of note in the country was already either
publishing its own guide or had signed a deal with with a Quadrant 3 monthly.

The biggest winner of all: Peter Funt's *On Cable*, which by
now had grown to well over one million in circulation, serving
more than one hundred different systems.

Though Meigher and the Goon Squad jet-hopped the country looking for deals, the effort came to nothing. The cheapest
Sunburst edition carried a 30 cents per month price tag, while
other publishers offered guides that began at a mere 10 cents
per month. The impossibility of the situation was simply com-
pounded by the company's Hatfields and McCoys woes: if ATC
would not sign a Sunburst deal, why would anyone else?

At the June 10th meeting, Munro had claimed the power
to compel ATC to sign. But the ramifications of that power were

limited. For unless Sunburst were priced low enough to be competitive in Quadrant 3, *only* ATC could be induced to buy it. And without more circulation volume than that, the cheapos *still* would lose money.

By mid-August, the dirge of doom grew louder each day, as executives rushed to disentangle the project from as many printing and supplier contracts as possible. Yet even as they did so, more equipment arrived. In one incident a man in overalls entered the Operations Area and announced to a DEC hand, "I got a computer outside on the loading dock, who's going to sign for it?" It was another part for the kludge, built in Los Angeles, shipped to White Plains, and now a high-tech hot potato for which no one could be found to take delivery.

Meanwhile, the kludge itself began giving forth death rattles. By now, twenty-one different systems had signed distribution deals for the weekly magazine, and just as Anne Davis had predicted, the number proved too many to be managable, as everyone from the DEC-hands to production staffers at the printing plants began mixing up listings data among the various systems. At a press run of only 282,000 copies (nearly four-fifths of which were being given away free), the kludge had carried *TV-Cable Week* as far as it could. Barring a motengator, it was, as everyone knew, the end.

Through it all, Meigher would periodically return from his travels, bringing assurances that he was getting "excellent feedback from the MSOs," that "TCI was very interested," that talks with Drew Lewis, head of Warner-Amex, had "gone well." It was the same performance that Zucchi had put on for over a year, and the audience was tired of applauding.

In this environment of tumult and uncertainty, people's moods swung between extremes of sadness to a strange giddiness at the stupidity of the situation. This was particularly so for the managing editor. At one point, Burgheim wandered into a colleague's office, apparently ready to discuss something, when he suddenly threw his clipboard and notes on the floor and announced, "Aw shit! We've *proved* we can do this cocksucker!" then scooped up his notes, laughed oddly, and headed out. At the door he turned with a desperate look and asked, "Tell me, are *all* companies as fucked up as this?" then headed off down the hall.

On another occasion, Burgheim and some editors went to dinner at a nearby restaurant. Halfway through the meal, he picked up a sugar envelop, examined it carefully, then declared, "You know, this could be a whole new Time Inc. business: restaurant-specific sugar packets."

Nor was the period any easier for Dunn or Labich, the only other two original senior management players who had survived to the end. Many Time Inc. staffers must live with long hours at the office, particularly the writers and editors of Magazine Group, where 3 A.M. closings have been part of the given circumstances of employment for generations. But few Time Inc.'ers ever endured the grueling work weeks and psychological pressure experienced for more than two full years by the members of the task force. Often, twelve-hour days that ran through the weekend became a routine that stretched on for weeks at a time, sometimes months. At the end of that ordeal, both Dunn and Labich were subjected to humiliation and embarrassment as the Goon Squad took command.

Dunn especially suffered. For here he was, a young man not one month out of business school before he found himself racing on the most glamorous track in magazine publishing, putting together the business and financial plan for the most talked about venture in the industry. Yet step by step, Dunn had seen the world of the business school classroom crumble, as ambitious executives clashed over technologies they did not bother to master, in pursuit of a market they had never tested.

It was, as he put it to a colleague over drinks on the night before the magazine's closure was officially announced, like pulling back the curtain on the Wizard of Oz and finding not a grand company of which he had been proud, but a group of little round men acting out of self-interest.

It was cool September evening, and the two sat in a sidewalk cafe watching moviegoers queue up across the street in the gathering darkness. Abruptly Dunn turned as if seized by a thought and said: "My school was Harvard and its motto is 'truth.' " Then he paused as if weighing the implications of that fact, and declared—more perhaps to himself than his companion: "In the end, I'm not sure how much truth mattered." Then Dunn drained off the last of his drink and got up and left.

TWENTY-FOUR

Say Goodnight, Gracie

THOUGH TIME INC.'S foray into the television listings guide business was a lost cause by June 10th at the latest, it was not until three months later that Time Inc. President Dick Munro felt he had conclusive evidence that the project needed to be shut down.

It was a trying time for Dick Munro, that summer of 1983. He had been pursuing a dream by which he had hoped to lead his company through the remainder of the decade and perhaps into the next century. The dream was technology, inchoate yet gripping, with its unimagined vistas of abundance and opportunity.

When Dick Munro was named president of Time Inc. in 1980, he inherited a problem not of his own making: the *Washington Star* newspaper. The paper had been acquired by the company more than two years earlier in a moment of what looked to be whimsy, as a prestige voice in the nation's capital. The newspaper had lost money from the start. Munro decided to shut it down. He could see no point in doing otherwise, since the world of print journalism already seemed in his vision vulnerable to the more dynamic culture of high-tech. When a reporter for *Editor & Publisher* asked him whether electronic banking, shop-at-home, and other looming high-tech consumer products represented a threat to print journalism, Munro answered, "Well, it would seem to me that the one area likely to be hurt most is your daily newspaper." Not long afterward, the *Washington Star* was folded.

Munro's company then began to develop an electronics information service it called teletext. Time Inc. was not the only company drawn to that product. By the turn of the decade, many of the largest and wealthiest corporations in the country had begun teletext development programs: IBM, Sears, CBS, and others. Time Inc. wanted to be in this league, and it joined them.

Meanwhile, Munro had authorized (and then expanded) another high-tech project, subscription television, to serve as an alternative distribution system for HBO. With STV, which involved relaying signals from a satellite directly to the at-home viewer, HBO would not be dependent on cable distribution networks, but would become available to every television household in the United States.

For Munro, these were the ingredients of the new Time Inc., and by the spring of 1983 they had been joined by another: *TV-Cable Week*, the hybrid venture that spanned the worlds of old and new, that bridged the gulf between ink and electrons.

Then on June 10 Munro had gone to White Plains; Zucchi and Dunn had briefed him on Denver; and the earth moved.

Normally a smiling and happy man, Munro by summer's end had grown preoccupied and anxious. As the weeks passed, the grim news from Sunburst was not the only blow to stun him; now he could see that STV and teletext had also been products of self-delusion.

Begun as mere "tests," the two programs had affixed themselves barnacle like to the corporate budgeting process. By the summer of 1983, the STV experiment had spread to three cities, and accumulated losses totaling $87 million; teletext had barely begun and expenditures already approached $25 million. In both cases the reasons were identical: no efficient technology to deliver the service, and worse, no market demand—the same problems that were killing *TV-Cable Week.*

For Munro, it was a time of self-doubt, and he began to speak to colleagues of a Time Inc. "arrogance"; had the company gotten into this bind by a smug, know-it-all attitude of its top executives and managers?

On a more practical level, Munro later confided to friends that he would "go home Friday wondering who I'll be working for on Monday." The reason for his brooding: the upheaval on Wall Street. The publicity surrounding *TV-Cable Week*'s woes had begun putting the company's stock through gyrations. From a high of $77 per share on June 17th, the stock slid steadily to a low of $60 on July 22nd—even though the market itself held firm during the period. Four days later came Zucchi's ouster, Meigher's appearance, and the start of Sunburst. Said an analyst for one Wall Street firm of the prevailing investor sentiment, "We've been getting calls all day, clients asking us why Time Inc.'s stock is off 10 points in one week. People are running scared." This was followed by even stranger swings. As news spread that Sunburst had no more substance to it than "the weekly" did and signs emerged that Time Inc. was ready to close down everything, relieved investors began bidding the shares back up again. Then, predictably, analysts began to wonder what magic new "future earnings stream" would replace *TV-Cable Week*—and the stock started to slide all over again.

Such gyrations almost instinctively unleashed thirty-fourth floor fears of an unfriendly takeover move. Rumors flourished that American Express was interested; that a Wall Street raider like Carl Icahn or T. Boone Pickens would buy the company, then break it into pieces and resell the parts. There was even a memorable moment involving Rupert Murdoch, the acquisitive Australian publishing tycoon. When executives of Murdoch's New York-based holding company, News America

Publishing Company, actually turned up in the Centroplex Building, the news hit like a thunderbolt. Within minutes of their arrival, word reached the thirty-fourth floor in Manhattan where one agitated official scurried about declaring, "Murdoch's in White Plains! He really is!" (In fact, the executives had come to see about subleasing the project's space for Murdoch's own publications; upon seeing the huge size of the premises, they lost interest in a sublease and continued looking elsewhere.)

For the executives of *TV-Cable Week*, the project's final weeks raised the most anguishing concern of all: how to explain everything to the magazines 251 employees, most of whom had been recruited from other companies, few of whom had hopes of employment elsewhere within Time Inc., and nearly all of whom had believed Time Inc.'s "deep pockets" press releases and proclamations. Now these people were about to find out the truth: that Time Inc.'s five-year commitment had been a public relations ploy to impress Wall Street, not potential employees. Among the staff were those with newborn babies or newly expectant wives. Others had given up apartments in New York and bought homes in northern Westchester County. Still others had relocated not from New York but Chicago, Atlanta, and points even further distant.

On and on the stories went. Everyone had a personal life, with expectations, hopes, and anxieties—and weighed against the reassurances of their superiors that Time Inc. was a company that "looked after its own," was the visible chaos all around them. It was not a scene to inspire confidence—in anyone.

These were the 251 individuals Time Inc.'s top men now had to look in the face. What would they say?

By far the most distraught was Burgheim. Zucchi, Dunn, Brauns, the others, they had all been fools, and he had been among them—perhaps in a way the biggest fool of all. For Burgheim had truly *believed* in the project, and he had driven himself to the limits of his endurance, both physically and mentally, to see it succeed. One day a week or so earlier Labich had mused to Ling that he supposed everyone had been "a little guilty of something" in the failure—a remark Ling had promptly passed on to Burgheim. Thinking about it now made him want to wretch. A little bit guilty? Guilty of what? All Burgheim had done was the best he knew how, under conditions of surreal difficulty—conditions created in the final analysis not by him or any of his colleagues but by the company's top brass.

As the situation had crumbled, Burgheim had fumed at the uncaring attitude of his boss, Grunwald, and he had felt no more kindly disposed toward Sutton, whose hunger to rush the magazine to market suggested the precise polar opposite of the editor in chief's indifference.

But most of all, Burgheim dwelt on the magazine's young M.B.A.s, who somehow seemed to epitomize the financial and management obsessions that had characterized the project from the start—eager young achievers from the fast-tracking 1980s. But when he thought of them now, no longer giving slide show presentations to the bedazzled brass but floundering amid the ruins of their efforts, a different image came to mind.

Burgheim saw himself thirty years earlier as a Harvard junior, sitting in a lecture class in international affairs. It was an autumn day in 1953, cold and blustery, and wind swept across the Charles River from Boston. But the cold had not deterred students from filling the hall to capacity. For the Korean truce was now in place, America was in the process of reasserting its hegemony in world affairs, and the man giving the lecture was emerging as one of Harvard's most impressive young thinkers. Listening to him talk, Burgheim felt himself carried away by the man's clarity of perception and grasp of the issues, and he wondered how long it would be before the teacher would turn to government and begin employing his talents to help guide America's relationships with the world. The scholar: McGeorge Bundy. Now, thirty years later, America had experienced Vietnam, and Time Inc. had had its *TV-Cable Week.*

And yet, for all the blood-drenched imagery, Burgheim toward the end had begun to feel the malice drain from him. He had stood up for what he believed in: editorial independence, quality of the product, value for the reader. He had done what he thought was right. And thinking this way, it came to Burgheim that every once in a while it really can happen: the whole army can be out of step but you.

The date was Friday, September 16, 1983. For nearly two weeks, rumors had swirled that the company was going to close down the project following the next meeting of its board of directors. So, when staffers had read in the previous day's *New York Times* that "the fate of Time Inc.'s newest magazine entry, *TV-Cable Week*, is expected to be decided today at the company's regular monthly board meeting" there seemed no point in continuing the deception any longer; the jig was up.

Now it was the next morning, and on all three floors of *TV-Cable Week*'s offices, the only people working were the DEC-hands. Of the many deadlines that brought together the magazine, theirs was the last—noon on Friday—when the final plain-vanilla edits were fed into the kludge, checked for accuracy, and dispatched electronically to the printing plants.

While the DEC-hands worked everyone else stood around and gossiped. The word was out: there would be an announcement later that morning in an unfinished fifteenth-floor storage area. But who would make it? Would Munro show up? Would Grum? Would Sutton? How about Grunwald?

At about 11 o'clock Ling and Labich were notified that the men from midtown had arrived, and began going from office to office telling people to gather downstairs. It was eerie, for although the staff knew what was coming, there was a palpable feeling of helplessness anyway, as if everyone were being herded together for a final roundup.

Down the winding spiral staircases the people filed, first a few at a time, then by the dozens. The storage area, as large as

a high school gymnasium, had been set aside for expansion as
circulation climbed. Now, at the end, it recalled the beginning,
reminding people what all three floors of the project had looked
like six months earlier—from the raw, concrete floor, to the
piles of sheetrock and partition board, to the open ceiling out
of which hung electrical wires and batts of insulation.

Packing one whole side of the chamber was the staff, som-
ber-faced and silent. They were staring across the room at three
men: President Munro, Editor in Chief Grunwald, and Group
Vice President Sutton. Executive Vice President Grum was
nowhere to be seen. Nor, for that matter, was Group Vice President Gerald Levin.

Sutton was a study in discomfort. In contrast to his press
conference performance the previous August, when he had
dominated the proceedings and kept steering his answers
around to the size of Time Inc.'s commitment and its "deep
pockets" staying power, he now stood so far off to one side as
to be practically hidden behind a pile of construction debris.

Munro spoke first, revealing that in New York an announcement would be released shortly that *TV-Cable Week*
was terminating publication. Said he, quite obviously deva-
stated by what had happened, "This thing proved a hell of a lot
harder and tougher than we had expected."

Next to speak was Grunwald, looking like contrition itself:
"A short time ago, we stood here giving you a pep talk on
your terrific success. Unfortunately, though 'terrific' your work
is, 'successful' the magazine is not."

Then Time Inc.'s editor in chief paused in apparent reflection and added what seemed the most forthright observation he
had made to anyone regarding the nature of his involvement in
the project. "Praise is the last thing you need at a time like this,"
Grunwald said. "But I must observe that if *we* had been in
charge of *TV-Cable Week* Magazine, we could not have done
what you achieved. You met impossible deadlines, with improv-
ised technology, with rigid standards of quality and style."

Incredibly enough, there it was; right up to the very last

hour of the project the message apparently still had not gotten through: Grunwald *was* "in charge" and had been so all along —as had Sutton, and ultimately Munro himself.

Time Inc.'s editor in chief concluded with a kind of "we're all in this together" afterthought: "I'm sure I speak for all of us when I say please feel free to call on myself or Ralph Graves anytime." Yet, so that everyone should clearly understand who was *not* welcome to follow up on that fraternal offer, Grunwald closed his remarks with these words: "For non-Time Inc.'ers, I can only say that I am sorry that your experience with this company has not been a happy one, and I hope that you will take away at least some fond memories and usable skills."

Off to one side stood Burgheim, looking smaller and more forlorn than ever. As Grunwald finished his remarks, the distraught little man held over his head a copy of the 25th—and last—cover of *TV-Cable Week,* which was even then going to press at printing plants from Illinois to Georgia. He began turning it before the audience as if to reassure people (or perhaps just himself) that there had been a point to all they had done. It was a sadly fitting gesture, for, in fact, no one seemed to notice it, or to care.

Epilogue

IN THE ANNUAL COURSE BULLETIN of the Harvard Business School these words appear: "The primary mission of the Harvard M.B.A. program is to prepare its students to assume general management responsibilities. This means developing in its students characteristics of an effective general manager."

The Harvard Business School began that mission in 1908, the first institution in the nation to confer upon a student a graduate-level degree in business management. Though the school initially restricted itself to training in specific fields such as printing and textile manufacturing, it soon broadened out into the teaching of "business management" as a universally applicable concept to a broad range of companies. It did so in the belief that, as each succeeding edition of the course catalogue repeats, "Business management is a profession, as worthy of serious study as traditional professions such as law or medicine."

Over the years, a philosophy of organizational behavior has developed around that premise. It is a philosophy that presents "business" as rational in nature, and sees its "management" as being made possible by means of certain scientific truths of economics and social behavior.

In the twentieth century, American business has produced great champions of that proposition: Alfred P. Sloan of General Motors, Robert McNamara of Ford, and many others. In his way, each has stood for the wisdom of the Harvard Business School course catalogue—that business comprises a rational world, that man is a rational animal, and that both can be managed by means of rational principles so as to "maximize performance."

Few social philosophies have had a more powerful impact on the national life. In our age of bureaucratic growth and corporate giantism, the dominant new breed has ceased to be that of the middle-management individual portrayed by William Whyte in *The Organization Man.* Instead, the new breed has become the professional business manager, a person possessed of transportable skills as useful to the administration of a hospital as to the Pentagon.

The nation's campuses now turn out such people in vast numbers. Between the Great Society watershed of 1966, and midway through the first term of Ronald Regan in 1982, teacher enrollment at colleges and universities declined by nearly 40 percent, to 732,000. But during the same period, students enrolled in business programs rose by almost 300 percent, to 2.6 million. Today, one out of every five students on an American college campus seeks a degree in business, the largest single group in all of higher education.

At their pinnacle sit the M.B.A.s, some 59,000 of whom now enter the executive ranks of American business each year. These are the new elite of the corporate age, trained not in any one business but in the financial and marketing abstractions that are common to all businesses.

With their rise has come a whole new financial orientation to American business—not the development of new products and processes for the marketplace, but the manipulation of financial environments. As Robert Reich, a one-time policy chief at the Federal Trade Commission, says of these "paper entrepreneurs" of the 1970s and 1980s:

"They innovate using the system in novel ways: establishing joint ventures, consortiums, holding companies, mutual funds; finding companies to acquire, 'white knights' to be acquired by, commodity futures to invest in, tax shelters to hide in; engaging in proxy fights, tender offers, antitrust suits, stock splits, spinoffs, divestitures; buying and selling notes, bonds, convertible debentures, sinking-fund debentures; obtaining government subsidies, loan guarantees, tax breaks, contracts, licenses, quotas, price supports, bail-outs; going private, going public, going bankrupt."

That is quite a list, but it hardly exhausts the new financial lexicon. Since Reich's comments in 1980, even more jargon has been added to the language of business: leveraged buyouts, corporate greenmail, golden parachute deals, shark repellant strategies, scorched-earth ploys, Pac-man schemes—the list grows and grows, all of it to help business managers who know little about individual products or markets make their firms grow bigger without necessarily helping them to become better.

Such was the business school orientation that gave rise to *TV-Cable Week*—a product conceived not for readers, or even for any known market, but developed by two young Harvard M.B.A.s, Jeff Dunn and Sarah Brauns, neither of whom knew much about the cable television industry or its customers, but both of whom were eager to move ahead rapidly in their careers by making use of the analytical techniques taught at the Harvard Business School. In this they succeeded beyond their wildest imaginings, at least for a while.

Yet when the very techniques in which Dunn and Brauns had been schooled warned them not to proceed further without a careful and elaborate market test, the two young M.B.A.s found themselves unable to make their reasoning understood by their superiors. They did not realize it, but they had become pawns in a corporate power struggle.

The root of that struggle traced to yet another expression of financially oriented corporate management: the cult of "growth by numbers" and the rise of the business conglomerate. In its way, the corporate conglomerate is the final elaboration of professional management theory, a business enterprise in which the focus of decision making is not the customer or the marketplace but Wall Street, the stock market, and earnings per share.

In the Video and Magazine groups of Time Inc., one had just such a conglomerate environment, composed of two separate and essentially unrelated business enterprises, both in direct competition for corporate resources. Though neither understood the business world of the other, both quickly saw in *TV-Cable Week* a source of power in the corporation as a whole. In their struggle to grab it, executives of the two groups soon found that the magazine was not a source of power but rather, in the words of one corporate director, a publishing "tar baby" that stuck everyone who came near it.

Corporate executives "managed" their way into *TV-Cable Week*, but someone had to "lead" them out of it. And this required talents that few in top management seemed willing to exercise. In this, Time Inc. simply reflected a trend that has spread through more and more of American business, as those at the top have learned to substitute image for substance, management for leadership.

One sees the result in many ways: in the celebration of business executives as media figures (Lee Iacocca, Frank Perdue, Tom Carvel); in the yearning for the appearance of importance as a surrogate for its substance *(Dressing for Success, The Corporate Power Look);* in the spread of executive "style" counseling. Says one such counselor, an ex-Colorado beauty queen who offers "charisma lessons" to executives, "The difference between a good executive and a great executive is 20 percent competence and 80 percent style."

But charisma is not something that can be measured or

taught in a classroom; it flows from within the leader himself. In *National Defense,* author James Fallows observes that management is not leadership. Management can be approached as an academic discipline; one can be taught to analyze data, to weigh alternatives, and to make a decision. But leadership is something else. It is a subjective chemistry filled with human variables. It takes more than the ability to analyze data to make a leader; one must be able to motivate those who are being led, to reach their emotions through command presence, force, and example. And one must be willing to accept responsibility for one's decisions. Faced with the most difficult situation in the corporation's history, Time's brass failed to rise to the challenge.

The company's brass also proved indifferent to the issues of quality and respect for the reader, issues that had obsessed Burgheim from the start. As with leadership, quality is not a concept that can be reduced to a mathematical abstraction and measured. Quality is an ethical consideration, implying a subjective judgment of relative worth, and professionalism is the measure of one's commitment to the concept for its own sake, a commitment that seemed to grow weaker, the higher up Time Inc.'s organization one looked.

Saving face proved to be a major thirty-fourth floor concern in the project's aftermath. When a television reporter asked Grunwald to comment on the failure, Time Inc.'s Editor in Chief said, "Well, everybody is entitled to one Edsel," then looked ready to answer the next question on any different topic. When a trade reporter asked Executive Vice President Clifford Grum which management official had been responsible for overseeing the project, Time Inc.'s second-in-command answered, "There was no *one* man in charge; it was a group effort," then looked ready to end the interview if the reporter should press further.

One measure of power in an organization is a person's salary, and in this regard Time Inc.'s top executives enjoyed largesse no different from that bestowed upon the brass of most other large corporations. In his three years as the company's president and CEO, Munro failed at virtually every new venture he authorized, eventually accumulating losses that totaled nearly 10 percent of Time Inc.'s entire net worth. Meanwhile, corporate debt increased, earnings per share stagnated, and investment analysts began to view the company as lacking in direction.

Yet his weak performance did not stop Time Inc.'s five-man Compensation and Personnel Committee, each member an outside director of the board, from bestowing on him regular annual salary and stock bonus increases anyway. On the day *TV-Cable Week* went out of business, Munro's annual salary and bonus package totaled $710,907.00, the highest in the corporation, and he held rights as well on $2.5 million in exercisable stock options. He was the first chief executive in the company's history to have been made a millionaire on a track record of entrepreneurial failure.

Munro's experience is typical of what is happening with more and more top officials of U.S. companies. Unlike the situation in Japan, where the salary range between the shop floor and the executive suite is often no more than a multiple of ten, the gulf in the U.S. is enormous and is widening. In 1977, only five executives of publicly held corporations had annual salaries in excess of $1 million; by 1983 the number had grown to 38, of which 18 had annual salaries of more than $2 million. As Mark Green, an activist lawyer and president of the Washington, D.C.-based Democracy Project observes, "The American system of executive compensation reminds one of Mark Twain's comment on bourbon—too much is never enough."

When companies excessively compensate their top managers, they do more than just drain the treasury; they also sap the morale of the staff. People know when their bosses are incompetent or weak, for they see evidence of it every day at the office. Six- and seven-digit salaries for such people simply looks like plundering the kitty, and breeds cynicism at every level.

In the case of Time Inc., the spectacle of rewarding failure was aggravated by the executive job shuffle that followed the shutdown. Zucchi, removed from the project by Sutton to make room for Meigher, and demoted to associate publisher of *People* Magazine, came to work one day to find that Sutton had put Meigher in his life all over again, now as his actual boss, *People*'s publisher. Said Zucchi with his usual cut-through insight: "I think Kelso's doing a tap dance on my head!"

Carmen Siringo's old boss, Bob McGoff, got a similar surprise from Sutton. Having battled with Labich for two years over technology, McGoff now found that Sutton and Grunwald had jointly named Labich editorial technology director for all Time Inc.'s magazines, making McGoff his deputy. Said McGoff woefully, "Labich, can you beat it!"

Since most project staffers knew little of the efforts Brauns and Dunn had made to prevent *TV-Cable Week* from ever launching, it seemed bizarre when the group vice president named Brauns a director of strategic planning for Magazine Group, and made Dunn general manager of *Discover,* another financially troubled Time Inc. publication.

For his part, Grunwald did little to find positions for *TV-Cable Week* writers and editors with other Time Inc. publications, seeming throughout to wish the problem of the magazine would simply disappear. The last senior management member of the project to find work: his own appointee to the task force, Burgheim, who was left to languish for months in an office for transients before being assigned to an editing position at *Life* Magazine.

For Time Inc.'ers as a whole, the most surprising assignments involved the men at the top. Though few knew the full details of the project's mismanagement, all knew that in some way it had failed because Video Group and Magazine Group had not cooperated with each other from the start. Hints of the struggle would appear in press and magazine articles from time to time, as when Sutton told a writer from *Rolling Stone* Magazine that he did feel certain apprehensions about Levin's "video soldiers marching on his kingdom."

Yet on the eve of the magazine's closure, Munro had chosen to elevate the two men most closely involved—Sutton and Levin—to positions on the company's board of directors. It was a move that he thought would somehow give the directors "less tunnel vision," but it looked to the employees like simply rewarding failure. The *Gallagher Report*, a gossipy newsletter for media executives, summed up the situation quite accurately: "Turmoil Inside Dick Munro's Time Inc.: Chief works to squelch rumors of takeover. Meanwhile, executive power struggle shapes up between magazines, video group for control of 'new' Time."

The effect on the staff was quick and obvious. When the company began its United Fund drive with posters featuring photos of officers urging employees to "give the United Fund Way," a Sutton poster soon sprouted illustrative graffiti: a black eye and the quote "No thanks, I gave $47 million at the office."

Levin as well had problems to confront. Fond of beginning press interviews with a caveat: "Everything I say about this industry might be wrong," Levin in the months following the shutdown turned out to be right. Not only had ATC refused to buy *TV-Cable Week*, but Video Group's "churn" problem now returned, as HBO subscriber growth began to ebb while fees to the studios began to rise. Within three months of *TV-Cable Week*'s closure, Video Group planners had begun to readjust their growth targets down sharply, and by the following autumn Video Group had laid off seven percent of HBO's employees.

Behind all this lay a decade and a half of conglomerate drift —a confused and directionless slide that climaxed in *TV-Cable Week*. During the 1970s, many companies experienced similarly aimless growth, acquiring whatever seemed a potentially profitable business prospect, accumulating debt, boosting cash flow, searching for whatever it took to make earnings per share rise on Wall Street. In its way, Time Inc. was one of these companies. Though they never achieved the broad diversity of an ITT or a Textron (with more than one hundred different and unrelated enterprises in its corporate family), Time's brass did yearn for the same "growth by numbers" that built the empires of Harold Geneen (ITT) and Royal Little (Textron).

Time Inc.'s founder, Henry Luce, in the closing days of World War I met another young Yale man his age, Briton Hadden, while the two were undergoing officers' training at an army camp in South Carolina. A friendship developed, and from that friendship grew a publishing venture the two proposed to call "Facts." Hadden died in 1929, but the weekly magazine he and Luce had six years earlier brought to market as *Time* Magazine was already beginning to change American journalism.

Behind the success of *Time* lay the energies of many talented people and a vision of its founder: of editorial independence, and respect for factual accuracy. In the half-century that followed, a corporate culture grew around these premises—the notion of "church and state." No memorandum issued from Henry Luce to spell out its philosophy, but as time passed the notion acquired a kind of sanctity in the minds of employees— that the editorial pages of Time's publications comprised a covenant with the reader, that they were above corruption or the taint of commercialism, that a company could not influence the slant of an article by spending (or withholding) advertising dollars—in short, that the business and editorial sides of Time Inc.'s publications were as independent and noninvolved in each other's affairs as if the corporation were separated into the worlds of church and state.

In time, this notion acquired structural form in the corporate organization chart, as two independent chains of command emerged, with the business and editorial sides of Time Inc. reporting separately to the company's board of directors—the business side through the company's president and CEO, the editorial side through the editor in chief. But real corporate power resided in one man, the company's founder, Luce, who made clear to all where he thought the true locus of leadership lay, at various times giving himself the titles of president and chief executive officer before settling in 1939 on the designation of editor in chief, which he held without change until his death in 1966.

Behind every successful corporation is a collection of shared values that form a social philosophy, the corporation's culture—how a company does what it does, and why. No strategic planner can reduce corporate culture to an analytical "decision tree" about what new business to acquire, merge with, or expand into. People are simply people, and when one company acquires another it automatically acquires the corporate culture that goes with it, that is imbedded in the hearts, minds, and souls of its employees, often in subtle and deep ways that the employees themselves do not realize.

Like many other corporations during the 1970s, Time Inc. lost sight of that fact, expanding into fields that had nothing to do with the cultural premises upon which the corporation rested—into forestry, heavy industry, cable television, Hollywood moviemaking. *TV-Cable Week* was the final fruit of that process, a confused effort, presided over by a weak top executive, to bring to market a publication that sought to unite the two separate worlds of church and state, of mammon and art.

On his last day at *TV-Cable Week* Dan Zucchi came into an editor's office and sat in a chair. He looked haggard from the events of the summer, tired to his bones. He wore dark slacks and his shirt was open at the collar. He had yanked his tie down and to the side. He sat for the longest time, slumped back, his head against the wall, gazing at the ceiling as the hum of the kludge seeped through the floor.

After many minutes, Zucchi spoke. One might have expected something deep and evocative, an insight that captured the essence of what the last year and a half had meant to him, what it had been like to be a regimental commander in a corporate war—a war that should never have been fought, that had no heros or even winners, that was yielding nothing but woe for all its combatants. Dan Zucchi looked about sadly, and in distant, slow words declared, "You know, I filled every damned part of the business plan except one. I never got hold of Burgheim."

Then Zucchi stood up, shook hands with the editor, and turned about and left the room.

It was the last the editor ever saw of Dan Zucchi, but not the last time he pondered that remark. For in its way, what Zucchi had said was what *TV-Cable Week* had been about all along: the lonely struggle of one man, Richard Burgheim, to defend the values upon which his corporation had been built.